EVERNEATH

BRODI ASHTON

EVERNEATH

SIMON AND SCHUSTER

A **simon pulse** book

Simon Pulse and its colophon are registered trademarks of Simon & Schuster UK Ltd

First published in Great Britain in 2012 by Simon and Schuster UK Ltd
A CBS COMPANY

This paperback edition published in 2012

First published in the USA in 2012 by Balzer + Bray an imprint of
HarperCollins Publishers.

1 3 5 7 9 10 8 6 4 2

Simon & Schuster UK Ltd
1st Floor,
222 Gray's Inn Road
London
WC1X 8HB

Simon & Schuster Australia, Sydney
Simon & Schuster India, New Delhi

A CIP catalogue record for this book is available from the British Library.

ISBN: 978-0-85707-459-1
Ebook ISBN: 978-0-85707-458-4

Printed and bound by CPI Group (UK) Ltd, Croydon, CR0 4YY

www.simonandschuster.co.uk
www.simonandschuster.com.au
www.simonpulse.co.uk

To: *my dad.*
A quiet man.
A fierce warrior.

EVERNEATH

THE EVERNEATH.

*History books call it the Underworld. Or even hell.
But I know it's neither. It is really called the Everneath,
and it's not a place for the dead. It's a place for the
Everliving—beings who have discovered the secret to
eternal life. It's a place for their Forfeits—the humans
who give up everything to nourish the Everliving. It's
the world caught between this one and the next, a layer
between Earth and hell. I know because I was a Forfeit.
I would give anything to change this.*

PROLOGUE

TWO WEEKS AGO

I was picturing his face—a boy with floppy brown hair and brown eyes—when the Feed ended.

At first I didn't know what had happened. I didn't know where I was or why it was so dark. I knew only that the pain inside me—the feeling that I was being drained from the inside out—had subsided, and now everything was numb. Maybe I no longer existed.

"It's over," Cole whispered in my ear.

I wanted to answer, but my mouth wasn't working.

"Nikki, try to open your eyes."

That was why it was dark. My eyes were closed. I'd been squeezing them shut for I don't know how long. The muscles around them had forgotten how to relax, so it was some time before I could pry them open.

When I did, they stung, like a fresh wound exposed to cool air. After a hundred years they had forgotten how to produce tears.

It was still dark all around us, but as I worked on my eyes, the black forms that had bound me to Cole began to peel away, as if an oil slick were lifting from my skin.

I could see.

I looked at my arm, from my shoulder down to the elbow, and a little lower, to where it disappeared behind Cole's back. My skin was so pale. Almost blue. I was wearing a black tank top. I tried to remember putting it on but came up with nothing.

"Nikki. Try to stand up."

I shook my head, surprised that I could move my head at all. The Shades, with their black, fluid forms, had cocooned us so tight for so long. Cole's head was next to mine, his chin resting on my shoulder, his blond hair touching my cheek.

"You can take your time."

"Mmm," I said. It was all I could manage.

I started with small movements, flexing my fingers and my toes, shocking my hibernating muscles awake. Cole did the same. I could feel his fingertips pressing into my back, restarting the circulation.

I worked up to my knees, my legs, my elbows, making small movements against Cole's body. But where I tried to separate my legs from his, the skin stung. It was as if we had been sewn together, and I was ripping us apart.

I groaned in pain and pulled him tight against me again.

He let me. "I know it's going to be hard, Nik. We'll just take it slow, okay?"

I nodded, and he held me for a few long minutes before we tried to separate again. This time, he rubbed the affected skin as we went, and I had a brief memory flash of a woman ripping a Band-Aid off my knee, and then rubbing it to ease the pain.

But when I tried to focus on the image, it slipped away and I was in the dark again.

I shook and reached for Cole, but this time he grabbed my wrists, gently and firmly.

"Nik, I'm sorry. The Shades say the Feed is over. I know it feels weird, but we have to get used to it."

I wasn't sure I believed him. Without his embrace, my body felt empty and hollow, as though we were one person, divided. Except it wasn't an even division. He had taken away everything that made me . . . me. And I would only be *me* again when I was next to him. I wasn't sure my body would survive on its own anymore. I was no longer whole.

Even though I was trembling, I sat up. My legs dangled over the stone ledge of our alcove and I looked around. We were in a giant cavern, the walls of which were filled with hundreds of alcoves just like the one we were in, but they were all empty.

Somewhere in the back of my mind, I knew we were the last ones to start the Feed, so we were the only ones left. Stairs built into the rock zigzagged up the walls, leading to the alcoves above us. The ground was covered in a sea of black sludge that swelled and pulsed like a lake in a storm.

More Shades. Hundreds of them. Maybe thousands.

"They're stretching out too," Cole said from behind me. They should be. The Shades had been wrapped around us for the entire century, unmoving, funneling my own energy directly into Cole.

Cole.

I turned my head until I could see him in my peripheral vision, deeper inside the alcove. His was the only voice I'd heard for the past hundred years. The only name I knew anymore. He rubbed his eyes, trying to pry them open with his fingers. "This part never gets easier," he said.

I faced forward again, looking out over the dark ground. I had this niggling feeling that I was forgetting something very important. The more I tried to figure out what it was, the more my heart pounded. If I could just remember, my heart wouldn't explode.

And then it hit me. When I'd opened my eyes, I'd forgotten the face. *His* face. That's what it was.

I closed my eyes again, and there he was. Hair that flopped forward in a tangled mess. Big brown eyes that could search me out in any crowd. Callused hands that could lead me anywhere.

I couldn't remember the name that went with the face. I'd lost it years ago.

"Nik?"

Cole shifted so that he was sitting beside me. He had shaken off the shroud of a deep sleep. "Nik, look at me." There was a strange urgency to his voice. I twisted my head to look at him and was struck by how attractive he still was. I had been in his arms, but I hadn't seen his face for a century. It was the same. His blond hair framed his dark eyes—eyes that were wide open now, in surprise. His gaze roved over my face, my body. "How did you do it?"

"Do what?" My voice sounded strange. I wasn't really paying attention to what he was saying because I was thinking about being wrapped up with him again. Being whole again. I started to lean toward him, but he put his hands on my shoulders and studied me.

"You . . . you're still the same *Nikki*. You survived." He cupped my face in his hands, and then turned it left and right, as if he couldn't believe what he was seeing. "I found you."

"What do you mean?"

He shook his head with a strange smile on his lips. "I mean, I've searched for you—for someone like you—for thousands of years." He tilted his head back and gazed up, as if he were thanking the cavern ceiling for something. He clasped my hands so tightly it hurt. "You have no idea what this means. This. Never. Happens. Nik, you don't have to go to the Tunnels. You can stay with me. Become an Everliving."

He jumped off the ledge and stood on the ground, the Shades there making way for his feet. He reached out his hand. "Come with me, Nik."

I looked at his hand, and then up at his face. "Where?"

"Out of here." He gestured to the giant cavern. "You can live forever like me, and you won't have to go to the Tunnels."

His face involuntarily grew hard. It seemed even immortals were scared of the Tunnels.

I reached for his hand, then hesitated as I remembered that face. The one with the brown eyes. The boy with the hands that fit mine just right. I'm not sure how, but I knew if I went with Cole, I'd never see that face again. The boy with that face was not an Everliving.

He was a human, and he was on the Surface. Where I'd left him. I knew it like I knew I needed air to live.

"No," I said. I pushed away from him and stood up on my own. Somewhere in the back of my mind, I knew I had another choice. "I'm going home."

The Shades at Cole's feet whipped into a frenzy at this. "Wait," Cole said, the realization of what I'd said sinking in. "Wait! She doesn't know what she's saying!"

But they didn't change course. One Shade rose from the whirlpool and, in front of my eyes, morphed into the shape of a dagger, driving itself into my shoulder. It felt like a hot poker, searing through my flesh. As I screamed, other Shades gathered round. They snatched me up, and in a whirlwind of black, I flew through the air as the sound of Cole's voice grew faint behind me, shouting my name.

I landed with a *thwump* on a surface that was cold and hard, the side of my face smashed against what looked like industrial tile floor. I could smell ammonia, and it was so strong it made my eyes water.

Where am I?

I wasn't in the Everneath anymore; the light was too bright, the odors too strong.

I rolled over onto my back and found myself staring into fluorescent lights that weren't lit, yet I had to shield my eyes. I looked around. On my right, a mop leaned against the wall in the corner, next to a brown wooden door with a NO ADMIT-TANCE sign. On my left were rows and rows of potato chips and candy, a couple of soda fountains, and a counter with a cash register.

It was a store—a convenience store, probably—and despite the brightness of the place, it was the middle of the night. I realized how dark the Feed cavern must've been if even the middle of the night was too bright for me here.

I shifted, and a sharp pain shot through my shoulder, still tender from where the Shade had stabbed me.

I closed my eyes and pictured the boy with the brown hair, and as I took in my first really deep breath of Surface air, a name to match the face came to me. A name I'd been trying to cling to for a century.

"Jack."

ONE

Park City High School.
Five and a half months of my Return left.

It was too soon.

But, really, I'd been gone for a hundred years. Everything about my old life would feel like it was coming at me too soon. Especially high school. I stepped through the doors of Park City High and nearly choked on the smell of fresh paint. I glanced around. None of the other students seemed to be affected by it, but it made my eyes water.

The halls of the high school looked the same, reminding me that aboveground—far above the Everneath—only six months had passed while I was away. Time moves differently in the Everneath. One hundred years to me was just months on the Surface. Everything was the same. And everything was different.

A banner hung above the entrance to the upper-class hall. PARK CITY HIGH: HOME OF THE MINERS. Right then a few large boys dressed in football jerseys and jeans ran under the sign, jumping and high-fiving the Miner's chisel as they went.

Junior year. A waste of time in one respect, considering I'd never make it to the end of the year, let alone graduation. I only had six months before the Tunnels came for me.

But I needed to be here. Needed to glimpse, for a moment, the life I had before. The year I should've had. To see Jack one last time, despite how we left things. To see my family again.

This was my chance to say good-bye. It was a chance I didn't get last time.

I scanned the hallway, searching for his face, but looked down quickly after catching a few questioning stares. I knew he was here somewhere in the building. The thought gave me goose bumps.

At least I had enough emotions left inside me to even get goose bumps. Blushes and chills didn't take much— I'd recovered them about a week ago, along with all of my memories. But it was the stronger emotions, the ones that produced laughter and tears, that eluded me still.

I glanced down at my schedule. First-period English litera-ture. As I checked the room numbers at the tops of the doors, curious whispers floated along the hall behind me, hanging in the air above my head.

Isn't that Nikki Beckett? She looks awful. . . .

Is she still using?

Has to be. . . . What else would do that to a person?

Poor Jack.

Does he know she's back? Does he know she's strung out?

When I found the right room, I clutched my books to my chest, lowered my head, and walked through the door.

Someone—probably the new English teacher—called from near the front of the classroom. "Miss Beckett, is it?"

Hearing my own last name did strange things to my heart. Made it beat a little faster. A little harder. It had been so long since I'd had a last name. For a hundred years, Cole had called me only by my first name. It was how the Everliving treated their Forfeits—if you didn't have a last name, you didn't have a life outside the Everneath. Nothing to want to come back to. Maybe that was why he was so surprised that I chose to Return.

I stopped just inside the doorway and lifted my head toward the teacher, keeping a few strands of hair in front of my eyes as I nodded in response.

"Welcome." She hesitated as she took in my appearance. People did that a lot. My dad told me it was because I looked like a malnourished animal, ready to sprint. I'd lost a lot of weight, and my dark hair no longer held any curls. "The principal told me to expect you. I'm Mrs. Stone. I see you have the textbook."

I nodded again.

"There's an empty chair in the back there, and here's a supplemental book on mythology." She pointed toward the rear of the classroom, but I kept my gaze on her. "You'll have to work hard to catch up with the rest of the class."

I turned and shuffled down the middle row until I reached the empty place at the back. Once seated, I took out my notebook and pencil and leaned forward over my desk so my hair created a curtain on either side of my face.

I could do this.

But I could taste the curiosity in the air. Literally. Cole used to tell me that the Everneath would change me—make me more in tune with the emotions of others because I was so empty of my own. Now that I was back, I could "taste" emotions hanging around me.

Certain emotions were stronger than others, and would hit me when I wasn't ready. Like when my dad told me he was so happy I was back and that he didn't blame me, but his disappointment in the air tasted as strong as a clump of salt.

It wasn't so easy to identify most of them, except when an entire group was feeling the same thing.

Like now. Thirty people in a room, all curious.

But as the class settled in for the lecture, one emotion, separate from the curiosity, floated to the top of the rest. I couldn't figure out what it was. It would've been easier if I'd been prepared.

"Hi," a familiar voice said from the desk next to mine.

I startled.

It was him.

Jack.

The boy who had gotten me through hell.

I wasn't expecting him to be in my first class of the day. Here he was, my reason for Returning, but any words I used to know got caught in my throat. I wanted to run toward him and away from him at the same time, laugh and cry at the same time. Instead I froze.

All this way, just to see him, and I'd never planned for what to do next.

Jack's voice sounded flat. Or more that he tried to make it sound flat. Maybe I was the only one who would've picked up on that.

I kept my head down, took a deep breath, and picked the easiest of the words that were stuck in my throat. I exhaled as slowly as I could, and the word slipped out. "Hi."

The word had no accompanying voice to it. Just the escaping air behind my lips.

He turned away from me to focus on Mrs. Stone. I wondered how I was going to get through the hour.

I took notes furiously, transcribing every word Mrs. Stone said. Since my Return, my emaciated muscles made my hands shake, and I looked for ways to keep them busy. It was part of the reason I took up knitting. In the two weeks that had passed since I walked out of the Shop-n-Go and back through the door of my father's home, I had knitted an entire wardrobe's worth of clothes, a few dog sweaters for my neighbor, and a handful of toaster cozies.

Mrs. Stone spoke animatedly about the role of the hero in mythology. When she asked the class for their favorite stories or figures from myths, several students raised their hands. A large kid in the back said, "Hercules." Another boy, wearing a

MATHLETES ARE ATHLETES TOO shirt, said, "Aphrodite."

People laughed. I didn't know why. It seemed to be an inside joke and I was an outsider.

Then a blond girl in the front row raised her hand and said, "Hades and Persephone."

I couldn't help flipping forward in the textbook to the story. I didn't know why it would be anybody's favorite. According to myth, Hades, the god of the Underworld, fell in love with Persephone, kidnapped her, and tried to make her his queen. When he tricked her into eating six pomegranate seeds, she was bound to the Underworld for six months out of every year.

Kidnapping and imprisonment. It was a horrible myth. I wondered where her hero had been.

Jack's leg bounced up and down, distracting me. I wanted to reach over and put my hand on his knee and tell him everything would be okay.

But that was impossible. I stared harder at my paper and tried not to think about Jack's leg.

The bell to end class startled me, and I dropped my pencil. It bounced on the floor, toward Jack's desk. I froze. Maybe he hadn't noticed. I'd wait and get it when the rest of the class left. I stayed perfectly still. The room cleared out, but I couldn't sense any movement from the desk next to mine.

Before I could stop myself, I looked up.

He was there, motionless, holding my pencil in his hand, watching me. My eyes drank in the sight of him, even as my body fought the urge to bolt. His hair was the same rich brown color, but it was longer and shaggier than before. And his face had lost any signs of baby fat, making me think his mom had stopped forcing meatball sandwiches down his throat like she used to during football season.

His eyes were exactly as I'd remembered, exactly as I'd pictured every day for the past hundred years. Chocolate. But there was one difference: a single steel post pierced one of his eyebrows.

It wouldn't have belonged on his face a year ago, but it somehow fit the face looking at me now. This face was edgier. This face had been through something.

He was beautiful.

I started to tremble. It took all of my strength, which wasn't very much, not to run out the door.

He'd obviously waited for me to look at him. Like his voice, his face held no easily identifiable emotion to pinpoint. No love, no hate. He held out my pencil for me.

I reached over and grabbed it, my fingers brushing lightly against the palm of his hand. I could hear my own intake of breath. He didn't flinch in the slightest. He didn't draw his hand back.

"Mr. Caputo? Miss Beckett?" Mrs. Stone called from the front of the classroom. "Are you waiting for something?"

"No, Mrs. Stone," Jack said, keeping his curious eyes on mine. "Just saying hi to an old . . . friend."

I gathered up my books and tried not to think about how it used to be.

LAST YEAR

September. Six months before the Feed.
Six months before I went under.

"Hey, Becks!" Jules, my best friend, called out to me from the end of the hallway. Most of the students clearing their lockers for the day turned to look. Jules had a way of grabbing attention. "You going to the game tonight?"

I was about to answer, but another voice rang out from just behind me.

"She'd better," Jack said as he wrapped an arm around my waist and pulled me back against him. I could smell the fresh leather on his letterman jacket as I crunched against it.

"Why is that?" I asked, smiling and instantly warm in his arms. I still couldn't get over the fact that Jack Caputo and I were . . . together. It was hard to think the word. We had been friends for so long. To be honest, he had been friends with me and I had been secretly pining for him since . . . well, since forever.

But now he was here. It was *my* waist he held. It didn't seem real.

"I can't carry the team to victory without you," he said. "You're my rabbit's foot."

I craned my neck around to look at him. "I've always dreamed of some guy saying that to me."

He pressed his lips to the base of my neck, and heat rushed to my cheeks. "I love making you turn red," he whispered.

"It doesn't take much. We're in the middle of the hallway."

"You want to know what else I love?" His tone was playful.

"No," I said, but he wasn't listening. He took his fingers and lightly trailed them up my spine, to the back of my neck. Instant goose bumps sprang up all over my body, and I shuddered.

"That."

I could feel his smile against my ear. Jack was always smiling. It was what made him so likable.

By this time, Jules had snaked her way through the throng of students. "Hello, Jack. I was in the middle of a conversation with Becks. Do you mind?" she said with a smirk.

Right then a bunch of Jack's teammates rounded the corner at the end of the hallway, stampeding toward us.

"Uh-oh," I said.

Jack pushed me safely aside just before they tackled him, and Jules and I watched as what seemed like the entire football team heaped on top of their starting quarterback.

"Dating Jack Caputo just might kill you one day." Jules laughed. "You sure it's worth it?"

I didn't answer, but I was sure. In the weeks following my mother's death, I had spent nearly every morning sitting at her grave. Whispering to her, telling her about my day, like I used to each morning before she died. Jack came with me to the cemetery most days. He'd bring a book and read under a tree several headstones away, waiting quietly, as if what I was doing was totally normal.

We hadn't even been together then.

It had been only five months since my mom died. Five months since a drunk driver hit her during her evening jog. Five months since the one person who knew all my dreams disappeared forever. Jack was the reason I was still standing.

Yeah, I was sure he was worth it. The only thing I wasn't sure about was why *he* was with *me*.

TWO

NOW
Lunch. Five and a half months left.

At lunchtime, my lunch sack and knitting needles in hand, I tried to weave my way through the crowded halls as fast as I could, searching for a quiet place to eat.

I turned a corner and a small group of cheerleaders broke out into some random rally song. The noise ricocheted off the metal lockers and rang in my ears and in my brain.

I ducked into an empty classroom and took a few deep breaths. It was hard for me to believe I had ever gone to school every day. How could anyone survive so many people in one place? Everything here was loud.

Even in this room, electric morsels of energy reached me, triggering my hunger, reminding me of where I'd been and how much of my own energy had been stolen. I closed my eyes and allowed myself a moment to wish that I had my own emotions back, that I wasn't so empty.

I realized how much had changed. On the other side of

a century, I had wanted to feel less, not more. Maybe most teenagers wouldn't think like that, but when the drunk driver killed my mom, I wanted more than to stop feeling sad. I wanted to stop feeling. Period. I wanted it so bad that when Cole offered to make it happen, I went to the Everneath with him. Willingly.

Now I knew what really happened when emotions were gone. Cole bought himself another hundred years of life by draining me, and in the abyss left over there was no peace. Only an emptiness that made me ache as if my insides had been scraped out.

I peeked out into the hallway again. The crowds had thinned, but not enough. I wanted to go home. Or at least someplace quiet. But I'd promised my dad I would finish out the day.

Last year, I'd left my dad in the heat of an argument. I threw despicable words at him and then walked out and never came back. This time, I was determined to do things better. I would not leave him, alone in a room, with echoes of the things I never should've said frozen in the air. I didn't have control over much during my Return, but I could control how I would leave the people I loved.

He asked me to stay in school, and so I stayed.

When my heartbeat had regulated, I ventured out of the classroom and found the corner of the darkest hallway on the second floor. I wedged myself in the nook between a drinking fountain and the brick wall.

Homecoming euphoria wafted through the halls. I could taste it.

I focused on the wall beside the fountain. Blocked out everything else. The paint was peeling away. It had come loose in one large patch, perfectly intact, and was just hanging there.

I wanted to rip it off, but I didn't. If I left it alone, maybe it could somehow fall back into place without cracking.

Last year, I'd counted down the days to the homecoming football game, crossing off the squares on my calendar. But last year was over a century ago.

This year, I wouldn't be wishing away time.

I stared at the peeled paint. Nobody noticed me here. I'd found my spot.

LAST YEAR
Homecoming. Five months before the Feed.

The clock counted down from thirty, and the student section chanted each number. Park City and Wasatch had been in-state football rivals for decades, and this year, with Jack at the helm, the Park City Miners had the chance to take the "Boulder" home for the first time in ten years.

The Boulder was a piece of granite, brought down from the summit of nearby Mount Olympus, and it held more significance than any state trophy. Once, Kasey Wellington, the Park City tight end, had stolen the Boulder. His parents let him rot in jail for three days for shame. The only way to get the rock is to earn it.

When the clock reached ten seconds, Jules grabbed my hand. "This is it!" she shouted over the roar of the crowd. Jack's older brother, Will, was on the other side of me. He reached for my other hand, a proud smile on his face for his little brother. Then he offered me a swig of the silver flask he'd started carrying around in his coat ever since he'd turned twenty-one.

I gave him a disapproving look, and he shrugged good-naturedly, took a sip, then shoved it back in his pocket.

I wondered if Jack's mom knew how much her other son was drinking.

Seven seconds. In big moments like this, each of the five senses becomes more acute. I knew the smell of mowed grass and mud, and the chill of the icy rain on my skin, and the sound of Jules screaming in my ear, would be grafted onto my soul and become part of the irremovable things about me. The stuff that memories are made of.

I breathed in.

Three . . . two . . . one . . . The bleachers shook as hundreds of fans jumped. It was so loud I had to cover my ears. Then the mass exodus from the stands started. Jules and I joined the rest of the school, scaling the wall that divided the fans from the field. Throwing my legs over the top of the barrier, I turned around and started to lower myself to the turf below. Two strong hands grabbed my sides, lifting me off the wall.

My feet didn't even touch the ground. With his hands at my waist, Jack flipped me around so I was facing him and pulled me tight, my head above his, our noses inches from each other.

His smile was dazzling. It always had been, but before, I was just admiring it from afar as he flashed it toward Lacey Greene or one of his other girlfriends.

Tonight it was for me.

"We did it, Becks!" He spun me around.

"Congra—" I couldn't get anything else out, because his lips were on mine. His mouth tasted faintly of salt. The eye black on his cheeks was no doubt smearing onto my face, but I didn't care. We had this moment together, and I knew it would be over too quickly.

After all, he was the hero. Soon his teammates would be carrying Jack off the field on their shoulders. I knew if I wanted to date the quarterback, I'd have to share him on a night like this.

NOW

My lunch nook.

My knitting needles darted back and forth as they worked. My lunch sack sat untouched on the hard tile floor beside me. The drinking fountain next to my shoulder shuddered to life, cooling the water.

I liked the white noise and solitude my nook gave me.

"Nikki?"

I paused the frantic knitting, but I didn't look up. Maybe whoever it was didn't mean me.

"Becks?"

Maybe not. Two feet appeared next to my lunch sack. How had she tracked me down?

I looked up. The girl looking down at me hadn't changed at all. She was still beautiful, her round face as cherubic as ever, her long blond hair falling in curling cascades over her shoulders. That hair always looked like a snapshot of a waterfall, as if it should be moving.

She was uneasy. I could sense it.

"Hi, Jules—Julianna," I said.

She smiled sympathetically and sank to the ground so she was facing me. I set my knitting down.

"Jules," she corrected. "You call me Jules."

I tapped the floor with my fingers, closing my eyes for a long blink. I felt one of the knitting needles being placed back in my hand, and when I opened my eyes, Jules set the ball of yarn in my lap. She fingered the flowers on the hat I'd nearly finished.

"This is gorgeous, Becks," she said. My nickname felt like warm coffee traveling down my throat, heating my insides. "When did you learn to knit?"

"Two weeks ago." My fingers automatically began their work again.

"You always were a quick study."

I smiled. She used to hate the fact that school came easy to me.

Right then the bell rang, ending the lunch hour. I shot up to my feet, startling Jules. I couldn't help it. Everything seemed louder here.

"Whoa, Becks. We still have five minutes," she said.

"Sorry. I just . . ." I didn't know how to finish.

Jules squeezed my hand. "It's okay. I can only imagine what you've been through."

She didn't say it, but it sounded like she believed the rumors that I'd run away and ended up in rehab. At least she wasn't asking me for the full story. I'd rather people believed the rumors than have to try to explain that I'd been in some version of the Underworld for a hundred years. I didn't need everyone thinking I was crazy, too.

I didn't speak to anyone else for the rest of the day.

When I got home from school, my dad was in the living room with a woman in a gray suit he introduced as Mrs. Ellingson. She said she was there as my friend. I told her I didn't need friends.

She asked me to pee in a cup.

Later that night my dad called me into his study. I knew whatever he wanted was serious, because the study was where all of our serious talks took place.

He was finishing up an email when I went in, so I sat quietly and looked around. The room smelled like leather. The dark wood walls of the study were covered with pictures of his accomplishments. His graduation ceremony from law school. His inauguration as mayor of Park City. Cutting the ribbon for the renovation project at the Egyptian Theater on Main Street.

There was only one family picture in the study, taken for our Christmas cards two years ago. My mom and dad sitting on a couch holding hands, me and my now ten-year-old brother, Tommy, standing behind them.

Poor Tommy. He was happy I was back, but he didn't know what to do with me. It took him a full week to realize I was in no condition to throw the baseball with him like I used to. He always seemed to be waiting for me to say something. Anything. And then he'd leave disappointed. I loved him, but I didn't know how to fix all of the things that were broken in our family.

My dad's desk was scattered with papers, many of which showed bar graphs of the latest polling numbers for his reelection campaign. I wondered if the mess surrounding me affected those numbers, but I was afraid to ask.

"How's the campaign?" I said.

He held up one finger, eyes still on the monitor. "Just . . . one . . . minute . . . and send." He shut the laptop, and then clasped his hands together and placed them on his desk. "The campaign's fine. It's in Percy's good hands. But that's not what I wanted to talk to you about."

I didn't think so.

He shifted in his chair, and the taste in the air only

confirmed what his body language was telling me. My dad was nervous.

"Now that you're back, I thought we could discuss expectations. Specifically, what I expect from you, and what you expect from me."

It couldn't be a coincidence that the first time we talked like this came after a visit from Mrs. Ellingson. She'd probably given him a pamphlet titled "Defining Expectations: How to Reconnect with Your Strung-Out Teenage Daughter" or something like that. But I'd promised myself to make things easier on my dad, and if this was what he needed . . .

"I'm listening," I said.

"Good. Here is what I expect from you. Number one: you will attend school, every day, and you will keep up on your studies. Agreed?"

I nodded. "Yes."

"Number two: you will submit to random . . . testing from Mrs. Ellingson. Agreed?"

It sounded like he was hesitant to use the actual word *drug*. Maybe if he didn't say it, it couldn't be true. "Agreed."

"Number three: I've arranged for you to do community service at the Road Home Soup Kitchen, starting next week. You will serve one lunch hour for every day you were gone. Clear?"

"Clear," I said.

"The *Trib* is sending a photographer."

A photographer? To cover me slopping soup? Percy Jones,

my dad's campaign manager, had probably arranged it. "Okay," I said.

"Now your turn. What do you expect from me?"

I smiled and answered as honestly as I could. "Nothing."

Apparently, that option wasn't in the handbook, because my dad looked a little flustered. Before he could recover, I went over and kissed his head. "Good night."

As I walked away, I decided I would try to do everything I could to appease my dad in the little time I had left. I wished my mom were still alive. She would know how to comfort him now, and after I was gone.

The lights in Tommy's bedroom were off, so I crept down the hall to my room. I opened my door as quietly as I could and shut it behind me without turning on the light.

I clicked on the lamp above my desk, illuminating the open English lit book. As I sat down, I thought about how I would be on display at the soup kitchen tomorrow.

"Why are you doing this, Nik?" The deep voice came from inside my room, near my bed. I gasped and shot out of my chair.

Cole.

THREE

NOW

My room. Five and a half months left.

He wasn't supposed to be here. I wasn't supposed to see him again.

"Won't you look at me?" he said.

Cole's voice. I'd know it anywhere. The sound of it took me back to those long days in the Everneath, where the only things that existed for me were Cole's voice and his touch.

I felt my pulse quicken all the way to my fingertips as a million questions flooded my head. Why was he here? What did he want?

But before I could say anything, I started toward him. I didn't even realize I was doing it until I had almost crossed the entire room and made it into his now open arms. His presence made me aware of the emptiness inside me, as if the only way we would have a complete soul would be if we were together. A couple more steps and I would feel whole.

I froze.

What was I doing? I couldn't be near him again. I couldn't let myself trust him again. Following him to the Everneath had been my choice, but he'd made me think he would help me.

I hated him for letting me believe I had no other option.

"Strange, isn't it, Nik? The connection between us now." He grimaced and cocked his head to one side, as if he were waiting for me to close the distance between us. When I stayed perfectly still, he added, "You don't have to fight it."

Deliberately I placed one foot behind the other and backed up until I was sitting in my chair and gripping the sides to stay in place. I swiveled around so my back was to him and I was facing my desk again. I could think more clearly if I wasn't looking at him.

It scared me that I hadn't noticed him. If it had been anyone else waiting there, I would've been able to sense extra emotions, but Cole survived on stolen ones. Those were harder to sniff out. I listened as his footsteps came closer.

"You're going to ignore me now?" He sighed.

My hands started to shake, but somehow I had the presence of mind to open my book. Running would be pointless. If I could just get through this, then maybe he would leave me alone.

I stayed completely still.

"Mythology," he commented, looking over my shoulder, reading from the top of the chapter. "I could help you with that, you know. If you'd let me."

"I'm sure you could," I mumbled. "You were there."

"Ah, she speaks."

Reluctantly, I turned toward him, and he shifted the guitar that hung from his shoulder to his side. When Cole Stockton had first come to Park City more than a year ago to play at the Sundance Film Festival with his band—the Dead Elvises—the school buzzed with excitement. Especially since the second guitarist, Maxwell Bones, had been dating a senior at Park City High, Meredith Jenkins. I'd met Cole through Meredith.

At the time, I thought he was mysterious and rebellious, but kind too. I knew better now. It was all part of the lie. Concerts were nourishment for Cole and his band. They could snack on the heightened emotions of a captive audience. It was an easy way to steal the energy he needed to survive between Feeds.

"How did you get in here?" I said.

"The window. The lock's broken." He brought his guitar forward then and picked through a haunting melody, as if adding mystery to the broken lock.

"You shouldn't be here."

Cole's lip pulled up in the same smirk that had hundreds of teenage girls swooning last year. "She was the original breath of life, you know."

"Who?"

"Isis." He pointed to the open book behind me.

"I thought Persephone was the first."

"She had a lot of different names. I used to tell you about Isis and Osiris. Don't you remember? Or is it all gone?" He blew out a breath that smelled of ash, and then started to strum background chords. "Osiris was the first man who tried to straddle the line between the mortal and the immortal worlds. The first of the Everliving. The search for immortality nearly killed him."

He struck a minor chord.

"Then along came Isis." He walked over to my open book and ran his finger along a painting depicting a man, naked and lifeless on the ground, and a woman with wings hovering over him. "Isis breathed life back into Osiris." He paused and looked at me. "Just as you did for me."

Cole made eternal life sound as simple as breathing, but I knew better.

I slammed the book shut. "That painting looks nothing like what I went through in the Feed."

"If you think the Feed was bad, wait until the Tunnels come for you."

"It can't be much worse."

He looked at me, his eyes boring into my own. "Yes, it can. I came here to show you. Something I should've done in the Caverns."

Before I could protest, he placed his hands on either side of my head and I felt something whoosh inside. Immediately my bedroom melted away. Everything around me went pitch-black. My chest was crushed, as if it were in a vise, and when I fought for breath, I inhaled a handful of dirt, and choked.

Buried alive.

I fought and clawed at the heavy dirt weighing down on me,

until my fingertips felt air. I dug my way out and fell in a heap on muddy ground. But I wasn't outside. I was in a long, dark tunnel with walls of coal, hundreds of pale hands sticking out, flailing. I tried to crawl away, but the hands grabbed my ankles, my legs, my arms, and dragged me back inside the walls.

I opened my mouth to yell at Cole to make it stop, but the black rocks poured in, covering my tongue and pushing toward the back of my throat. The whole thing felt too real. The stones in my mouth cut the inside of my cheek, and I tasted blood. This was no vision. I was trapped.

I screamed, but I couldn't hear a sound until the nightmare had completely disappeared and I was back in my room with Cole, his hand over my mouth.

I blinked, trying to reconcile what had just happened in my head. He gave me a look, like *Are you done screaming?* I nodded and he lifted his hand. The vision had left me light-headed, and I started to sway. Cole caught me and held me close to him, my head on his chest. Where I should've heard his beating heart there was nothing.

"Those are the Tunnels, Nik. Those are what you chose, over me."

The Tunnels. The Everneath's final claim on every last drop of energy in a Forfeit. I knew they were bad, but Cole's shared vision left no doubt.

"Why are you here?" My voice sounded breathless.

As if it should've been obvious, Cole said, "I came here to offer you eternal life. *Again.*"

I pushed away from him. "I already made my choice."

"Yes, but it's obviously the wrong choice. Return with me. To the Everneath. And we'll live in the High Court. And you won't be a battery in the Tunnels. You could be a queen."

"The Everneath has a High Court?"

"Of course. It's where Osiris and Isis ruled. Hades and Persephone. Every realm in every dimension has people who give orders and people who take orders. And I'm tired of taking orders, Nik."

I grimaced. "That has nothing to do with me."

He paused and let out a little sigh. "Then I'm saying it wrong, because it has everything to do with you. I want what Hades and Persephone had, and I can't do it without you. The only time the queen of the Everneath has been overthrown is when an Everliving has found his perfect match. I've spent my whole life—and it's a long one, trust me—looking for my perfect match, and it's you. I knew you were different from the first moment I met you. The first moment you placed your hands on mine. You remember?"

I nodded. It had been the night we first met.

"Your cheeks turned red, and I was gone for you." He shook his head, and his lip quirked up in a smile. "I know you felt it too. The connection between us. It started even before the Feed."

I looked away, because my cheeks were getting warm thinking about it, and I couldn't let him see it. Remembering that night was pointless. I was a different person now. "It doesn't matter what I felt then. I didn't know who you really were."

I glanced up. He raised his eyebrows and said, "It wouldn't have made a difference."

He held my gaze with eyes so intense I couldn't look away. He was probably right. From the moment we met, I had been drawn to him. At the time, nothing would've changed my decision to go with him. I just hoped I was stronger now.

I turned away, and then he pulled his guitar forward and picked a smooth, soft melody.

"You've had plenty of Forfeits," I said. "What exactly makes me different?"

"I wish I knew. I really do." He let out a deep breath and stood up as if he would leave. "Think about it. I'm offering immortality. You could be like me."

"Tell me one thing. If I went with you, became an Everliving, would I have to Feed off others the way you Fed off me?"

He hesitated for a moment, then nodded.

"I thought so. I would never do to someone else what you did to me. I'd rather be a battery in the Tunnels." I tried to infuse my voice with authority, but the attempt made it crack.

He smiled. "You don't belong here. And you don't belong in the Tunnels." He leaned closer, swinging his guitar around to his back. "You saw what I just showed you." I shivered as I remembered the vision. "We could go now, and leave it all behind. Look at you. This world will kill you."

Cole was right. Returning was harder than I'd imagined, but I couldn't let him know that. His eyes locked on mine.

"Please, Nik." He ran a finger down my cheek.

I blinked my eyes to break his gaze, and turned back around to my book. "I'm already dead. It's *your* world that killed me. Just go."

He placed his hand on my shoulder, his fingers grazing my collarbone, causing the black scar on my shoulder to sting. The mark was shaped like a stab wound—a thin oval with pointed ends—and it was in the same spot where the Shade in the Everneath had transformed into a knife and sliced me. It'd never completely healed.

"You were supposed to . . ." He paused, and when he spoke again his voice was gruff. "You were supposed to forget your life here."

I nodded, wincing from his touch on my shoulder. "I forgot most of it." I *had* forgotten almost all of it, and if I hadn't remembered Jack's face, I probably would've gone with Cole.

"Why would you ever choose to Return? You could've just gone straight to the Tunnels. Why, Nik?"

I flipped a page of my textbook.

"I don't have to answer you. I don't owe you anything."

"Hmm." His gaze hardened. "You know, I was wondering about your brother, Timmy."

I eyed him warily. "Tommy. What about him?"

He shrugged. "Nothing much. It's just that I've never Fed off a child before, mostly because children's emotions haven't matured to their full potential. I always thought of them as unripe fruit. But now I wonder if it would be more like eating veal."

I stood up and grabbed his arm and pulled him away from the bedroom door. "Don't."

"Don't what?"

"You know what. Leave Tommy alone." My voice was stronger than it had ever been since I Returned. "I'll answer your question, if you promise to leave my family alone."

"You'll answer my question?"

Just get through this, I thought. "Yes."

He cocked his head, as if he was taking his time to consider the offer. Finally, he sat on my bed. "Deal. Why did you come back? And remember, it doesn't count if you're not honest. And, Nik." He paused, his gaze boring into me. "I'll know if you're lying."

I took a breath. "I came back to see my family again." Jack was family too. "And to say good-bye . . . better. Last time, I left during a fight, with no explanation. At least this time I can leave them a note, so they don't waste their time thinking I was kidnapped or something."

Cole moved forward a little. "Be serious. You don't really believe there's a *good* way to say good-bye forever, do you?"

I didn't answer. He was giving voice to thoughts I'd been trying to bury, because I knew how selfish I was being in Returning.

He sighed. "I'll tell you this much, Nik, you may have survived a century in the Everneath, but you won't last six months on the Surface. You'll be begging me to take you away again. I promise. There's too much pain for you here."

I squeezed my eyes shut as I listened to the sound of my bedroom window opening. He paused.

"Your mark."

My hand flew up to the black daggerlike mark on my collarbone. It was still warm. "What about it?"

"It's the mark of a Shade. You have a Shade inside you now." Seeing my expression, he quickly said, "Don't worry. It can't hurt you. But eventually that Shade will want to be reunited with the Tunnels. It's like a magnet for them."

I'd thought it was just a scar. I suddenly wanted to tear at the skin on my shoulder. Rip it until there was no dark left. It couldn't be true.

"Why are you telling me this?"

"In case you start thinking you can hide. The Tunnels will find you. They can't be outrun. They can't be overpowered. And as long as that mark is on you, they'll find you."

"Why do you care if I try to run?"

When he spoke, his voice was soft. "The Tunnels can track you. But I can't."

I couldn't listen anymore. Whether it was true or not. "Get out. Just get out."

He nodded. "I'm gone. But watch your mark. It will grow bigger as your time on the Surface winds down."

He slipped through the window and was gone.

I sprinted to the mirror hanging on the back of my closet door and pulled the collar of my shirt aside.

Cole was right about my mark. I hadn't noticed before, but

it was getting bigger. What if it wasn't just a scar? What if it *was* an actual Shade inside of me? A tracking device, growing, counting down the time I had left.

And there was nowhere I could hide.

FOUR

NOW

The soup kitchen. Five months, one week left.

I tried to forget about Cole's visit. He didn't come back the rest of the week, and I thought maybe he would give up. At least, I hoped.

That Saturday, my shift at the soup kitchen started. I was relieved to be put to work. There was no way to make up for all the pain I'd put my family through, but service to others was a start—my last chance for any sort of redemption, if it existed.

When I got to the shelter, the manager of the soup kitchen met me outside the doors, and another a man with a serious camera was there. I felt like turning and leaving, but I couldn't disappoint my dad anymore. I had to get through it.

The manager came toward me, hand extended. "Nikki, right? Your dad told me to expect you. I'm Christopher." Smile. *Click.* The flash of the camera went off as Christopher took my hand.

"Nice to meet you," I said.

Christopher leaned in and said in a quiet voice, "Just ignore this guy. What matters is that you're here to do some good."

I immediately liked Christopher. His breath smelled like peppermint and tobacco, and tattoos of vines and wire crept out from underneath the collar of his shirt and snaked along his neck. He ignored the photographer and led me inside to the dining hall, which smelled like a cafeteria mixed with a thrift store.

It wasn't hard to learn the ropes at the soup kitchen, and after ladling the first few bowls, I hit a groove. The photographer took the required pictures of me with a ladle in my hands. Then he took off.

As the line of people grew, I could no longer study faces and wonder how they ended up waiting for handouts at a soup kitchen. I just slopped chili and tried to keep my ladling hand from shaking.

Most of the people trudged along silently, which is why I was surprised when I heard an older woman say to me, "You are absolutely beautiful."

I looked up from the vat of soup. "Me?"

"Yes," the old woman said. Deep wrinkles filled every inch of her face. The skin around her eyes was pinched in the corners, as if she'd spent years squinting. Despite this, her eyes looked clear and fresh. Her withered hands reached out to take the soup; they seemed so brittle I worried the bowl would be heavy enough to snap them. "You're not old," she said.

"Oh," I said, a little puzzled. "I guess not. I'm seventeen."

"I'm eighteen," she said. She straightened up as she spoke, making herself a little taller.

Christopher, who was standing next to me, dealing out the bread, chuckled. "Hi, Mary. How are you today?"

The woman—Mary—kept her eyes on me when she answered. "Just fine. Can you believe how young she looks?"

I turned to Christopher, who winked at me reassuringly. "Yeah, she looks seventeen."

A loud crash made us both whip our faces toward Mary, who had thrown her bowl of soup to the linoleum floor.

"I'm eighteen." Her lower lip trembled. "I'm eighteen, I'm eighteen . . . or maybe I'm nineteen. Wait, who's the president?" Her words melted into sobs, and she seemed to forget where she was. "Who's the president?!" she wailed. Then she jerked her head up and looked at me with clear, dry eyes, and out of nowhere she said, "You broke a heart."

My breath caught in my throat. She said it with such conviction, for a moment I had a hard time believing it was just a random comment. It was like she could see inside me, to the guilt that was there. But she couldn't know. It wasn't possible.

Christopher made his way around the counter and put his hand on her shoulder.

"C'mon, Mary," he said. "Let's go sit down and have some lunch. Together."

One of the other volunteers—a girl maybe a few years older than me, with two French braids on the sides of her head—handed me a couple of rags, and we mopped up the floor.

"Don't worry about her," the braid girl said.

"What's wrong with her?"

"Dementia or something. The first time I met her, she kept saying she was lost. Asked me over and over to help her find someone's daughter. I had no idea what she was talking about."

"Someone's daughter?" I asked.

"Yeah . . . Penelope or Priscilla or something." She made one last swipe at the floor and then gathered up the rags into a big ball in her hands. "She wouldn't stop talking about it."

"Who is Penelope's daughter?"

She shrugged. "She never said. Maybe it's a friend she used to know. Poor woman."

Penelope's daughter. Strange. Maybe the braided girl was right, that it was an old friend. Or maybe it was nonsense.

Once the lunch was over and the chairs were stacked away, Christopher told me that Mary had been coming to the shelter for about a month and she seemed to be suffering from dementia.

I guess I sort of knew how she felt. But I decided if I saw her again, I'd ask her about Penelope's daughter. Maybe I could help her figure out what she was looking for.

There was nothing I could do to make up for everything I'd done, but if I could help just one person finish these next six months better off than she started them, that would be something.

Home.

My mother used to make pancakes every Sunday morning. After she died, my dad avoided the kitchen each week. Now that I was home, I decided to reinstate the Sunday tradition.

I put a kettle of water to boil on the stove and then I looked out the window. Tommy was sitting in the chestnut tree, holding a fishing pole.

Tommy. I thought of all the things he'd been through in his short life and all the loss he'd experienced. He was so confused about where I'd gone and why I was suddenly back. I owed him more than I was giving him. Maybe not an explanation, but I had to try to make it better.

I watched as he balanced on a thick branch, raising his fishing pole and swishing it forward and back. Ten o'clock to two o'clock. I smiled. He was giving his latest batch of homemade flies a "test run."

I put a tea bag in my mug and set it on the counter. Then I went outside, creeping around the side of the house to where the chestnut tree towered over our tall wooden fence.

Tommy didn't see me at first. I watched him send a cast out, expertly avoiding branches and flowers. I couldn't think of any other ten-year-old who would consider this a fun Sunday morning, but Tommy always was different from other kids in the neighborhood, and sometimes those other kids teased him for it.

I looked at the rough bark on the tree and the wooden slats nailed into the trunk for climbing. I used to climb the tree too, with Jules. We would sit at the top, where the summer pruning created perfect flat seats. We'd pluck the spiky chestnuts, leaving their green outer shells intact, and throw them at the neighbor boys.

I always took particular care in aiming for Jack's head. He told me later that he rode his bike by my house on purpose. I asked him if he liked pain.

Jack, Will, Jules, and I became inseparable. Stayed that way for a long time, until Will left for the war right before Christmas.

A fishing fly landed at my feet.

"Hey, Nikki," Tommy called out from his perch. "What do you think? Would you take the bait?"

I picked the fly up and squinted one eye as I examined it. My hand started to shake, and the fly slipped from my fingers. "Definitely. She'll fly true."

"Wanna come up and cast with me?"

I thought about my trembling hands and the spasms that had plagued my weak muscles since my Return. Hanging from branches wasn't a good idea. "Thanks, buddy, but I don't think I'm much for climbing trees lately."

"You're no fun anymore," Tommy said, sounding disappointed.

"I'm sorry, Tommy."

"Everyone says sorry," he said. "I'm tired of everybody being so sorry. I just want things to be normal."

I didn't say anything, because my first instinct was to apologize again.

"Now that you're home, can we be normal again?"

How was I supposed to answer that truthfully? I knew my Return would be difficult, but as I watched Tommy playing in the backyard, hoping for something that could never happen, I was struck by how painful it had become. It hurt to see the life I'd never have.

"Can't we, Nikki?" Tommy pressed. "Be normal?"

"Yeah."

I'd started to walk away when he added, "You can pick a fly. From my personal collection in my room."

I knew how precious his collection of favorites was. I forced a smile. "Thanks, Tommy. How about I pay you for it?"

He smiled wide, then started to reel in the line as I turned to go.

FIVE

NOW

After school in Mrs. Stone's classroom. Five months left.

A week passed and my mark doubled in size, to two fingers wide. One morning, Mrs. Stone offered to help me catch up since I'd started school almost a month later than everyone else.

She'd assigned the class thirty-page "practice thesis" papers, due in the spring. I decided the finished paper would go to my dad, to give him some sort of physical evidence that for six months I was here and making an effort.

When I showed up in her classroom after school, she was talking to a student at her desk. I didn't get a good look because I kept my head down and went directly to my normal seat in the back, even though every chair was empty.

I pulled out my textbook, ignoring the conversation at the front. Until I heard Jack's voice.

"The deadline's not for a couple of months," he said.

My heart sputtered. I glanced up. Jack's back was to me, so I watched, grateful for the chance to stare at him.

"That's fine," Mrs. Stone answered. "I stay late most days, so you're welcome to work here—then I can help you when you need it. But don't you have football?"

"Practice doesn't start until three thirty. So that'll give me an hour." Jack peeked toward the back of the room and I ducked my head. "I really appreciate your help."

"I'm happy to see you taking more of an interest in English," Mrs. Stone said. "Those competitive college programs are looking for well-rounded applicants. Too much math and science isn't nourishing to the soul."

I smiled at her enthusiasm, flipped through the pages of my book, and took my notebook out of my bag.

I didn't hear his footsteps, so his voice startled me.

"Hi," he said.

I dropped my notebook.

Jack sat down beside me in the same seat he used during class. I couldn't move. He reached to get my fallen notebook and held it out for me.

"Thanks," I said. This time there was a little sound behind the word.

I should have asked him about his project. Or his football. Or the weather. That's what old friends would do. But the words weren't there, so I turned back to my open lit book.

"You missed the big game Friday," he said.

Was he expecting a conversation? I couldn't do it. I knew he didn't have feelings for me anymore. It was one of the reasons—the main one—I'd gone with Cole. At the time, his betrayal shattered me, but the Feed had since taken away the hurt. It didn't matter anymore. But did I dare let him in again?

I could feel his eyes on me as he waited. The wait seemed very long, to the point where it would have been uncomfortable for anyone else.

And yet he sat, watching me.

Waiting.

Patient.

Still.

By this time, I'd almost forgotten what he said. Something about missing something.

"Yes," I said.

"Now you've done it." His tone was quietly playful.

I couldn't help it. I looked up at him questioningly.

"You've added a third word to your repertoire. *Hi, thanks,* and now *yes.*" His lips turned up at the corners, and the heat rushed to my face. He noticed. "At least that much hasn't changed."

I turned back to my notebook, my hands trembling.

He leaned toward me. "Now that we have our first conversation out of the way, do you want to tell me where you've been?" From the way he spoke I knew his smile was gone.

I could feel little beads of sweat form on my forehead.

"You left me. Without a word," he said. He sounded tentative, as if he were trying to keep his voice even. I took in a deep breath, but I couldn't figure out what he was feeling. There wasn't one singular emotion that was stronger than the others. "Don't you have anything to say to me?"

He waited. My heart felt like it would burst through my chest into a million little pieces, and I could see this wasn't going to work.

I started to close my book.

"Don't—" he blurted, and I froze. "Don't go. You don't have to talk to me. I'm the one who should go." His voice sounded achingly sad. I could hear him packing his bag.

Say something. Say something. "Um . . ."

Jack paused, as if further movement might stop my words.

He was the reason I came back. I couldn't scare him off. As hard as it would be to talk to him, it would be much harder to watch him walk out that door. "No," I said. I took a shaky breath. "You don't . . . have to leave. Please."

He took his book back out and put it on his desk. I followed, setting my own books out.

"Thank you," Jack whispered.

We didn't talk for the rest of the hour.

Jack didn't try to speak to me the following day. Or the day after. Or the day after that.

But he was in Mrs. Stone's classroom, in the seat next to mine, every day for an hour after school, the only sounds coming from our pencils scratching against our papers. And the days passed like this quickly. Too quickly.

I stole glances at him. Sometimes he tucked his hair

behind one ear, but mostly it hung loose around his face. Sometimes he had stubble, as if he were shaving every other day. Sometimes I was sure he could feel me staring. His lip would twitch, and I'd know he was about to turn toward me, so I would hurry and look at my paper.

And sometimes I would read the same sentence in the textbook over and over, and at the end of the hour, the only thing I'd learned was that Jack liked to tap his eraser on his desk when he was stumped, and when he would stretch forward, his shirt lifted, exposing a tiny bit of skin on his back.

I fooled myself into thinking it could go on like this indefinitely, us being together without any questions.

But on one of these afternoons, someone called Jack's name from the hallway. I fought the urge to look up, because I knew that voice. It was the same one that told me bangs were definitely "out" on my first day of middle school. Lacey Greene.

After that I'd spent the rest of sixth grade growing them out. I learned early on that it was safer for girls like Lacey Greene not to notice you. Sure enough, Lacey didn't notice me again until I started dating Jack last year.

"So, Jack, this is where you've been hiding out," she said. I couldn't see her face, but I imagined it working hard to look indifferent. I lowered my head closer to my notebook.

"Hi, Lace," Jack said. He tapped his eraser on the desk.

"What's so important that you've been skipping out on the the Ray?"

The Morning Ray was a hangout for students after school. We used to go there every day. I almost felt her eyes cutting over to me.

"Mrs. Stone said I could work on my personal essay here. For applications." *Tap, tap, tap.*

"I thought those weren't due for a few months," she said.

"That's right," Jack answered.

It was quiet for a few moments. Jack wasn't going to elaborate. I tested the air, but I couldn't really sense anything. It was more a lack of emotion than anything else.

"Just remember senior year is supposed to be fun, Jack." She paused and then added, "You used to know how to have fun."

Her voice held implications. I wondered how things had ended up between them after football camp, and if she blamed me. I could've blamed her. But it was so long ago.

"Thanks for the reminder, Lace." *Tappity tap.*

I heard her footsteps echo as she turned and walked away, and the tapping stopped. Whatever their past, there seemed to be nothing between Jack and Lacey now.

"Becks?" A different voice called from the hallway.

I looked up to find Jules standing in the doorway. She pointed to her hat, the red one I had knitted.

"I love it. Thanks."

I smiled and raised my fingers in a little wave. Jules hadn't joined me for lunch again, but she stopped by my nook nearly every day. A couple of days ago, I put the hat in a sack and gave it to her.

Jules glanced from me to Jack. "Hey, Jack," she said.

"What's up, Jules." I could hear a grin in his voice as he spoke her name, and where moments ago the air was empty, now the space around us seemed charged with something sweet. Affection, maybe. I couldn't tell if it was coming from Jack or Jules. Or both.

Something tore at my heart a little, at the thought of Jack and Jules together. Maybe I was imagining it. Tasting the air was still so new to me, I didn't know which emotions belonged to the people around me and which ones were mine.

Jules turned and left. I could've sworn her cheeks were a little flushed.

Jack shifted toward me. "So, Jules gets a smile, huh?"

I could feel his eyes on me, waiting for a response. He hadn't tried to talk to me since that first day, and his voice directed at me again did strange things to me. Made my stomach flutter. Of course, Jack had always had that power over me.

I kept my eyes down, but I couldn't stop my lips from turning upward.

"I see that," he said. Jack always saw everything.

LAST YEAR

Christmas Dance. Three months before the Feed.

Jack took me to the Christmas Dance.

It snowed the day of the dance, making the Meier

Farmhouse and Dance Hall look like something out of a painting, the lights on the roof glowing under sheets of white. And when Jack led me onto the dance floor and grasped one of my hands and tugged it up behind his neck, then placed his arm around my back, soft and low, I thought life couldn't get better.

He pulled me close against him, our hands clasped next to his chest. The cedar from the farmhouse mingled with Jack's aftershave, making a sweet, rustic scent.

"Becks, remember the first time we met?" he asked, his lips grazing my ear.

Of course I remembered. The events of that day were permanently etched into my brain. "You mean, the time you nearly beheaded me with a baseball?"

"I had to do something to get the new girl's attention."

"A simple 'hello' would have worked."

He pulled me in tighter, as if that were possible. "Why did we wait so long to do this?"

"Um, because you were making your way through the entire cheerleading squad?"

He looked at me for a few moments, then shook his head and leaned in to brush his lips along my shoulder.

I closed my eyes. If this was what I could expect for the rest of my high school years, I never wanted to graduate.

Ever.

Later that night, I was alone in the girls' bathroom. I'd just shut my stall when the bathroom doors opened. Several voices were in the middle of a conversation, and it sounded like one of the girls was fighting back sobs.

"You're seriously, like, a hundred times prettier than she is," one girl's voice sounded loudly.

"Yeah. I mean, if her dress didn't have those straps, she'd have nothing to hold it up."

My cheeks went red as I glanced down at the thin straps on my shoulders. But what were the chances they were talking about me?

"Ignore them both! You're at the Christmas Dance with Jake Wilson," another girl gushed.

I froze. I'd seen who was on Jake's arm as he entered the hall. Lacey Greene.

"Shut up, Eliza," a new voice said. Lacey. It sounded like she was talking through tears. "That doesn't help. I was supposed to be here with Jack."

Crap. They *were* talking about me and my pathetic straps.

"But you guys broke up months ago . . ." another girl said before her voice faded away.

"It was just a break, Claire, and he knew it." She sighed loudly. "I gave him everything. He told me he loved me. And the second that little slut gives him one opening, he takes off."

"She didn't—" one girl started to say, but then she stopped.

"If it makes you feel any better, Lace, he'll be over her fast. She has no backbone. She'll give it up, and he'll get tired of her, like he does everyone else. Then maybe he'll come back to you."

My hands started to shake. I wasn't just another girl; the gossip was overblown. Jack wasn't going to get tired of me. Was he? He'd told Lacey he loved her. Was she lying?

I realized I was leaning against the stall door, my hand over my heart as if I could hold it in. Even if he did tell her he loved her, he was here with me. That meant everything, didn't it?

The truth was, I didn't know. I'd never had a boyfriend, and Jack obviously had more experience than me. I didn't want to be like the others, but that didn't stop me from wanting to be with him. It didn't stop me from wanting him to want me.

I didn't have an answer for that one, but at least I could show them backbone.

I flushed the toilet and swung the door open wide, staring straight ahead to the mirrors above the sinks. Their chattering stopped immediately, and they watched in silence as I marched over, washed my hands, took my time drying them, looked in the mirror, applied lipstick, and finally made my grand exit.

I hoped they were too busy looking at my determined face to notice my wobbly knees.

Jack was waiting for me when I opened the bathroom door. He grabbed my hand and whisked me away to the dance floor again, as if we were wasting precious seconds.

I tried not to let those girls bother me. The fact that Jack had dated Lacey Greene was common knowledge. Jack had dated everybody.

Everybody. Like really, *everybody*. Crap. What was I doing?

"Jack?"

"Mmmm?"

The band was playing a softer song, mellow and slow.

"Why did you ask me out when you did?" I tried to sound casual.

"What do you mean?"

"I mean, did something specific happen to make you ask me out?"

"Yes," he said.

"What was it?" Had I thrown myself at Jack Caputo? Had I done something to get in Lacey's way?

"You remember the first game of the season?"

"Yeah," I said. It was Jack's first game as starting quarterback, the youngest starter in school history. I remembered sitting in the second row, directly behind the team bench.

"After I threw for the first touchdown of the game?"

"Yes." I still couldn't figure out where he was going with this. Had I flashed him or something, and blocked it out of my memory? I was pretty sure I wasn't holding up any large signs declaring my love or anything.

"Our defense took the field, and I was on the bench. When I turned around to look at the fans . . ." He paused.

Oh no. "What did I do?"

He smiled. "You looked at me. Not the game." He sighed, as if reliving the memory.

I felt my face scrunch up in confusion. "That's it?"

"That's it." He shrugged. "It was the first time I thought there might be a chance. I asked Jules about it."

I bit my lip. "Apparently she doesn't understand that trusty sidekicks aren't supposed to spill secrets."

In a flash, I was suspended in the air, the back of my head inches from the ground, Jack's face a breath away from mine, his lips in a wicked grin.

I gasped, more from surprise at the sudden dip than from fear.

"There are no secrets between us, Becks." His smile remained, but his eyes were intense.

I couldn't answer.

He held me there for a few seconds more, then slowly raised me up, keeping me in his arms.

I bit my lip. "Then, can I ask you something?"

We stopped dancing for a moment, and he frowned. "Uh-oh. That doesn't sound good. Shoot."

"You and Lacey . . ." My voice trailed off.

"Me and Lacey . . ." he said, waiting for me to continue.

"Did you break up with her?"

"*That's* what's bothering you? Yes, we broke up."

I thought about what I'd overheard in the girls' bathroom. "Does she . . . know that?"

Jack smiled. "I hope so. She was there."

As if the conversation were finished, Jack pulled me close and we started to dance again. Then he said in my ear, matter-of-factly, "She'll get over it."

***

When he pulled up to my house after the dance, we could see the silhouette of my father in the doorway. "I think I'll say good night here," Jack said.

"My dad's not so bad."

"Oh yeah, he was great . . . right up until the time I started dating his daughter."

I'd seen how my dad had become considerably colder toward Jack. There were little clues, like the other evening when out of nowhere he told Jack about how every football player he went to high school with had gotten fat after graduation. We'd been talking about what to make for dinner.

"Okay," I said. "Maybe next time." I leaned over to peck him on the cheek, but he grabbed my face in both of his hands and kissed me. His breath tasted like the mints the chaperones had passed out when the dance was over, and when he parted his lips against mine, I shivered, but not because of the cold. I pressed against him even more and hoped the dark inside the car obscured my dad's view.

But I knew better than to push it. As I was about to break away, Jack put his hands behind my waist and pulled me even closer, practically lifting me over the center console, so I was sitting in his lap.

I pulled back. "My dad's going to love that—"

He put his finger over my lips, cutting me off. "Please don't talk about your dad when I'm kissing you. Besides, unless he's enacted a law against it—"

"Which he may well do after tonight," I interrupted.

He smiled and then brought my face to his again for a few moments before finally releasing me.

"After that kiss, we'd better dream of the same thing tonight," he said with a smirk.

My face got even warmer, but I tried to speak in a calm voice. "I'll probably dream my usual dream, where I show up to school without any clothes on."

"Me too." Jack chuckled. I gave his shoulder a playful shove.

He popped out of the car and went around to open my door, being careful to avoid any actual contact with me as I stepped out. I waited until his car had rounded the corner before I walked up the pathway and opened our front door.

"Careful, Nikki," my dad said.

"What do you mean?"

"I just don't want to see my girl so overwhelmed."

"I'm fine, Dad," I said.

"I know," he said. "It's just that even though I'm totally old and unhip, I remember what boys in high school were like. Especially the kind like Jack Caputo."

"What kind is that?"

"The kind that doesn't even walk a girl to the door."

I rolled my eyes. "Well, he would have, but he had to go drop off his other dates. There were three of us." My dad finally cracked a smile. "Good night, old man," I said, giving him a hug.

"Wait a sec, honey. Did I do that okay?"

I pulled back. "Do what okay?" It hit me then that this was my first dance since my mom died. I felt a little guilty that I hadn't realized it before. It was just that the night was so perfect. Before he could explain, I said, "Yes. You did great."

"Night, Nikki."

The next morning, I found a note in my jacket pocket. I unfolded it and read two words, written in Jack's handwriting.

Ever Yours.

SIX

NOW

My bedroom. Four and a half months left.

I walked into my house after school with a smile on my face. Even the smallest interaction with Jack, and the fact that he noticed my blush, was enough to send me into orbit.

But as I got closer to my bedroom, the mark on my shoulder began to tingle.

Cole was here.

I opened my bedroom door slowly.

"It's been over a month, Nik." Cole was sitting on my bed, strumming his guitar. And as usual, I tried to ignore him. There was nothing I could do about his visits, but that didn't mean I had to make it easy for him. Without looking at him, I took my books out of my bag and placed them on my desk, turned the lamp on, and opened my notebook.

I scratched my mark.

He strummed a little louder, but I still didn't turn. "You won't last. You must see that."

"Find somebody else to entertain you," I said.

"There is no one else."

I turned a page in my notebook and started writing again. "There's always someone else. You've been Feeding off Forfeits for hundreds of years. Get a new one."

"You don't give my job enough credit. It's really hard to convince a girl to follow me. The average pickup lines don't work so well. 'Hey, wanna get coffee? And then spend an eternity getting the life force sucked out of you?' They don't go for it. Think about it, Nik. Would you have come with me if it weren't for Jack being such a—"

"Don't blame Jack," I said, even though I wondered if deep down, a tiny part of me wanted to blame him too.

"You're still defending him?" His voice bounced off the walls, seeming extra loud. And then he started strumming again. "He left you before you ever left him. He'd never take you back."

The words stung. "I don't want him to take me back."

"You don't have to lie to me," he said. He knew me too well.

I swiveled around in my chair. "I'm serious. You're right. He deserves better."

"You expect me to believe you? You would choose the pain of a Return, and for . . . what? Just to see him? For a few moments? Not to get with him?"

I nodded defiantly. Besides, Jack wouldn't want to get with *me*. Cole was right. He'd left me first.

Cole sighed. "Then you'll get hurt. Again. And so will he. You were broken before I ever took you to the Everneath. Remember how you were when you showed up on my doorstep? That had nothing to do with me. You came broken and that was the fault of this world. Not mine."

I nodded again, a little less aggressively. "Why do you care if I get hurt?"

All he said was, "I hate to see it. Whether you go with me or not, I don't like you getting hurt." But his face seemed to say more. As if there were something he wasn't telling me.

Before I could ask him about it, his iPhone vibrated in his pocket. He pulled it out, read the screen, and then walked over to the window. "We'll finish this later."

"Tell me why you care," I said.

He put his hands on the windowsill. "Because it's you. Despite what you think of me, your pain will always be my pain."

"There has to be more to it than that. What aren't you telling me, Cole?"

He grinned. "How are you so good at reading me when you can't read anyone else around you?" He sighed, and as he climbed out the window, he said, "I love it."

He pulled the window down before I could say anything.

I slammed my book shut, frustrated. He practically admitted he was keeping something from me, but what was it? Why did he care if Jack hurt me? Why was he hiding something from me when my fate was already sealed?

I closed my eyes and put my head in my hands. Cole's visits drained me, but right now he held all the cards because he had all the information, and I didn't know anything.

I raised my head. That was my problem—I didn't know enough about the Everneath and the Everlivings. Cole obviously had secrets he was keeping from me, and I could only think of one reason he would do that—he had a weak point. Cole valued his power. I had to assume he would conceal anything that posed a threat to that power.

I put my books away and grabbed my coat. I didn't know if finding out more about Cole and the Everneath would get me anywhere, but I had to take a chance.

I decided to follow him.

There was only one way out of our neighborhood, so it wasn't hard to guess which way Cole went.

The evening air had an early winter bite to it, and I wondered how Cole could stand riding his bike in this cold. Once I got out to the main road, I looked toward the left, the direction that would lead to town, and saw the unmistakable narrow taillights of a motorcycle. It had to be him.

I kept my distance. I wouldn't learn anything if Cole saw me. The road was long and straight, and I didn't have trouble until we got closer to town and he made a few sharp turns, one right after the other. I lost sight of the motorcycle, but I kept going in the direction of Main Street, keeping my eyes glued to every side street and every alley, so I almost missed his bike.

It was in plain view, in the parking lot of a convenience store right off Main.

Not just any convenience store. *My* convenience store.

The Shop-n-Go. The same place where the Everneath had spit me out. I flipped my car around and pulled over about a block down the road, then killed the engine and crossed the street on foot. I was so concerned about being seen, I actually tiptoed.

As I got closer, I could see Cole through the store window, near the entrance. I crouched down behind a wall that separated the shop from the dry cleaner's next door, and watched.

Cole pushed the door open and came outside, and I ducked down even further. But I could still see him. He leaned back against the brick wall of the store as if he were waiting for something. He took the guitar pick out of his pocket and stared at his hand as he rolled the pick over his fingers. It was a typical Cole move. I'd seen him do it many times since the night we met.

I was close enough to hear him breathe. What was he doing here?

The door opened again, and I heard a man's voice.

"It's done." He was talking to Cole. The voice was familiar. I couldn't see him—he was behind a pillar.

"Good." Cole's voice. "Keep it up."

"Why?" The other voice sounded exasperated. "We're already ahead of our quota. And it's not getting easier. This guy took a lot more persuading than usual. Poor bastard was

clinging to life. Was convinced he had a granddaughter somewhere out there."

"I don't care. If we fall behind, the queen's people will start
asking questions," Cole said. "And if that happens, that means
more attention on us, and a better chance someone will find
out about Nikki and report back to the queen."

At the mention of my name, I took in a quick breath, and
then covered my mouth so they wouldn't hear me.

"Won't it look suspicious if we flood the queen with food?"

"No. She'll be too high on energy to question anything. It's
only when she's hungry that she gets curious."

They were quiet for a moment, and I silently prayed they
would keep talking.

"Fine," the other voice said. "It had better pay off."

"It'll be worth it."

I heard one of them sigh but didn't know which one. "So
when's it going to be your turn to bring an offering?"

I heard Cole's unmistakable chuckle. "When you find
someone as strong as Nikki, I'll do the same for you."

"You saying Meredith isn't strong?"

They both laughed at this.

Meredith. She'd been a year older than me at school. She'd
dated Maxwell—the Dead Elvises' second guitarist—and
become his Forfeit. What had happened to her?

Their voices were growing softer, and I realized they
were probably walking away toward the parking lot. Then
the engines of two bikes roared to life, and they peeled away.

One went up the street, and the other passed me on the way down. I pressed even farther back in the shadows but I could still see his face when he went by, confirming what I'd already guessed.

It was Maxwell.

Once I couldn't hear their bikes anymore, I stood up and looked at the shop. What did they mean, Meredith *wasn't* strong? I wondered where Meredith had ended up, if she was still alive, if she had come back to the Surface, or if she was deep in the Tunnels. And why didn't Maxwell make her the same offer Cole made me?

Right now my only clue was the Shop-n-Go.

I went inside. The clerk at the register looked like he was a couple of years older than me. He didn't even glance up from the paper he was reading.

I walked toward the back, trying to see anything out of place, any clue as to what they were doing. The only thing I noticed was the strong smell of liquor. When I rounded the final corner, to the place where I'd landed when I'd returned, I found nothing. No person covered in sludge. No doorway going down. It looked the same as before. It could've been any spot in any convenience store, except the smell of alcohol seemed to be strongest here.

I crouched down and touched the tile, wondering how in the world I'd passed through it when I Returned. It felt dry and cold, just like it looked.

But as I was close to the ground, something caught my eye

on the floor under the nearest rack of goodies. A brown bag, concealing what looked like a bottle. It was turned on its side, surrounded by a puddle of light brown liquid. The last of the contents dripped slowly out.

I stood up and searched the shop. It was empty of customers, except for me. I crouched back down and looked at the bottle, which had to have been dropped recently. Someone was just here, minutes ago. It couldn't have been Max's or Cole's. They rarely drank anything harder than beer. They didn't need to.

I didn't know what it meant, if anything. But whoever dropped the bottle, he wasn't here anymore. I walked up to the counter, to where the clerk was still reading his paper, sucking on a lollipop. His name tag said EZRA.

"Excuse me. Did you see anybody in here?"

He took the sucker out of his mouth, but he didn't look up. "When?"

"Just now? In the back?"

"Nope."

I watched him. I probably could've broken out in a full-on tap dance right then and he wouldn't have noticed.

"Are you sure? Maybe a guy with a paper sack, with a drink in it?"

He finally looked up, totally bored with the conversation. "You mean the old homeless guy?"

Now we were getting somewhere. I tried not to sound crazy. "I don't know. Did he have a bottle?"

He gave me an exasperated smirk, like I wasn't making sense, which I guess I wasn't. "There was an old guy, came in with another guy a few minutes ago. But they left."

Another guy. Maybe he meant Maxwell.

"Was the other guy younger? And tall? With black hair? And a black jacket . . . ?" My voice trailed off as the guy slowly wrinkled his forehead.

"What are you, a detective or something?"

Yes. A seventeen-year-old detective. I smiled and tried to look normal. "I'm just looking for my friend."

He narrowed his eyes, then went back to his paper. "They came in and looked around. Then they left. Didn't buy anything." He put the sucker back in his mouth.

"They *both* left?" I'd only seen Maxwell come out of the shop. No old guy.

"You don't see them here anymore, do you?" The guy was definitely done with me. He put in his earbuds and pulled out an iPod.

"Thanks for your time," I said, even though it was obvious the guy couldn't hear me. I left the store and climbed back into my car, my breath coming out in foggy puffs.

An old man who may or may not have disappeared, and Maxwell talking about an offering. It sounded so ominous. Or it sounded like nothing.

My brain was spinning as I drove home. I tried to make sense of it all, but there were still so many questions, and I didn't know if anything I'd learned could help me, but what had I expected when I followed Cole? That he would lead me to a magic key that would unlock my salvation?

I wished I knew exactly what I was looking for.

One thing I did know—Cole didn't want the queen to find out about me. I tucked this piece of information in my back pocket. Maybe it would come in handy.

SEVEN

NOW

School. Four months, one week left.

An entire week passed and I still couldn't get the Shop-n-Go out of my head, so I was a little flustered when Mrs. Stone asked about my paper in her room after school.

"Do you have the theme of your thesis picked out, Miss Beckett?" she said as she took the seat in front of me.

Jack leaned closer. It was crazy how any movement from him sent shivers down my spine.

"Yes," I said.

"What have you decided on? Modern-day parable, or modern-day myth?"

"I decided to write a myth."

"Have you figured out a topic? A moral conundrum?"

"Yes."

"What is it?"

I heard Jack's chair creak.

"It's about how there's no such thing as redemption,"

I whispered. "How you deserve what you get, and no higher power can save you."

Mrs. Stone didn't answer immediately. The only sound in the room came from my own breathing. "What about heroes?"

I hunched over and scribbled a few lines on my notebook. "There are no heroes." Sure, it wasn't an optimistic paper, but it was the only thing I could write passionately about.

She was quiet for a moment again. When she spoke, her voice was gentle. "Okay. I'm excited to see what you put together."

I nodded.

"And, Mr. Caputo? Everything going well with the personal essay?"

I could only assume he nodded, because Mrs. Stone returned to the front of the classroom. My right hand started to tremble, and I clenched my pencil and began scribbling.

"You don't really believe that, do you?" Jack's voice was soft.

I lifted my head, allowing my eyes to meet his for the first time in weeks. "It doesn't matter what I believe." I looked down at my notebook.

"Wait," he said.

I turned back. "What?"

He shrugged, then spoke in a low murmur. "Just stop hiding behind your hair for a minute."

I closed my eyes, but I didn't turn away. "You're making things difficult, Jack Caputo," I whispered.

"At least you remember my name."

I remembered everything. The first time he called me his

girlfriend. The first time he told me he loved me. The first time I started to question whether or not I'd be able to hold on to him. The first time I knew I had to come back to see him again, at whatever cost.

LAST YEAR

January. Two months before the Feed.

I was Jack's and he was mine. I was getting used to the idea.

"Three whole months, Becks. You've been with Jack Caputo for *three whole months*," Jules said to me in between bites of her turkey sandwich. "What are you doing to celebrate?"

"I don't know," I said, tracing the wood grains of the cafeteria table with my finger. "I don't think Jack's the type who keeps track of anniversaries. Besides, three months isn't exactly a long time."

Jules flipped her hair over her shoulder. "Are you kidding? He's never admitted to having a girlfriend before you, so three months is like fifty years in Jack Caputo years."

I rolled my eyes. "So now we're counting in dog years?"

Jules gave me a knowing look, and we both giggled. "So, Becks, is tonight . . . *the night*?"

She paused, and I caught her meaning. "No!" My cheeks flushed, and I lowered my voice. "No. No, nothing like that has . . . no."

She raised her eyebrows. "Don't hold out on me. It's Jack Caputo."

"Stop saying his first and last name, like he's some sort of god."

"He is. At least in this school. And mythological beings like him need the physical pleasures of—"

"Stop!" I said, cutting her off. "I'm not talking about this anymore."

She gave me a disappointed look. "Fine. Just promise you'll tell me everything."

"I promise."

After lunch, I took the route that would lead me past Jack's locker. When I turned the corner, I stopped dead in my tracks.

Jack was leaning back against his locker, his head resting on the metal, his eyes squeezed shut. His face was tense. But that's not the reason I stopped.

Lacey Greene was standing right by him, close, leaning her shoulder against the locker next to his and talking animatedly. The way she was standing, she was almost forcing his arm to touch her chest. Even I wouldn't have stood like that with Jack.

Then again, maybe that was my problem. Whatever she was talking about, it was definitely not a good time for me to interrupt. But I was his girlfriend. If anybody could interrupt, wouldn't it be me?

I gripped the strap of my bag that was over my shoulder and walked toward them. The closer I got, the more I could hear Lacey.

". . . so then *I* suggested each spirit team member could be assigned *two* players, and that would cover every—" Her voice cut off when she saw me.

At the silence, Jack opened his eyes. His gaze met mine, and his face broke into a wide grin, the tension that was there moments ago melting away.

"Sounds great, Lace," he said absentmindedly, keeping his eyes on me. "Do it."

He pushed off the locker and grabbed me in a tight embrace.

"Hi, you," he said. The words came out in a contented sigh. Lacey no longer existed for him, but I had a clear view of her behind Jack, scowling. I squeezed my eyes shut and buried my face in his shoulder, inhaling the clean, leathery scent of his jacket, mixed with something else that was . . . so Jack.

"Hi," I said back.

He released me, but only a little, so he could see my face.

"So, we celebrating tonight?" he said, the grin still in place.

His hair flopped over his eyes, and he ran a hand through it so my heart flitted inside my chest.

Celebrating. I narrowed my eyes. "Did Jules talk to you?"

"She reminded me it's our three-month anniversary, and girls like stuff like that, don't they?"

I remembered what Jules had said at lunch, and studied my hands, which were suddenly fidgeting. "No. Not me. I'm fine, um, not doing anything. At all."

He chuckled and put his arm around my neck, steering

me down the hall. "That's what I love about you. So easy to please." His nose touched below my ear.

I gave a nervous giggle and couldn't get rid of the blush as he drove me home. When we reached my driveway, he squeezed my hand. "How about we go night skiing?"

Huh. Boots, layers of clothes, awkward skis. Perfect. "That sounds great."

"Good. I'll pick you up in a half hour."

I climbed out of the car feeling slightly relieved. As I walked up the sidewalk to my front door, Jack rolled down his window. "Becks!"

I turned around.

"Bring a change of clothes tonight. My uncle has a lodge on the hill he said I could use anytime. We'll stop there for hot chocolate afterward."

Crap. I forced a smile and waved as he took off. It was times like these I missed my mom the most. But even before the crash, would I have talked to her about this kind of stuff? She'd been open about most things, but loudly quiet when it came to sex. Maybe she had been waiting until I got older, and never got the chance.

Later that evening, I'd skied the hill until I thought my ears would fall off from the cold. Jack kept suggesting we head in, but I insisted on skiing until every last light on the hill was out. By the time we made it to his uncle's lodge, it felt like it was two o'clock in the morning. But it was only ten. My curfew wasn't for three more hours.

"You can go change in the bedroom, and I'll try to start a fire," Jack said as he rubbed his hands together and searched for the light switches.

"Great," I whispered. I clutched my bag of clothes and tiptoed across the orange shag carpet of the living room and through the bedroom door.

Once I'd shut the door behind me, the trembling began, and not just from the cold. I dumped my clothes out on the bed. Pink yoga pants and a white sweatshirt.

"Just breathe," I whispered to myself.

I peeled off my freezing ski suit and the layers of thermal cotton underneath, then rubbed my arms to get the circulation going. I was in my bra. And there was only one thin door between me and Jack.

I hurried and pulled on my fluffy rabbit outfit. My feet were still cold from the mountain, so I kept my thick green wool socks on. Catching a peek at myself in the old mirror hanging on the wall, I nearly choked out a laugh. After hours stuck under a ski hat, my dark hair now looked like it had been sucked into the vortex of a tornado, and the clothes made me resemble a cotton-candy marshmallow. It made me relax enough to open the door.

When I emerged from the bedroom, Jack was crouching next to the fire, his back to me and a mug of hot chocolate in his hand.

"That looks cozy," I said in a timid voice.

He turned at the sound and—taking in my appearance— immediately spit hot chocolate all over.

"What?" I demanded.

With an obvious effort to compose himself, he forced his lips into a frown and wiped his chin with the back of his hand. "Breathtaking."

I raised an eyebrow, and his lips started to quiver, and then there was no stopping him. The laughter came in waves.

"Well, that's not exactly the reaction I was going for," I said.

"Isn't it?" he said, gasping for breath.

I put my hand on my hip and tapped my foot as he inhaled deeply and rubbed his eye with the palm of his hand. "Finished?" I asked.

He shook his head. "I love you."

"I'm sorry?"

"You heard me." He stood and walked toward me.

I glanced down at my sweats, and then back at his face. "Did you not notice my getup?"

He halved the distance between us. "Oh yeah. I noticed," he said, like it was the sexiest thing he'd ever seen. His lips curled up into a smile.

"Okay, so that's not the reaction I was going for either," I said, taking a small step backward as he closed the gap between us.

He grabbed my hands in his and his grin disappeared. "Becks. I think I know what you're worried about, but I meant what I said. I love you. And I would never push you."

My entire body turned red. "But don't you mythological higher beings"—I tried to remember how Jules had put it—"need . . . the . . . um . . ."

Jack looked confused, and then he chuckled. "Please don't even try to finish that sentence."

The nerves had taken over, and there seemed to be a short between my brain and my mouth. "But you've had . . . the . . . I mean, I know I'm not . . . the . . . first . . ."

"Becks. Please." He pulled me over onto the couch, in front of the fire. "Look, my history isn't exactly a secret." He shrugged. "I'd change it if I could."

I wrapped the drawstring of my sweats around my index finger. "Okay," I mumbled.

"Don't hide your face from me." He placed his fingers lightly under my chin and urged my gaze up. "It's you. And I don't want to screw it up."

Could he be serious? I didn't know whether to believe him or to assume I really did look that undesirable. Jack had a rep for easy one-nighters. How long before he grew tired of waiting for me?

It didn't matter. Right at that moment, I knew my dad was right. I was totally overwhelmed by Jack Caputo. There would be no going back.

I took his arm and put it around me so I could curl into his chest and hear his heartbeat, which despite his calm demeanor, was racing. He held me close and tight, as if he were tucking a football.

He pressed his lips into my hair. "I love you, Becks. I've never felt like this."

I nodded against him, still unsure if I could believe him.

I thought about Lacey and the way she was standing next to him. "You've never been in love?"

He let out a quiet breath, and I felt him shake his head. "Easy to say. Harder to feel." He ran his fingers through my hair and tucked a few strands behind my ear. With a lighter voice, he said, "Out of curiosity, what would you have said if I wanted to . . ."

"I would've said no."

"Yeah?"

I nodded. "I'm glad you didn't, because that would have been awkward."

His chest shuddered with laughter.

EIGHT

NOW

The soup kitchen. Four months left.

My days on the Surface started to stack up and run together, so I wasn't sure how many Saturdays had passed before I saw Mary at the soup kitchen again. I'd been looking for her as I ladled chili into soup bowls, because I wanted to ask her about that Priscilla's daughter the braid girl was telling me about.

My need to help her was stronger than I could explain. It's not like she was the first senile person I'd ever met, but ever since she told me I'd broken a heart, I felt a sort of connection to her, as if her dementia gave her a unique insight into people's souls.

I knew that wasn't possible.

When I'd served about half the tub of soup, I saw her in the line. As she reached for a tray, an old silver bracelet slid down her arm and settled on her wrist. It was the only jewelry she wore and looked heavy on her frail wrist. It must've been an heirloom or something.

"Hi, Nikki," she said when she reached my station.

I didn't remember telling her my name. "Hi, Mary. How are you today?"

"Can you eat with me?"

"Um . . ." I glanced at Christopher right next to me, and he nodded. "Sure, I guess."

Maybe he considered this another aspect of service, beyond ladling soup. I dished myself a bowl and followed Mary to one of the long rectangular tables in the dining hall. We took the two seats on the end, facing each other.

"I'm sorry about the other day," she said. "The little scene I made."

"It's okay."

"I just . . . sometimes I get confused." She broke her bread into tiny little pieces and placed them in her soup.

"I understand."

She looked at me with strangely hopeful eyes. "Do you?"

"Sure, Mary." I considered telling her my great-aunt had Alzheimer's, but decided not to. Maybe she'd be offended if I compared them.

She waited for me to say something else, so I felt it was a good time to ask her. "Mary, one of the girls here told me you were looking for somebody's daughter?"

Her eyes darted back and forth, as if she were nervous about being overheard. I wondered if it was a secret.

I lowered my voice. "Is that right?"

She didn't answer, so I pushed a little. "I could try to help you find what you're looking for. Was it Penelope's daughter?"

Mary went from looking frightened to suddenly trying to stifle a laugh.

I guess it did sound a little ridiculous. Once she'd regained composure, she said, "I don't remember anything about that."

"Oh." She was quiet again. Obviously if she knew something about it, she wasn't going to offer it. I changed the subject. "So, where are you from?"

"Here. Park City."

"Do you have family?"

"Just my mom."

I tried not to look skeptical. She had to be at least eighty years old. Maybe she meant her mother was still here in spirit. Or that she'd been raised by a single mom. I changed the subject again, because I didn't want to be the one to break the news that her mother was probably dead.

"That's a pretty bracelet," I said, pointing to her wrist. "Where did you get it?"

She deftly moved her hands under the table, a reflex action. "It's been passed down through my family for generations." She took a bite of soup and roll. "To the women," she added. "But you can't have it."

"Oh. Well, it's beautiful," I said.

The lunch line was starting to thin out. Mary swallowed, took a drink of her water, set the cup down, and leaned forward. Her hands started to shake. "Help me, Nikki."

The statement came out of nowhere. "Um, okay. What can I do?"

"I'm confused. I was ready to go. And now I don't know what to do." Was she talking about dying? "What's waiting for me?" she asked.

I slowly shook my head. "Honestly, I don't know."

"But what do you believe?"

A year ago, my Christian upbringing would have told me the answer: paradise. When I used to ask my dad where he thought my mother was, he would tell me she was above, looking down on us. But now that sounded like another lie people tell themselves to feel better. I knew nothing of heaven.

"I don't know what's waiting for you," I said. Her face fell. "But it has to be better than this life," I added. "It just has to be."

Her shoulders relaxed, and I realized how tense she had been. "Thank you."

As we were cleaning up after the lunch rush, the braid girl came over to me. "Sorry you got stuck with Mary today."

I bent down with a dustpan to scoop up some crumbs. "It was fine. I feel sorry for her. I tried to ask her about Penelope's daughter, but she just seemed confused."

"Persephone," braid girl said.

I popped up. "What did you say?"

Braid girl shoved a bite of leftover roll into her mouth. "It was *Persephone's* daughter," she said with a full mouth. "I remembered. Only she said it all formal, like *Daughters of Persephone.*"

She tied her trash bag and took it out back, and I was left in the middle of the floor, holding my dustpan.

Daughters of Persephone?

Too weird.

The following week, I couldn't get Mary and the Daughters of Persephone out of my head. When I got to the soup kitchen on Saturday, Mary had already been through the line and was sitting at a table with a woman I didn't recognize. She looked like she was my father's age, maybe a little older. Her clothes were the kind I'd expect at an art gallery, not a shelter kitchen.

I waved to Mary. She looked at me, but she didn't wave back. Her head was lowered, and her shoulders sagged as the woman sitting across from her did most of the talking.

I slid into my place by Christopher. "Sorry I'm late."

"No problem. I'll just dock your pay," Christopher said with a little wink.

I served up a couple of bowls, but I could tell I had missed the lunch rush. "Who's the woman sitting with Mary?" I asked Christopher.

He looked up from his bread basket. "Don't know. Haven't seen her here before."

"She looks familiar, though, doesn't she?"

He squinted. "Maybe a little. Something about her, but I don't think she's ever been here before. Look"—he pointed with a piece of bread—"she's not eating. Maybe she's just here to visit Mary. Many of our patrons still have family, you know."

I watched for a few minutes. Mary wasn't talking much, except to give a one-word response or to nod. I glanced at the tray in front of her. She hadn't touched it. I noticed Mary's wrist. She wasn't wearing her bracelet.

She didn't look happy, and I hoped the woman would leave soon so I could talk to Mary and make sure she was good. Toward the end of the lunch hour, the woman stood. Mary leaned toward her, as if to hug her, but the woman turned and walked away before she could. Once she was gone, I went to Mary's table.

"Can I sit down?" I asked. She looked at me and motioned toward the chair. "Are you okay, Mary?" I said.

"Yeah, I guess."

"Who was that woman here with you?" I asked. "Was she family?"

Mary looked at me warily, and nodded. "She's my mother." She slumped a little in her seat and looked at my face. "You don't believe me," she said.

I put my elbows on the table and tried to sound understanding. "It's not that, Mary. We all get confused."

Mary nodded. "She's mad at me."

"Why?"

"I have something that belongs to her. That's the only reason she came. It's the only way I could get her to talk to me."

"What do you have?"

She took her spoon and dragged it through the soup. "I'm not supposed to talk about it."

"Why not?"

"I've already disappointed her enough."

I reached over and put my hand on her arm. I understood about disappointing people. "Friends forgive each other."

She looked up from her bowl. "I don't think you believe that any more than I do."

I drew my hand back, and Mary stood and grabbed her tray.

"Wait," I said. "I wanted to ask you about the Daughters of Persephone. Maybe I could—"

"Stop trying to help," she interrupted. She turned around and took her tray over to the garbage. I sighed. Maybe she was beyond help.

NINE

NOW

My bedroom. Four months left.

$\mathcal{T}$ime's flying for you, Nik." Cole was sitting in the darkest corner of my bedroom, his guitar lying silent beside him. I wasn't sure why he only ever showed up in my room. I didn't complain anymore. His visits were my chance to learn more about the rules of the Everneath.

The scar on my shoulder began to prickle, as if it were waking up. It did that whenever Cole was around. I wondered if the Shade inside me could feel the presence of an Everliving.

Cole couldn't know I thought about any of this. I nodded and flipped through my notebook on top of my desk, trying to fight the urge to go sit next to him. Now that I was prepared for the pull between us, it was easier to ignore it, but it never went away.

"Is it everything you hoped it would be?" Cole said.

"It's everything I allowed myself to hope for," I qualified.

He sighed, then grabbed his guitar and picked out a classical melody. I thought it was Bach, but I wasn't sure. "Where's your family?"

So we were going for small talk now? I turned around. "My dad's at his campaign headquarters and Tommy's at my aunt Grace's."

He picked through another few measures of the melody. "So you came back to be with your family and friends, and yet you sit alone most nights."

I turned back to my desk.

"It doesn't have to be like this, Nik." He leaned his head against the wall with a soft thud. "I can take you now. You've only seen the Caverns and the Tunnels—and yes, those places are all about the awful—but the rest of the Everneath isn't like that. It's like the Elysian Fields."

I gave him a quizzical look. "Elysian Fields?"

He rolled his eyes. "You haven't been doing your homework. The Fields are a place of light, of happiness, where nobody is dying the slow death of mortality. And all of the good emotions inside you are expressed outwardly in your surroundings. *I* think it's heaven."

"Except for the part where you have to steal energy from other humans to survive."

He was quiet for a moment. When he spoke again, his voice was muted. "It's a small price to pay for heaven."

"Show me," I said.

He blinked. "What?"

"Show me. Like you showed me the Tunnels. Only this time, show me the Fields."

He glanced away as he considered it, and then shook his head. "It's too hard."

"Why?"

"Because I'd have to use my own energy." When I protested he continued. "Too much time has passed since I've been in the Everneath. I don't have any extra energy to waste giving you the five-cent tour."

His refusal made me want to see the Fields even more. I sat down next to him on the floor. "Please, Cole. Help me see what I'll be missing."

He frowned and sighed. "Enough with the sad eyes. I'll do it. But it'll have to be a quick glance only."

I nodded.

"Hold still," he said as he brought his hands to my head and placed them on either side. "You don't have to hold your breath, Nik."

I hadn't realized I was. I let out a sigh and heard him chuckle softly, and then my bedroom melted away. I was standing in an open field, surrounded by light. A soft breeze with clean air—not the dank stuff in the Caverns, but clean, crisp air—ruffled through my hair. I looked at my hands. They were no longer sickly pale.

I filled my lungs with air, expanding them to capacity, and then even further. I was so caught up in the delicious air, I forgot where I was, or how I'd gotten there. All I knew was that my bare feet longed to be running. I took off toward the center of the field, the length of my stride growing with each step until I thought one more step and I would be able to push off from the ground and never land. It was the sweetest feeling, as if nothing would ever burden me again. One more step and I would fly.

But I didn't get to try. Too soon, the field disappeared and I was back in my bedroom, acutely aware of how hard my chair felt against my body and how heavy the air was here. It was like coming down from a high.

Cole struggled for breath beside me. He lay down on his back, put his hands over his eyes, and tried to even his breathing. He looked like he'd just crossed the finish line of a marathon.

"Are you okay?" I asked, distracted. I wanted back inside the vision.

"Nothing a little mouth-to-mouth won't cure," he said, but he couldn't muster the energy to laugh at his own joke. "You're no good for me, Nik," he said in between gasps.

"What do you mean?"

His breathing slowed a little and he looked up at me. "I can't say no to you."

I scoffed. "If that were true," I said, "you'd find a way to let me stay here. For good." I knew it was impossible; when you choose to be a Forfeit, you belong to the Everneath, and the pact is as strong as any other force in the universe. Defeating it would be like defying gravity, a power beyond Cole. Maybe I said it to show how weak he really was.

He closed his eyes. "You know I can't challenge the Shades."

He was telling the truth. The Shades only cared about the harvesting of energy, and in the Everneath, their word was law.

"The vision . . . did it work?" Cole asked hesitantly. He breathed easier now, and sat up next to me, watching me for my answer.

"I saw the Fields."

He waited as if he expected me to go on and on. When I didn't he said, "And were they as amazing as I told you?"

"Better," I said. I didn't continue, because I wasn't sure of my own strength. If I could press a button right now, here in my room, that would take me straight to the Fields, would I be able to refuse? I didn't know.

"So are you coming with me?"

"Would I have to drain people?" I reminded myself it always came back to this.

"Why do you get hung up on things that don't matter?" He grunted in frustration. "Nik, if you come with me, together we could make a run for the throne, and that would mean you wouldn't have to drain people."

I raised my eyebrows skeptically.

"Other people would do it for you if you were the queen. That's the power of the High Court. The queen's deepest fantasies become reality. She never has to search for her own food."

"You're saying slaves would do it for us."

He nodded. I thought back to the night at the Shop-n-Go,

how Maxwell had talked about making offerings to keep the queen and her court fed. How the old man, who may have disappeared that night, was reluctant to go.

"Do you have to do that for your queen? Do you . . . bring her sacrifices?"

He hesitated and then narrowed his eyes, and I worried I'd said too much, but then he gave me a mischievous grin. "I'd tell you if I could, but I can't. I mean, I'm physically bound not to tell you. Unless, that is, you say you'll come with me. Then I can tell you everything."

I let out a small sigh. I didn't want him to know I'd seen him at the Shop-n-Go, because I wanted to learn more first.

"Look, Nik. I can't lose you. We can be partners. With you by my side, and with the band backing us, we could take over. I want you by my side in the High Court."

"What does that even mean? We'd be . . . together? Like, *together*, together?"

Cole gave a sly smile. "We'd rule hand in hand. And as far as being *together*, we'd be as together as you'd allow."

Annoyingly, my cheeks got all warm, and I turned away, frustrated at my reaction. I stood and went over to my desk chair to sit down.

Cole chuckled. He pushed himself off the floor and walked closer to me, and the Shade at my shoulder pulled toward him. I wanted to hit it.

"Stay over there," I said.

"Why?" He held his hands up, all innocent-like. "Does my

nearness affect you? That's what happens when you spend a century with someone."

I had to keep him away, so when he'd gotten close enough, I scraped my fingers down the strings of his guitar, the resulting noise loud and disjointed. Anger flashed in his eyes as he jerked it away from me. Finally, a true reaction.

I smiled as if I had discovered some sort of weakness. "Leave me alone, Cole. I may be bound to the Tunnels, but I'm not bound to you anymore. You have no power over me."

"You have no idea what I can do," he said.

I leaned in closer and lowered my voice. "I've been with you for a hundred years. I know exactly what you can do."

"Did you know I could still Feed off you?"

Before I could stop him, he grabbed behind my head, pulled me toward him, and kissed me. For a moment, I didn't fight it. For a moment, I let him steal the deepest layers of my pain. Desperation replaced reason in my head. He seemed surprised that I hadn't pulled back, and he briefly opened his eyes, searching my face. I didn't move, and he kissed me again.

The moment became longer. With the touch of his lips, he literally removed my doubt, my guilt, my fears. I felt good for the first time in a long time. Cole could shield me from the pain of this world, and for that moment, I wanted to go with him.

No good-byes. No second chances. No disappointing the people I loved. Or at least I'd be in a place where I didn't care if I disappointed anyone.

But it wasn't real. And I'd been down that road before. I knew where it led. With my lips against his, I reached a conclusion I'd been trying to avoid: the easy path in this whole mess would be to go with Cole, and I couldn't let myself make the easy choice. I had to make the *right* choice.

With all the strength I could muster, I pushed him away from me.

His face was as shocked as mine felt, and his cocky grin had disappeared completely. "Nik . . . I—"

I held my hand up. "Don't. That had nothing to do with you." I forced myself to look him in the eye. I spoke deliberately. "It will never happen again."

His face grew hard, and he gave me a smile that made him look sinister. "We'll see about that." The smile stayed on Cole's face as he climbed out my window. "One of these days you should sample the emotions floating all around you. If you let me, I can show you how."

"I'd rather produce my own. I'll never steal from others."

"Never say never, Nik. I won't." He leaned his head against the window frame. "I'm not giving up on you." He shoved the window down and disappeared.

My fingers clenched the edge of my desk. His words sounded like a threat.

TEN

NOW

Mrs. Stone's classroom. Four months left.

The following day, Jack and I were sitting alone in Mrs. Stone's classroom, working, when Cole made good on his promise. A boy, maybe a year older than me, showed up in the doorway. He was tall enough that with a few more inches, his head could have touched the top of the frame.

Jack looked up from his desk, his pencil halted midword.

"Nik? Is that you?" The boy's voice wasn't familiar.

His face wasn't either. He looked like a typical teenager, with thick black hair that was purposely mussed up. His lanky body leaned against the doorjamb, casually. His ears had several piercings, as did his eyebrows, which framed dark, familiar eyes.

Eyes that didn't belong here. Eyes that I would know anywhere.

It was Cole. No question. But he had somehow changed his appearance, down to his hair and his skin.

Whatever he'd done, though, he couldn't change his dark eyes.

"Don't you remember me?" His lips curled upward. "Neal? From the party?"

I could feel Jack's gaze from beside me. I narrowed my eyes at Cole and shook my head.

"I'm not surprised, really. You probably don't remember much from that night," he said.

Mrs. Stone was out of the classroom. Cole probably timed it that way. I said a silent wish that she would return soon.

"You must have me confused with someone else," I said in a quiet voice.

"I'm sure I don't," Cole said. "Nikki Beckett. Seventeen. Sweet. Great little tattoo on her shoulder that tastes faintly of . . . charcoal."

My face flamed red and I could feel the tears behind my eyes, but they didn't come. What would Jack be thinking? I could hear him tapping his foot beside me.

"Go away," I whispered.

"That's not a nice way to treat an old friend. I go to school here now. I'm going to graduate someday, just like you." He took a few steps forward. "I'm gonna clean myself up. Just like you."

I could sense Jack shifting in his seat next to me. I bit my lower lip, leaned down, and shoved my books into my backpack.

"You're not giving up, are you, Nik?" Cole sang out, his voice an eerie melody.

I hoisted my bag over my shoulder, lowered my head, and scrambled to the door. He blocked the exit.

"Sorry, Nik," he whispered, barely audible. "You forced my hand."

"Let me go, *Neal*," I said, using his fake name.

"If only it were that easy."

"Let her by," Jack called out from his seat at the back.

Cole set his gaze on Jack, a snide lip curl on his face. I knew that look.

I put my hand on his arm. "Don't—"

"Quiet, Nik," Cole cut me off, keeping his piercing gaze on Jack. "Listen, friend. Little Nikki here doesn't want me to let her go. Trust me. She likes a guy to take charge."

Jack pushed his chair back, and I knew I had to do something. I ducked my head and threw my weight against Cole's arm, barreling my way past.

I didn't stop running until I had reached my little red, rusted Rabbit. Once I was inside, I put my head against the steering wheel and took in some deep breaths as I thought of a harsh fact I didn't want to face—if Cole was going to follow me everywhere, there was a good chance someone important to me would get hurt.

I shivered at the thought.

My bedroom.

"What was that?" I said, unable to keep my voice lowered. "How did you . . . change?"

It was later that night. Cole had shifted back to his regular form, blond hair and all. He waved his hand, as if he were swatting a fly. "It's not a big deal. Sometimes we can use our energy to alter our appearance. It's a waste, though. I only like to use it on special occasions."

"And today was a *special occasion*? Making Jack think . . ." What? I had no idea what he thought about it, but it couldn't be good.

I turned away from him and put my face in my hands. I wanted to hurt him.

He sat next to me on my bed, and when he spoke again, his voice was gentle. "I had to see what the big deal was. You Returned for this guy, but I have to admit, watching the two of you together . . . I'm just not seeing it."

My eyes started to sting, even though I was sure I hadn't recovered enough emotions to cry. I pulled my knees into my chest and rolled onto my side on the bed. "We're not together. I only wanted to see him again. Before I go."

"In that case, I did it for your own good, Nik," he said. I couldn't believe anything less right now. "Now that he knows what you're really like, it'll be easier to stay away from you. Besides, why would you want to live through pain like that? You'll lose everything again."

"What do you care?"

"I can't explain the need to understand your heart. But I've been feeding off it for so long, it's almost my own. I have to know, because it doesn't make sense why you would choose to Return."

"It wouldn't to you." I sighed.

"Tell me, Nik. Please."

I pushed myself into a sitting position, feeling defiant. "You want to know how I could pull off lying to you for one hundred years about forgetting everything? Because I had his face behind my eyelids. And I thought if I could see him, even just for a day, it would be worth the hundred years. One day is all I deserved, and I've had so many already. I've won. I've won!"

He shook his head and looked at me as if I were delusional. As if I didn't know what winning was all about. Then he put an arm around me and it was almost like he was mourning my life with me. "I don't understand the things you would give up for mortal relationships."

"You better hope you never do, Cole."

"Why?"

"All you know about is the search for the next energy source. Your only relationship is with something you can Feed off. If you ever understood what you were missing . . ." I shook my head and realized how much I wanted him to understand. Maybe then he would feel, for the first time, real pain.

"Why don't you help me understand, Nik?" He raised the corner of his mouth in a devilish smirk and tightened his grip around me.

I shook his arm away from my shoulders.

I remembered the first time I'd met Cole. On the other side of the hundred years. Did he know then that I'd end up following him? That I'd allow him to drag me to the Everneath?

LAST YEAR

February. One month before the Feed.

The line to get into Harry O's extended all the way to the sidewalk on Main Street, and up around the Park City T-Shirt Company building. But Jules walked past everyone like she had a VIP badge or something.

More than a few freezing people gave nasty looks as we went by.

"Are you sure we can do this?" I asked Jules.

She grabbed my hand and pulled me along. "Yes. I told you. Sean said we just give our names to the guy at the door."

Harry O's was hard enough to get into on a regular night, but during the Sundance Film Festival, it would've been easier to break out of jail than to break into Harry O's.

But Sean O'Neill was the great-grandson of the original Harry O. And he was in Jules's pottery class. And he had a thing for blondes.

He told Jules she could bring a friend. Jack was more than happy to stay home and watch the Jazz play the Nuggets. This wasn't his scene. It wasn't mine, either, but Jules begged.

Jules hesitated only slightly when she saw the large bouncer at the door, a big, thick man dressed in a tight black T-shirt and black pants, with a clipboard in his hands.

"Um, hi. We're supposed to give our names? Or something? Um . . . Julianna Taylor?"

He gave us a look that made me wonder if we were doing something totally illegal, and all I could think about was the fact that if we were arrested, my dad would never bail me out. But then he scanned his list, stopping his pen midway down.

"Julianna Taylor and guest."

I smiled when he said "guest," as if that were my name or something, but he didn't notice. He unhooked the velvet rope. We were in.

The place was packed with the most decked-out people I'd ever seen. The music blared, and I could feel the thrum of the base all the way to my heart. A few private booths with curtains lined the sides of the room, to accommodate the ultra-famous people.

Now that I was here, I realized I probably wouldn't see one other person I knew. There was nowhere to sit. Fewer places to stand. And even though I'd worn my best club outfit—okay, my only club outfit—I felt like an orphan out of *Oliver Twist* compared to everyone else. Jules scanned the crowd, probably thinking the same thing. Maybe I should've stayed home. Watched the game with Jack.

"Look! There's Meredith Jenkins." Jules was pointing

across the room to a large table of people. "How did she get in?"

Jules caught Meredith's eye and waved to her. Meredith nodded and then turned to the girl next to her, a girl I didn't know.

"Let's go over," Jules said.

"Um, she wasn't exactly inviting us."

Jules shrugged. "Where else are we going to go?"

We could just go home, I thought, but I followed Jules over. Meredith smiled as we approached, but she definitely wasn't making room for us or anything.

"Hi, Julianna, Nikki. How did you get in?" She didn't sound rude. Just curious.

"Sean put us on the list," Jules answered.

A few awkward moments passed, and I considered pulling Jules away and making a break for the exit, when a guy on the other side of the table stood up. And then I knew why Meredith was acting weird.

The guy was tall, dressed in a black T-shirt and jeans that looked distressed, but the kind of distressed that cost a lot of money. And I knew him. Not personally, but I knew who he was. I had both of his CDs at home, and his blond hair left no doubt in my mind. He was the guitarist for the Dead Elvises. Cole.

I glanced down the table. The entire band was there: second guitarist Maxwell; the bass player, Oliver; and the drummer, whose name I couldn't remember. Gavin, maybe?

How was Meredith with these guys? Then I remembered hearing something at school about how Meredith was friends with some musician. I guess it was true.

Cole looked right at me. "Here. We can make room." He stepped away from the end of his bench and motioned me over. Me. Not Jules. "We can fit you here. Mer, make some room for her friend, will you?"

Meredith gave Cole a confused look, then scooted over so Jules could fit one butt cheek on the bench. I slid onto the end of the other bench, where Cole had been, and then he sat next to me so I was sandwiched between Cole and Maxwell. My heart was pounding. I wasn't a crazed fan of theirs—I didn't have any tattoos of a skeletal Elvis anywhere on my body—but this was my first run-in with a celebrity. Even my fingertips were sweating a little.

Cole held his hand out to me. It was difficult to shake because we were sitting so close, and I made it fast because I didn't want him to remember me as the girl with the clammy hands. "Cole Stockton."

"Yeah, I know. I'm Nikki Beckett." He stared at me in silence for a few moments. I could feel my cheeks turning pink. "Um, shouldn't you guys be in one of those?" I pointed to the booths that were curtained off.

"Oh no. Those are for famous people." He gave me a smile that I could've sold on the internet for money. He wore a few silver bracelets and a necklace with a silver cross hanging on it. Each of his fingers had a tattooed design, like a ring, and in his hand was a plastic triangular object that he absentmindedly rolled over the tops of his knuckles. A guitar pick, it looked like. I'd only ever seen someone do that with a coin. "Beckett," he said. "Any relation to Mayor Beckett?"

"My dad. You know his name?"

He shrugged. "Saw him in the paper." He lowered his voice like a newscaster. "*Mayor Beckett Reads* Fluffle Bunny *to Kindergarten Class.*"

I smiled. "Slow news day, I guess."

"Is there any other kind here?" He winked.

No one else was really talking. Our end of the table just watched Cole and Maxwell, as if they were waiting on them. I wondered if that was how famous people felt all the time— like everyone around them was waiting for them to perform. But Maxwell wasn't doing anything, and Cole was only talking to me, and I was sure the music was too loud for anyone to really hear us.

Meredith's gaze kept darting to me. She looked annoyed.

I leaned in to Cole and lowered my voice. "So, are you and Meredith . . . ?" What would be a term a rock star would use? Dating? Together? Going out?

As I grappled with the words in my head, Cole just watched me with a smirk. He wasn't about to help, which flustered me even more.

". . . are you . . . you know?" I waved my hands in a circle, in what I thought was a fill-in-the-blank kind of way.

Cole crinkled his brow.

Seriously? How could I be more obvious? I sighed. "Never mind."

"No, don't give up." Cole was definitely smiling now. "Do you mean, are we . . ." He held up the index fingers of both his hands, and then put the tips together and made a loud smoochy noise.

I couldn't help laughing. "You're making fun of me."

He wiped the smile off his face with his hand. "Sorry. No, I'm not with her. But Meredith and Max are . . ." He started tangling his fingers together, twisting them around each other. My face went red, and I covered his hands with mine to make him stop, and then my face got even hotter because I was clasping his hands.

Thankfully a waiter appeared right then with new drinks. He must've known the tip would be good because he kept the drinks coming—some local draft for the band and sodas for the rest of us. Over the next hour, the bouncer let more people in, but it seemed like no one was leaving. I lost count of the number of people who'd come up to our table and asked Cole or Maxwell for their autographs. These fans had more guts than I would have had.

Cole signed napkins, scraps of paper, even one girl's arm, all the while keeping up a conversation with me. Like it was totally normal that he was asking about where I was going to college while he held another girl's arm flat on the table in front of him, poised over it with a Sharpie.

It was all very surreal. The music and the drinks and

Cole's voice blended together, and I soon forgot I didn't really belong here. But then a familiar man at the bar caught my eye. It was Carl Volker, the prosecuting attorney for the case against the drunk driver who killed my mom. The trial was set to start in a few weeks, and I'd been avoiding any news about it. A fresh wave of grief washed over me, and I stared hard at the shiny metal surface of the table, trying not to cry. It still surprised me how close to the surface the tears were. Whenever I was overcome with sadness—and it happened a lot since my mom died—I always tried to think of Jack and the fact that we were together now. It was my version of finding a happy place.

I pictured Jack at home, watching the game, his arm wrapped around me. I closed my eyes and smiled, and it was a few moments before I remembered I wasn't alone. When I did, I raised my head. Cole was looking at me with a strange expression on his face.

"Whoa. You are the happiest sad person I've ever met."

"Huh?"

"Or the saddest happy person." The corner of his mouth quirked up. "I'm not sure which." He leaned a little closer, to the point where I could smell his breath on my face. Beer and smoke. "Nope. Happiest sad person."

I tried a smile, so he couldn't see how close he really was to the truth. "I'm not sad."

"And she's not afraid to lie."

I felt my smile drop and I turned away. The second

guitarist, Maxwell Bones, was on the other side of me. I'd read somewhere that Bones wasn't his real name, but he changed it before he joined the band.

Maxwell had an iPhone that he'd been fiddling with all night, and he was reading a message.

"What's the news, Max?" Cole asked.

"The queen," Max said. I could've sworn I felt Cole tense at this. I tried to lean a little closer to read the message, but Max clicked the screen blank. "Says we owe her."

I felt like I was intruding on a business conversation, but there was nowhere I could go. I looked at Cole. His lips were pressed together.

He saw the look on my face. "Our . . . manager."

"You call your manager the queen?"

He gave a short chuckle. "It's more of a . . . term of endearment."

He and Max were quiet for a moment, making the music in the place seem even louder. Whatever the message was, whoever this "queen" was, it seemed to bother them.

"Mer!" Max called out suddenly. "To the dance floor!"

Meredith flashed a wide grin in response. I was about to scoot out so Max could pass by, but he just climbed on top of the table and held his hand out to Meredith. I guessed famous people could walk on tables whenever they wanted.

Cole nudged me with his elbow. "C'mon, sad girl. Let's turn that frown on its ass. Dancing makes everything better."

The entire table got up, and we made our way to the middle

of the floor. I noticed a bouncer place a RESERVED sign on the table after we were gone.

Jules and I stuck together, but after a few minutes I got carried away in the music, and the fact that I was dancing with the Dead Elvises, and it was a long time before I remembered my mom was gone and her murderer's trial would start soon.

ELEVEN

NOW
School. Less than four months left.

$\mathcal{I}$ wasn't sure how Jack would react after Cole had showed up at school as "Neal." I would've understood if he decided to completely ignore me, and maybe even ditched out on Mrs. Stone's classroom after school.

But I was *not* expecting him to seek me out at lunch. I was sitting in my usual nook next to the drinking fountain when he turned the corner. He sat down on the floor against the opposite wall, facing me.

I stared hard at my knitting needles, their frantic pace nearly making them blur. What was he doing?

"Jules told me where you've been eating lunch," he said.

I nodded, but I didn't look up.

"Is this okay?" he asked.

I wanted to say no, but that answer would have required further explanation, and I didn't want that. So I nodded once.

We ate in silence. I worried about what we would say to each other, but it never came up. He didn't say another word.

When I got to Mrs. Stone's classroom after school, Jack was already there. As I sat down, he stood.

"Mrs. Stone?"

"Yes, Mr. Caputo?"

"Do you mind if I close the door? Sometimes the commotion in the hallway is a bit distracting, for me at least, and I don't want my friends thinking they can come in here and bug me."

I looked up at Jack's face, and then at Mrs. Stone's. Jack always had a way of sounding like he was in charge of any situation.

"That's fine, Jack. I'm happy to see you so dedicated." Her eyes shifted to me as she said the word *dedicated*. "I hope you won't mind if *I* go in and out? In the course of my teacher duties?" she said with half a smile.

Jack shook his head. "No. That's fine."

"Thank you, Mr. Caputo."

Jack went to shut the door, then sat back down, and it hit me that maybe he was acting this way because of the encounter with Cole. Was I reading it right? He was protecting me. If Cole showed up again today, he'd have to go through Jack. It made my heart race.

We worked in silence for the first half hour, but I couldn't concentrate. Did I really think I could choose to Return and then just watch Jack from a distance? He wasn't going to allow it. This wasn't fair to him.

I turned toward him. "Jack, you really shouldn't be—"

"Shush. I'm trying to work," he growled. He kept his head down, but his lips turned up slightly.

A soft chuckle escaped me. The first in a hundred years. Jack stared at me, and I gasped.

"What'd you say?" he asked.

I shook my head, my mouth slightly open. I couldn't have just laughed. I didn't even have the ability anymore, did I?

"It sounded like a laugh."

"No," I said abruptly. "No. It's not funny."

He raised an eyebrow at me. "Are you sure? Because it sounded almost as if you said something to me, and then I said something back that you found funny. And you giggled. I'm pretty sure that's what happened."

I took a few calming breaths. "No. That's impossible."

"Impossible that I said something funny?"

And there it was. I laughed again. "No. Impossible that I laughed."

His smile widened, and I laughed some more, at first because it was obviously *not* impossible, and then because I knew what it meant. I'd recovered enough to laugh.

Jack seemed amazed. "I think anything's possible, Becks."

And then the fleeting levity disappeared. He called me Becks. He believed anything was possible. I couldn't let him believe that. I was being selfish.

I didn't bother putting my books in my bag. I just grabbed them and took off. I could hear his footsteps behind me as I yanked the door open.

"I'll just follow you."

This made me freeze. "You don't know what you're saying."

He grabbed my wrist and pulled me around. "I let you go once, and you disappeared on me. Without a word. I'm not asking for it to be the same as it was, but I just want to know you again. Please. Can I know you again?"

I tried to wrench my hand free, and he let go of my wrist. "Becks, what happened to you? Do you even remember me?"

At that moment, I made a decision. Jack was grasping at the faint shadow of the life we'd had before, searching for a stronghold. I could see him doing it and I couldn't let him. I'd already hurt him enough. He said he'd moved on.

So I lied. The biggest lie ever.

"No." I looked at his eyes. "I don't remember anything."

He glanced away and nodded. "Okay. I get it." A ghost of a sad smile appeared on his lips, and my heart felt as if it were being choked. I fought to keep my hands at my sides. To keep them from pulling Jack to me. Placing them on either side of his face and forcing him to look at me again.

I shouldn't have come back, but looking at his face, I knew. Nothing could've kept me away. I was that selfish.

Last spring, he'd already left me before I left him. But all that mattered now was that neither of us deserved to go through it again. I had to keep him from getting close again.

Without glancing up, Jack turned and walked away. I let him go.

Then I remembered the last time I'd let that happen. And how it turned out.

LAST YEAR
April. Two weeks before the Feed.

Jack and I stood in the parking lot of the school, oblivious to the people around us hoisting their bags onto the waiting buses. It was spring break, and the only people at the school were the ones leaving for football and cheerleading camps, and the ones saying good-bye to them.

"It's two weeks, Jack. I think we'll survive," I said.

Jack clenched both of my arms, his fingers digging in almost to the bone. His brother, Will, had shipped off for basic training right after Christmas, and Jack was having separation issues.

"I'm going to need those." I glanced at my arms.

"I don't think I should leave you." He paused. "Especially this week, of all weeks."

Jack was referring to the ongoing trial of Kevin Reid, the man accused of hitting my mother with his car. The defense was wrapping up, and a verdict would be coming in.

"It's okay, Jack. I'm not even paying attention to it."

"I know you are."

I extracted one of his hands and placed it on my cheek, leaning into it. "Two weeks."

Neither of us noticed somebody approaching. "Okay, love-birds. The buses are waiting." Cole appeared beside us. His band had stayed on after Sundance. Apparently they were using a condo near the ski resort for songwriting. I'd run into him a few times since the night at Harry O's.

"Hey, Cole," I said. "What are you doing here?"

"Max asked me to drop Meredith off." He tilted his head toward the bus carrying the cheerleading and pep squads. I didn't see Meredith, but I saw Lacey Greene watching us from one of the windows.

Lacey had spent the week leading up to football camp telling everyone who would listen "What happens at camp stays at camp," which made it sound like camp consisted of a craps table, tequila-lime shots, and tangled sheets.

I tried not to let it bother me that she would be staying on the same campus as Jack.

"That's nice of you," I said.

"It was on the way. I'm making some silk screens for T-shirts at the shop," Cole said, gesturing across the parking lot toward the GraphX Shop down the street.

"Making your own T-shirts? Don't you have people for that?" I asked. "Like professionals?"

"Well, I usually travel with an army of professional T-shirt makers, but today I thought I'd go it alone."

Jack didn't take his eyes off me as Cole spoke. I wasn't sure he was even listening, or aware Cole was there.

"What are the screens of?" I asked.

"Elvis Presley as a corpse. You wanna come look?" Cole

gave me a grin as if he'd just asked if I wanted to see rainbows being made.

"You had me at 'corpse.'"

Jack chuckled. "Saying good-bye here. Remember?"

I turned to Jack, rose up on my tiptoes, and kissed his lips lightly. "Two weeks, Jack. It'll fly by."

I started to back up, but Jack grabbed my hand and pulled me close. "No you don't," he said. "The corpse can wait."

He gave me a kiss that was not quite appropriate for public view, and I would've been embarrassed if I hadn't lost the ability to think straight. His arms reached around my back, and he pulled me in tight against him so that my feet were barely touching the ground. And things started disappearing around us, just like they did every time Jack kissed me.

He pulled back. "What were you saying about two weeks?"

"That it will feel like forever," I said, breathless.

"That's better." Jack lowered his head so his forehead was touching mine. "Miss you."

"Miss you too," I whispered.

Somehow, he finally let me go, and Cole—who had stepped away during our kiss—stood next to me as I watched the bus cough and choke its way up the hill and out of the parking lot. Before it disappeared completely, Cole tugged on my arm.

"Cheer up, Nik. You can help me splash some shirts." He released a breath of air on my face, and suddenly I was overwhelmed with a strange feeling of loss. I couldn't explain where it came from. It was as if an electrical pulse had charged the air and penetrated my skin, and I was left with the sense that something was slipping from my fingers, and I couldn't hold on to it. I clenched my car keys in my pocket, but that wasn't it. Then I jerked my head back toward the buses, and all I could think about was the way Lacey Greene had been staring at me, and how Jack was on a bus with her. And how she was equating camp to a weekend in Vegas.

"You okay?" Cole asked.

I tried to shake the feeling away. Jack was mine. There was nothing to worry about.

"Yeah, I'm fine." I turned to follow him toward GraphX. "You don't have to feel bad for me. I'm not lonely."

"Don't be silly. I don't feel bad for you. You'd be doing me a favor." As he spoke, he winked at me, and I couldn't help feeling a tingle.

"Where are your groupies?" I asked, referring to the constant entourage that usually surrounded him.

"They get in the way. Especially when I'm working with paint. Too many cooks, you know."

"Oh." I slowed down. "Maybe you'd rather—"

"*You're* not a groupie," he interrupted. He put his hand on my back and urged me forward. That strange feeling of loss wasn't as bad now.

The inside of the workshop smelled like fresh paint and developing chemicals. Paint spots dotted the floor and most of the walls. Two silk screens were drying on one of the industrial counters. The image on the screen was a haunting portrait of

Elvis Presley, not necessarily dead, but not alive, either. The eye sockets were sunken and the cheeks hollow and ashen, the lips drawn back, exposing long teeth. Yet he cradled the microphone like a baby with one hand, and had just finished a strum on his guitar with the other. It was a beautiful rendition caught between life and death, trapped between this world and the next.

I fingered the silk screen carefully.

"Wow," I whispered. "This is amazing. Where did you find the original?"

"I drew it," he said offhandedly. He focused on the stack of T-shirts on the other counter, laying them out.

"Cole, you're messing with me! It's too . . ." I just shook my head as he turned to look at me. "No words."

He took a couple of steps closer to me. "I think that's the nicest review I've ever received."

And just like that, he was standing too close. I could see the glint of the iron ball on his tongue post, and before I knew it, I was staring at it.

He smiled and I quickly looked away.

"Okay, so, let's get started," I said, turning toward the T-shirts on the counter before Cole could see the pink on my cheeks.

We worked together in companionable silence for a while. I appreciated the delicate technique; the routine of the silk-screening process almost resembled an elegant dance.

"What are you going to do with the shirts?" I asked.

"We're selling them at the concert tonight."

"The Dead Elvises are playing tonight? Where?" I had only ever heard the band's CDs, since I never could afford a ticket during the festival.

"The Dead Goat Saloon, appropriately enough. We're trying out some new material." He paused as if a thought had just occurred to him. "You should come, Nik."

"I don't know." I was pretty sure my father would not approve.

"You don't have to be twenty-one." He must have noticed my skeptical look because he quickly added, "Only for tonight, though, since the band is mostly underage. We have special passes." His voice had turned persuasive.

I fidgeted for a moment, trying to figure out why I was hesitating. It was spring break, so it's not like it was a school night or anything.

"Besides, we need help selling our T-shirts." He picked out one of the smallest ones that had been drying on the counter and held it up to me, playfully assessing the look. "Nik. All you need to do is wear this tonight, and we'll sell out."

I glanced down at the shirt and then back up at Cole. "Yeah, I'm sure this is the look you were going for."

"You can make anything look good," he said softly.

When I got home, I called Jules and convinced her to go to the concert with me. I still wasn't sure they'd let us in, until our bus pulled up to the Dead Goat Saloon and we saw a bunch of students from Park City High. Anyone sixteen and older could enter with a special pass. The Dead Elvises packed the house, and the air was heavy with the smell of alcohol and sweat.

Jules and I stayed as close to the stage as possible, and as the concert wore on, I wondered if my hearing would be permanently damaged. But the music soon made me forget any pain. As I danced, I closed my eyes and tried to remember why I had been so sad that morning.

Jules tapped me on my shoulder and leaned in to yell something, but I couldn't hear her above the throbbing bass. Finally she gave up and pointed toward the back of the place and mouthed the word *bathroom*. I nodded and turned my attention back to the stage.

I never understood how guitar players could jump up and down while making sure their fingers struck the right frets and picked at the right strings. Cole made it look easy and natural, as if he were surrounded by a cushion of the music he was making; his movements were so graceful. He was at once severe and beautiful, and the more he played, the more I felt surrounded by that cushion as well, as if I could fall and never hit the ground, as long as he was playing.

I closed my eyes and let the music take over, and when I opened them, Cole was watching me. As our eyes met, he didn't look away, and he didn't try to hide where his attention was. For some reason I was determined not to look away first, and before I knew it I'd gravitated to the stage. People turned to look at me, as if the momentary bond between us was visible, and I couldn't take the attention. I finally turned away.

By midnight, I could barely stand upright. I hadn't had anything to drink, but everything around me still seemed to sway. The band played two encores, and then the music switched over to MP3s.

Jules hadn't made her way back to me, and I was about to search out the ladies' room when I felt a hand on my shoulder. I turned around.

Cole's face was pure energy, and he threw his arms around me and lifted me off the ground.

"Whoa, okay, you can put me down now," I said in between gasps for air. "My head was already spinning."

He smiled widely. "Sorry. I always feel like this after a set."

"Like what? Like you have the sudden urge to pick up teenage girls and throw them around?"

He laughed and put me on the ground again. It was obvious Cole was passionate about music, because he couldn't contain his euphoria. It was contagious.

Behind Cole, the rest of the band was packing their gear. Maxwell fastened the clasps of his guitar case, then jumped off the stage and landed right next to where Cole and I stood.

"Cole, we heading out?" Maxwell said.

"In a minute," Cole said, and he waved his hand dismissively. Maxwell looked from Cole's face to mine, and walked away with a strange smile on his lips. Cole didn't seem to notice. He looked past me. "Where's Jules? Wasn't she with you?"

Oh yeah. Jules. I was so caught up with Cole, I'd almost forgotten about her. "I thought she went to the restroom, but she hasn't come back. I should probably go look for her."

I started to walk away, but he grabbed my wrist. "Did you check your phone? Maybe she texted you."

"Oh, right." I pulled my phone out of my pocket, and sure enough, it showed a new text. "I didn't even feel it."

"What does it say?" Cole asked.

I squinted as I read the screen again. "She said she wasn't feeling well, so she got a ride home with Spence Eckhart."

Cole smiled at me. "Does that mean you're stranded?"

"No more so than before. We took the bus here."

"Well, I have a car. Let me drive you home." He threw one arm around my shoulders and leaned in to whisper in my ear. "I'm glad you came." His breath washed over my neck and my face, and I only had a moment to register the smell of cigarette smoke before my mind inexplicably flashed to Jack. How would I feel if he had his arm around Lacey like Cole had his arm around me? I wondered what he was doing right at this moment, if he was asleep, or if they were out partying somewhere.

Cole put his hand on my back, leading me toward the exit and the parking lot. I ran a few fingers through my frizzy hair, damp with sweat. Lacey's hair was always perfect.

Why was I thinking about Lacey? I trusted Jack.

TWELVE

NOW

Lunch. Three and a half months left.

Jack didn't come to Mrs. Stone's room for an entire week. He didn't try to speak to me during class. By lunchtime on the fourth day, I found myself going a little crazy. I knew it was better for him this way, but I longed to hear his gruff voice and see his brown eyes dart toward mine.

With my lunch sack in hand, I made my way to the school library. The windows on the north side overlooked the courtyard, where most of the students ate their lunches on sunny days.

If Jack was there, I would see him.

I found a seat near the windows and scanned the courtyard. The large table at one end, near the doors, still held all the big names in the school. The hierarchical seating chart, based on social standing, hadn't changed. But Jack wasn't with them. I kept looking, and finally found him sitting at a small table on the other end of the yard, across from a girl with long blond hair.

She turned briefly and I could see her face, confirming what I already knew.

Jules.

Jack and Jules had been friends before I left, but it was mostly through me. I wondered if they ate together every day now. Nobody seemed to notice them.

They inclined their heads toward each other, both of them pushing the contents of their lunches around on their trays, but neither of them eating.

Jack's lips were moving, and Jules mostly just nodded. At one point, she reached out and put her hand on Jack's forearm. She was so tender with him. I realized my hand was covering my mouth as I watched them. I had no right to be jealous, but I found myself squeezing my apple. I stared hard at the stem, and twisted it off before I dared to look up again.

Jack smiled and leaned back in his chair. At this movement, Jules pushed his sandwich toward him. Jack rolled his eyes and picked up the sandwich, took a purposeful bite, then set it down.

They both laughed.

I left the library and almost sprinted back to my nook. Were they together now? They spent a lot of time with each other, but they'd done that before I left too.

I didn't want to think it was possible, but then again, why shouldn't they be happy?

I had to get my mind off Jack. It wasn't doing anything to

make my Return easier. In fact, it had distracted me from figuring out what Cole was hiding.

I needed to go back to the Shop-n-Go. Continue my search for clues that probably weren't there. At least it would get me away from here and give me something else to think about.

Outside the Shop-n-Go.

I looked up and down the street to make sure no one saw me. In the daylight, the place looked so ordinary it was even harder to believe it had anything to do with the Everneath.

Through the window I could see the same bored guy—Ezra—at the counter. I felt in my pocket for change, so I could buy something and not look so crazy. He probably wouldn't even remember me.

I pushed the door open, making the bell chime, and walked past him. This time I couldn't smell any alcohol.

"Didn't expect to see you here again, detective," Ezra said loudly. I looked around. There weren't any other customers—he had to be talking to me.

As if to prove it, he said, "Still looking for the man with the bottle?"

I walked toward the counter. "Nope. Just shopping."

He gave me a skeptical look and went back to working on what looked like a crossword puzzle, as if he were too bored to argue.

I ignored him and wandered slowly down the aisle toward the back of the store to look at the tile again. My cheek had smacked against that floor the day the Everneath released me. Ezra was busy with his paper, and I made sure he wasn't looking before I stomped a few times on the floor. As solid as ever.

I rubbed my forehead with the palm of my hand. What wasn't I seeing? I turned away and kicked my shadow on the floor. How could something so ordinary hold the answers to anything at all, let alone anything that would help me? I crouched down and put my hand to the tile. Cold. I looked at my hand. The only thing it proved was that the floor needed a good cleaning. I was missing something. Or maybe I was trying to find clues where there were none to be found.

My investigation of the floor was so intense that I didn't hear the store door open, and I didn't notice that someone was standing behind me.

"What did you lose?" a familiar voice said.

I shot up so fast that I whacked the back of my head on Jack's chin.

"Ow." I rubbed my head as I turned around.

Jack had a hand up to his chin. I'd hit him just right. His lower lip was starting to bleed a little. "You're telling me. Sorry, Becks. Didn't mean to scare you."

"It's okay. Sorry about your . . ." I motioned to his face. A drop of blood trickled down his lip, and I reached into my bag and pulled out the closest thing I had to a tissue—a knit tea cozy I'd been working on.

"Here," I said. I brought the tea cozy to his lip and put his hand there to hold it in place. He held it there for a second and then pulled it away to look at it. Without a teapot under it, the cozy looked a little misshapen.

"What is this?" he asked, his lip twitching.

"A tea cozy."

"Of course."

We stood there in an awkward silence for a moment. I wondered if he was still mad at me. I couldn't tell from his expression, and I couldn't discern the taste of the energy in the air. I only knew there was a lot of it. I didn't know if I'd ever get better at it.

Jack gripped the tea cozy so tight, his knuckles turned white.

When I couldn't take the silence anymore, I said, "What are you doing here?" It sounded like an accusation.

Jack raised an eyebrow and let up on his death grip of the tea cozy. "I heard this place has great tile." He jerked his head toward the floor.

I gave a nervous laugh.

"Truth is, I saw your car out front," he said. My heart did a little happy dance. Maybe he wasn't so mad anymore. "So, what's so special about the floor?"

"It's not the floor. I was just . . . reaching for . . ." I crouched down again and grabbed the nearest thing off the bottom shelf. "These."

He looked at the package in my hand and raised his eyebrows. "Chocolate-covered raisins?"

I nodded.

"You don't like raisins."

He remembered. "They're, um, not so bad now."

He gave a little nod and shifted his weight from one foot to the other. "I guess everything changes."

I wanted to yell out, *Nothing changes! I still hate raisins!* But then I heard a loud motorcycle pull into the parking lot. I glanced out the window.

It was Gavin, the Dead Elvises' drummer.

What if he saw me here? I had to assume if Maxwell knew about me, then Gavin would too, and I didn't want him to report back to Cole that I was snooping around. And I doubly didn't want to involve Jack.

"I have to go," I said. I had to get out of there before Gavin came in.

"Wait, Becks," Jack said. He tried to grab my hand, but I yanked it away and pulled my hoodie over my head, all Unabomber, and started toward the door. Jack stood there watching me with a confused look on his face. "Don't leave."

"I'm sorry," I said, backing toward the door. "I am."

"What about your raisins?" Jack said.

I could see Gavin flip the bike's kickstand with his foot. "I don't want them anymore," I said. "You're right. They're gross."

I was almost to the door now.

"Don't you want this?" Jack held up the tea cozy. It was as if he were trying to make my escape even more difficult. Gavin was crossing the parking lot.

"No. Keep it."

Right as I shoved the door open, I heard Jack mumble, "I guess nothing says 'I'm sorry' like a tea cozy." Frustrated, he kicked the counter that held the rotating hot dog machine.

Then I made it out, and the door slammed shut behind me.

I ducked my head and passed Gavin just as he reached the door. He didn't seem to notice me, and I was pretty sure he hadn't heard Jack.

I avoided my car and walked up the street a little ways, sat down on the curb, and let out a breath of relief.

I hadn't learned anything new, except that another one of the Dead Elvises had an affinity for the Shop-n-Go. And Jack officially thought I'd lost my last marble.

I put my head in my hands. After several long minutes, I felt someone sit down next to me. I half expected it to be Jack, but when I looked up, I saw Mary. I'd never seen her outside the soup kitchen before.

"Mary," I said. "Hi."

Mary was looking straight ahead. She scratched her arm a few times, as if something there were bothering her. "I come here a lot too."

I grimaced. "Where? The Shop-n-Go?"

"Yes. I come here for supplies. The cashier doesn't notice things."

Great. She just admitted she's a shoplifter.

She patted my knee. "Okay. I have to go. I'm late."

"For what?" I asked.

Her face went blank, as if my question made no sense, and she scratched her arm again. "I hope you find it."

"Find what?"

"What you were looking for." She looked at me like I was the one suffering from dementia. She stood up and wandered down the street, pausing only to ask a couple of tourists for some spare change. I hoped they gave her plenty.

THIRTEEN

NOW

School. Less than three months left.

$\mathcal{M}$rs. Stone read through a rough draft of my paper, and one day after school she sat in the desk in front of me. "Nikki, you seem to have a chip on your shoulder when it comes to ancient myths."

"What do you mean?"

She smiled. "You place an inordinate amount of blame on some of the central figures of Greek mythology."

I was quiet for a moment, unsure of how to answer.

"Don't get me wrong. I love how you've seamlessly planted characters such as Persephone in a modern high-school setting. Superb." She placed the stack of papers on my desk. "But you, as the author, are letting your disdain show through."

"How?" I asked.

She gave me a wry smile. "Like when your modern Demeter, and basically everyone else who's even nice to your Persephone, gets killed or maimed by random acts of violence."

Oh yeah. I nodded.

"Now, if you intended to offer a scathing indictment of heroes, well, you're succeeding."

"I just think they were foolish," I said. "Made irrational decisions in hopeless quests."

"Maybe. But don't forget that what we can glean from these stories is not the string of decisions that got them into harrowing situations but what sacrifices did they make? Did Demeter give up when Persephone was kidnapped? Did she ever lose hope that she would get her daughter back?"

"That's just it, Mrs. Stone. She shouldn't have let herself hope, because she didn't really get her back. Persephone ended up ruling the Underworld anyway. I don't know why she wasted her time."

Mrs. Stone paused. "Now you're asking the right question. Why do we hope when all hope is lost? What if Orpheus had given up hope?"

"Who?"

"Orpheus. We'll talk about him later in the unit, but in a nutshell: The love of Orpheus's life, Eurydice, was taken to the Underworld. He was desperate to get her back, but no one ever comes back from the Underworld, right? Orpheus didn't give up, though. He followed her and pleaded with Hades to let her go. He played music for Hades and touched his heart, so much that Hades released Eurydice on one condition— that Orpheus never look back as they left."

Goose bumps appeared on my arms. I wasn't familiar with

the story, but Cole said most myths were rooted in some truth. Could it be that a mortal girl who was bound to the Everneath escaped? I stayed quiet, anxious for Mrs. Stone to go on.

"I'd like you to ask yourself, Who loses hope first? And who never gives up? Because it's not the supernatural abilities that set mythical characters apart." She leaned forward. "It's the decisions the *human* characters make, in impossible situations, that have us still talking about them centuries later. Heroes are made by the paths they choose, not the powers they are graced with."

I didn't tell her my opinion about the existence of heroes. I wanted her to talk about Eurydice again. "So this Eurydice escaped the Underworld?"

"Yes." Mrs. Stone paused. "For a moment."

"What happened?"

"Orpheus couldn't help looking back to make sure she was behind him. She was sucked back down." She smiled and patted the papers in front of me, as if she hadn't just obliterated my little ray of hope. "What you've done here is fine work. Good structure. Solid voice. But I think you can dig a little deeper."

I nodded, no longer paying close attention. No one could escape.

"Okay. We're good here. I can't wait to see your next draft, Nikki. Don't shy away."

When I left Mrs. Stone's classroom, I couldn't get my mind off the story of the two lovers. Which is why I didn't notice, at first, the small group of students gathered around something at the edge of the football field.

I watched the crowd as I walked toward the parking lot. I wouldn't have stopped, only I saw Jules standing there, and she turned to stare at me. Something in the way she looked at me made me want to see what was going on. As I walked closer, a couple more students turned to watch. As if they'd expected me.

Then a voice rang out from somewhere in the middle of the fray. Jack's voice.

"Leave her alone!"

Another voice. An all-too-familiar voice. Cole—as the dark-haired Neal. "She got to you, didn't she? And you want more. They always do."

Oh crap. I picked up the pace and pushed my way into the center, where Jack and Cole were facing off. I wanted to grab Jack, to wrap my arms around him and pull him away. But I didn't feel like it was my right, since he was angry with me.

So I stood in front of Cole.

"Stop it." I put my hand on his chest. Despite being an immortal, he had the physical strength of a regular boy my age, nothing more. He still could have flattened me, but he gave way and stepped back. And I realized my mistake. The way he gave in to me made it look like we were together.

Everyone watched. My face was sweating.

"I can't help it, Nik," he said with a smirk. "He's such an easy target."

Jack made a lunge toward Cole, but I stood my ground in the middle. I was about to get squashed.

"Jules!" I called out, as Jack collided with us. He tried to strong-arm me out of the way, but then Jules was there, tugging on his arm, trying to pull him off. I wondered why she hadn't tried to stop it before now.

"C'mon, Jack," she said. "Let's go. Please."

Jack didn't take his eyes off of Cole, but he let Jules lead him away. The crowd let out a collective sigh, probably disappointed there'd be no fight.

Cole turned to me as we walked and licked his lips. "Oh man, his humiliation is absolutely delicious."

"Stop it, *Neal*. Just stop it. None of this is going to help you get me back."

"It's not just about getting you back, Nik. Poor Jack is smitten. I feel sorry for the boy and what he's going to go through again. I'm doing this for both of you."

I shook my head in disbelief. "Leave Jack out of this. He wants nothing to do with me anyway."

"You're wrong, Nik. He wants everything to do with you."

We both looked over at Jack, who was letting Jules lead him to the parking lot. Jack's eyes cut back and forth between Cole and me. I felt like I was betraying him somehow.

"Poor Jules," Cole said.

I turned to look at him. "What do you mean?"

He raised an eyebrow. "Don't tell me you don't see it. She's in love with Jack. And she thought there was a chance, until . . ."

"I came back," I said.

He nodded, and then shrugged as he turned toward Jules again. "Now she doesn't know what to do. Maybe I can help her decide." He glanced at me sideways. "Do you think I'm her type?"

We'd reached his big black-and-silver motorcycle parked illegally along the curb.

"Don't say things like that, Cole. Please."

"Would that bother you?" He had a strange look on his face. Almost vulnerable. It had come so quickly, and it made him look like a different person.

"Yes," I said. He started to smile, until I added, "I don't want you anywhere near the people I love."

He was taken aback, but then he chuckled and was back to his old self. "You can end this anytime, Nik."

I didn't answer. I had underestimated how much damage he could do before I left. He couldn't hurt me, but he could hurt the people I cared about.

Cole sauntered the rest of the way to the motorcycle, swung a leg over, and kicked it to life. "Just say the word."

He revved the engine and looked past me, toward the parking lot. His expression became smug and he grinned as he pushed away from the curb. I turned to see what had captured his attention. Then it all happened quickly.

I heard Cole take off just as my eyes registered Jack in his black car, peeling out after Cole. Jules was left behind, calling out frantically after him. The chase was on.

Jules and I exchanged silent glances for just a moment. Then we both took off at a run toward my car.

"You drive," I said to her as I tossed her the keys. She snatched them out of the air. My driving was still a bit rusty. Maybe she could catch us up faster.

We didn't say a word to each other as Jules tore through the streets. She kept to the main road, probably figuring the boys had done the same. I hoped she was right.

We didn't see any signs of Jack's car or Cole's motorcycle.

"Look," Jules said. She pointed to an older couple on the sidewalk. They were looking farther down the road, toward a sharp bend, with obviously panicked expressions.

Jules sped up.

As Jack's car came into view, I let out a yelp of horror. The front end of his car was wrapped around a telephone pole. A few people stood near the car, looking in the windows and calling out to Jack. Some were already on cell phones.

I threw open the door and bolted out before Jules could even stop the car.

"Jack!" I called out as I pushed a man out of my way. Jack was slumped over the steering wheel. "Jack. Jack! Can you hear me?"

I pulled Jack away from the wheel. His eyes were halfway open, and his cheek started to swell and turn red. I turned his head toward me. "Jack. Can you hear me?"

His eyes fluttered. "Is the boy okay?"

"What boy?"

"The boy. In the street."

I turned to the man behind me. "Was there a boy?"

He shrugged.

"I almost hit him," Jack insisted.

"There's no one." I pushed his hair away from his eyes and took a closer look at his cheek. Maybe there really had been a boy in the street, but I also wouldn't put it past Cole to make one appear, if he had that power.

Jack's eyes opened fully, and he looked at me with half a grin. "You remember the first time I told you I loved you?" His words slurred together.

"Shhhhh. Don't talk. The paramedics are on their way."

"Do you?"

I touched his cheek and he winced. I could almost taste his pain, as if it were a tangible element in the air. I could feel my body hungering for the hurt. It was the first time since I'd Returned that I craved someone else's energy. Even at my lowest point, those last moments in the Everneath, I'd never felt a need for it. Until now. Until I was faced with emotions this strong.

He tilted his head toward me, and I jerked back. The taste in the air became bitter and sweet, a mixture of pain and longing.

"Tell me you remember," he said. "Please."

The pain was no longer coming from one source. It was behind me as well. I turned, knowing whom I would see. Jules stood a few yards back, watching us, and the look on her face made it clear that she had heard everything.

I ducked my head and walked back through the crowd. As I passed her, I said, "He needs you. He doesn't know what he's saying."

Sirens wailed in the distance. I glanced down at my hand, the one that had touched his cheek.

This had to stop. I had to stop.

FOURTEEN

My bedroom. Less than three months left.

The halfway point of my Return had come and gone, and I still wasn't any closer to saying good-bye. The only thing I had actually accomplished was getting Jack beat up. It was nobody's fault but my own.

When I got home after the accident, Cole was waiting for me in my room, as usual. But today was the first time I actually wanted him there.

"I'm ready to leave."

He sat upright. "You are? I . . ." he started, as if wondering what he should pack. Apparently I'd surprised him. "Sorry, I just . . . Wow. I thought you'd take a lot more convincing. Let's go."

He stood and held out his hand. I didn't take it. "I said I'm ready to leave. Not that I'm going with you."

He let his hand drop to his side. "What do you mean?"

I took a deep breath. "I'm ready to go to the Tunnels." At

my words, the mark began to writhe underneath my skin, like a muscle spasm.

A scowl replaced Cole's smile, and he sat back down on the bed and started playing his guitar as if I hadn't said anything.

"I want to go," I said.

"See ya."

He wasn't looking at me. I pressed my lips together and balled my hands into fists. "How do I do it, Cole?" He strummed another chord. "The Tunnels want me. They're going to take me anyway. How do I go there now?"

He shrugged. "My best guess? It's called the Ever*neath* for a reason, so aim that way"—he pointed toward the floor— "and go."

I sat on the bed next to him and grabbed his hand before he could strum another chord. He stared at my hand, wrapped around his.

"Please, Cole. This situation can't be good for you, either. You obviously aren't moving on. I don't know what's out there for you, but there has to be something more than this—hanging around me. Trying to convince me of something that will never happen."

He jerked his hand away and looked at me. "Once you choose to Return, there's no getting out of it early. Except to go with me. I can help you."

"You'd help me . . . lose my heart. Right? That's what it would mean to go with you. I'd lose my heart. And then to survive, I'd have to ruin someone else's life. Sentence them to the Tunnels."

Cole stood and walked over to the window. "I can't talk to you when you're like this. Let me know when the reality of your circumstances has sunk in. Then maybe I can help."

"Wait."

He paused. "What?"

"When we were in the Everneath, did you ever tell me about Orpheus and Eurydice?"

He narrowed his eyes. "No."

"But you said you told me all the stories of the Everneath. Why not—"

He didn't let me finish. "Because that one never happened." The iPhone in his pocket vibrated, and he stared at the screen. "I have to go." He started to climb out the window.

"Bu—"

"Nik, now's not the time for an education." He tilted his head toward my shoulder. The one that held the mark. "Time's running out."

He slid out the window, slamming it shut behind him with such force that the framed picture of me and my mom crashed to the floor.

I checked my mark. It had tripled in size. And it was still tingling from when I'd talked about going to the Tunnels early, as if the Shade beneath my skin had gotten jittery at the mention of its home.

I sank into my chair for a moment. The last time Cole was

here and he'd gotten a text, he'd ended up with Max at the convenience store.

I knew what I had to do. I'd been stupid to go to the store when Max and Cole weren't there. Maybe whatever happened at the store was triggered only by Max or Cole.

I sprinted out of my room and down the hall to the kitchen to grab my car keys. If there was a chance I could catch them both at the store, maybe I'd understand.

The Shop-n-Go.

I stopped up the street from the Shop-n-Go and walked the rest of the way. Cole's bike wasn't parked out front, and I wasn't at the right angle to see inside the glass windows of the store.

Maybe Cole wasn't here. Maybe the text was about something else.

I crept closer to the building, ducking down in case Cole was nearby, but then I rolled my eyes. Why would Cole be hiding out? Waiting to ambush me on the off chance I might be strolling down the street?

I made my way to the side of the store, where the windows gave me a clear view inside to the spot near the back. No one was there. No old man, no Maxwell, no bottle. From my position, I could look through the store windows and see the front door too. I decided to wait and see if either Cole or Maxwell showed up.

The thin hoodie I'd thrown on wasn't doing much to keep out the chill, and I rubbed my arms and bounced up and down, trying to get warm. After a few minutes of this, the front doors of the shop swung open. I stepped a little closer to the glass to get a clear view, and I saw Maxwell go in with a woman I'd never seen before. My breath fogged up the glass a little, so I wiped it down and kept watching.

The woman was blond, with a bad dye job and a few inches of regrowth. She wore a short skirt, a tight, sequined tube top that was missing every other sequin, and an overcoat that was a few sizes too big, as if it were made for a man.

She had black smudges below her eyes and streaks of mascara running down her cheeks. She didn't look like the usual Dead Elvises groupie.

Maxwell nodded to the clerk—Ezra again—as they passed, and Ezra waved lazily. The woman was staggering, and Maxwell put an arm around her to steady her. What was he doing with her?

They made their way to the spot by the chocolate-covered raisins, and I scooted back so there was no way Maxwell could see me if he happened to glance out the window. I couldn't remember there being anything behind me, so when I backed into something, I jumped.

Two strong arms wrapped around me from behind, pinning my arms to my sides.

"Hey, Nik. Thought you might show up." Cole's voice was at my ear.

I struggled to get out of his grasp.

"Let me go!"

"Why? You wanted to know what happens at the Shop-n-Go. Let's find out, shall we?" He forced me closer to the window. The woman was sitting on the floor, leaning against the racks of powdered doughnuts. Maxwell crouched down beside her and held out a small white object in the palm of his hand.

"What is that?" I said.

"Shhh. Just watch."

The woman looked up at Maxwell with a pathetic expression on her face, and then she nodded resolutely. Max handed her the object, and the woman brought it to her lips.

"No!" I shouted, and I threw my weight against Cole, trying to break free. I didn't even know what the pill contained, but coming from Maxwell it couldn't be good. I put my foot against the wall below the window and pushed off, but Cole absorbed the force and grabbed my wrist, pinning it behind my back and twisting to cause enough pain to make me freeze.

"Stop fighting, Nik. I'm not trying to hurt you." He let up a tiny bit. "Do you promise to settle down?" I nodded. "Good. I just don't want you to miss the one thing you've been dying to see."

The woman put the pill in her mouth and swallowed. She closed her eyes and sank further against the racks. Maxwell left her there and walked out of the store. The woman looked like she had fallen asleep.

And then something strange happened. Her skin developed a glossy sheen, as if she were suddenly covered in liquid. Her eyes shot open, and her mouth contorted into a silent scream . . . then she dropped through the ground.

What the . . . ? I blinked, trying to make sense of what I just saw. She'd slipped through the floor, as if she were a ghost. There was no gaping hole left behind, no fissure in the tile. Nothing left.

Cole eased his grip on my wrist and helped me stand. He held my hand in his, examining the welts he'd made on my skin. "Sorry, Nik."

I yanked my hand away, and he gave me an impish grin.

"No permanent damage."

I pointed at the window. "What was that? What happened to her?"

"I told you we have to make sacrifices to our queen. Feed the Tunnels. That woman you saw in there was a sad, lost soul, looking for an easy way out of her miserable existence. Maxwell gave it to her."

"The Tunnels? An easy way out?" I said, incredulous.

Cole nodded. "Think about it, Nik. It's a hell of a lot better than suicide. It's like suicide lite. She'll become a physical part of the Tunnels, and it will be a long time before she feels pain, because she has so many layers of self-loathing."

"What was the pill she took? Drugs?"

"You know we don't need drugs. That pill contained a few of Maxwell's hairs. You can't get to the Everneath without an

Everliving host. What do your mythology books call him? A ferryman? That pill is the ferryman who escorts humans to the Everneath. The sacrifice takes the pill, and she has part of an Everliving inside of her. It's the only way she can go through."

"Why does it happen here? What's so special about the Shop-n-Go?"

"You've heard of the River Styx?" I nodded. "There are several spots throughout the world like it, where the wall separating the Surface and the Everneath is thin. Paper thin. Legend calls these places rivers. A way to get from one world to the other. Entrances to the Everneath. This store was built over one of the rivers. Around here it's the easiest access to the Everneath."

"I don't remember you taking me here before the Feed."

"That's because you had a personal host—me. I can take you to the Everneath anytime. From anywhere."

"Then why don't you take me now?"

He gave me a smile that didn't reach his eyes. "Help you leave early? I'd never be able to live with myself." His voice grew quiet. "Even now I'm not sure I'll be able to survive without you."

I shook my head slowly. "Sacrifices. Offerings. Suicide lite. I'd say there's not much left you couldn't live with. There's no end to your evil."

Cole chuckled. "There is no evil. There is no good. There is only life, and the absence of life." He stepped in front of me and leaned in closer. I was up against the wall, so there was nowhere for me to go. "We are life."

I squeezed my eyes shut and leaned my head back against the wall until I could feel that Cole had moved away.

"So, Nik. You wanted a quick way to the Tunnels." He gestured toward the Shop-n-Go. "This is the gateway to the Everneath. It's like your own River Styx." He pulled me in front of the window so we had a clear view of the floor in the back of the store. "I won't take you there personally, but I'll give you a piece of my hair." He plucked one off his head and put it in my hand and closed my fingers around it. "All you have to do is go inside and swallow it."

He let go of my hand. "You'll slip through the floor, to the Fields, where hundreds of Shades will find you, wrap you in darkness, and carry you off to the Tunnels." He put his lips to my ear, so I could feel his breath on my neck, and whispered, "You were so desperate to go. Here's your chance. It's now or never. Are you going to take it?"

My breath fogged up the window as I thought about that woman, her face a silent scream, and then gone forever. I thought about my father, and Tommy, and the fact that I wasn't ready to say good-bye. There hadn't been enough time to make up for anything.

I thought about Jack, and how he was so angry with me, and how I wasn't finished with him. How his hand used to fit mine so perfectly, and if I left now, I'd never have the chance to feel it again. I couldn't leave him the way things were now.

And then I realized the truth. I left him once on the other side of the century. I couldn't leave him of my own volition ever again. The Tunnels were going to have to take me. I didn't have what it took to go early.

"You win," I said to Cole. "I won't go early."

He kissed me on the cheek and let out a sigh. "I don't know what I'd do without you, Nik."

I remembered when I'd said the same thing to him. I'd thought he was my hero.

LAST YEAR

The GraphX Shop. One week before the Feed.

"Have you heard from Jack?"

Cole and I were in the back room of the GraphX Shop again, making more T-shirts with the Elvis wraith picture. Cole had been right. On the night of the concert at the Dead Goat Saloon, the T-shirts had sold out, and a long list of people had signed up for more.

I agreed to help him, mostly because it was a good way to pass the time.

"He's not allowed to communicate with the outside world," I answered. "Something about keeping his head in the game."

Cole gave me a strange look. "Huh. Max heard from Meredith, but maybe she was breaking the rules."

I shrugged. "Did she have any good stories?"

"No," he answered immediately, and then he was quiet. We worked in silence for a few minutes. His guitar hung down

153

his back. Cole could be rock climbing and he'd probably still carry the thing.

"Do you ever take it off?" I said. "The guitar, I mean."

Cole laid a shirt on the counter and smoothed the wrinkles. "Nope."

"Why not?"

He picked up a folded shirt from the top of the stack and shook it out. "It's part of me. Would you go to school without your hand?"

"I don't think that's a useful comparison."

He laughed as he dragged the blade across the silk screen. "So, this thing with you and Jack."

"Yeah?"

He lifted the screen and examined the print before he looked up. When he did, he had a small smile on his face. "Is it love?"

The question threw me. It didn't seem like a friend asking a friend. It felt more like Cole was defining boundaries. But maybe that was just my imagination.

I took a deep breath. "Um . . ." I twisted toward the counter where the T-shirts had been stacked, but they were all gone. I looked at the floor. My fingernails. The paint. Everywhere but his face. Why was I fumbling all of a sudden? "Um . . . Where'd that come from?" I finally lifted my gaze to meet his. Could I possibly have been any more flustered?

He raised an eyebrow and reached toward me. I flinched back before I realized he was reaching behind me, to where a second pile of shirts was stacked. At my reaction, he held his hands up in an innocent gesture, then pointed to the shirts. "The shirts, Nik. I'm getting a shirt."

"Right." I shook my head and made a noise that sounded like a nervous giggle. "So, um, why do you ask about . . . me and Jack?" I couldn't bring myself to say the L-word.

He flattened the new shirt and then bladed another screen. "I don't know. It's just that the more time I spend with you, I don't know. I don't see it. You and him."

"You don't know him."

He shook his head and drew in a breath. "You know what? It's none of my business. You coming to the concert tomorrow night?"

"Where?"

"The Spur. It's already sold out."

"Well, then, no. I didn't buy a ticket."

He sighed. "Nik, you never need to buy a ticket. You could watch it from backstage if you want."

"Really?"

"Sure. It's no big deal."

"It is to me. My friends will be so jealous."

"You're only saying that to make me feel good."

"Shut up. You know how much people love you around here." I shook my head as I ran the paddle along my silk screen.

"Do *you* like me around here?"

I startled, and my hands fumbled with the paddle as my

155

cheeks went pink. I didn't realize there was a fold on the shirt. "Oh crap. Sorry, I messed this one up."

I held it up. It looked like Elvis's face had been cut in half and then put back together by Picasso. I was about to toss it, but Cole grabbed it from me.

"No way. This one is going to be famous someday. Like that upside-down airplane stamp."

I laughed, relieved the awkward moment had passed. He grabbed a Sharpie off one of the counters and quickly autographed the shirt. He was beaming at it like it was the coolest thing he'd ever seen.

"Cole, in case I haven't mentioned it, I appreciate you letting me tag along lately," I said.

He waved me away in response.

"No, really. Thanks. I don't know what I'd do without you. I mean, it's sorta been a difficult week for me—"

"With Jack gone?"

"No. Well, yes, that too, but . . . the man who was driving the car that killed my mom, he's on trial. And I'm trying not to watch, but it's everywhere. And everyone who knows me seems to think I want to talk about it, when really all I want to do is ignore it." I didn't know why I was telling Cole all of this. I hadn't even told Jules. "So . . . thanks for the distraction."

Cole brought the shirt over and put it in my hands. "I like having you around," he said. "It's too bad football camp will be over so soon."

At the mention of football camp, I thought back to his

short reply about Meredith, and for some reason I wondered if he was holding back. "That phone call from Meredith . . ."

He looked away. "What about it?"

There it was. Evasiveness. I could see it.

"Did she say anything about Jack?"

He didn't look at me. "Not that I can remember. Hey, the band is going to run the river this afternoon. You up for more distraction?"

I thought about pressing him, but why would he purposely hold something back? He'd probably think I was being paranoid, so I dropped it. "Are you sure they won't mind if I come?"

"No. Who doesn't want a fifth wheel? Although it would be better if you weighed a little bit more."

I grinned. "I'll eat a few cheeseburgers on the drive."

When I got to the upper banks of the Weber River, Cole and his bandmates were hoisting the raft off a large white van. They divvied up the life jackets, and then we were pushing away from the shoreline.

I knew the river well. The rapids were bunched up at the end of the run, so for the first half, I tilted my head back and let the sun warm my face. The weather was at that point where if the wind wasn't blowing and the sun was shining, it was almost too warm. The first half went by fast.

An intense winter and a late spring runoff had left the river deeper than usual, and most of the tourist rafts bugged out at the West Table cutoff, as the brochures suggested. Before the rapids got too bad.

Experienced locals were known to gamble on the level-five rapids just after West Table, but never with the spring runoff we'd had.

Which is why I kind of freaked out when—a half hour later—Cole and Maxwell steered our little raft away from the West Table shore, the final exit point.

"Uh, guys, we should probably . . ." I pointed to the disappearing shoreline and had a sudden panic attack. "If we all paddle backward—"

"Live a little," Maxwell said from his steering post at the back of the raft.

"There are serious rapids ahead." I waved my hand toward the approaching bend in the river. "And the canyon walls mean there are no banks."

"No way out, dude," the drummer—Gavin—said from near the front. "Sounds like a song."

Cole was behind me, and I clenched his arm. "Cole, listen to me. It's not a good idea." But what was he supposed to do? We were past the point of no return.

"Don't be scared." I couldn't explain the expression on his face. Like he was exhilarated by my fear. He looked away, a faint smile on his lips.

"Hey, Nik!" Maxwell jerked his head toward the front of the boat. "Is that what you meant?"

I turned to look. The Tube. The stretch of level-five rapids had gotten its name because of the smooth walls on either side of the river that made it impossible to stop. I'd been down the rapids once before. During a dry summer. There was a giant sharp rock in the middle that my uncle had deftly swerved around.

Today the water was so high, I couldn't see the rock.

"Stay to the side!" I shouted. "I know there's a rock in the middle."

But two eddies on either side of the river were forcing our boat toward the center.

"We'll be fine," Maxwell said.

"No, we won't!" I searched the rapids for an unnatural break in the water, hoping I could see the tip of the rock I knew was there somewhere.

Finally, I saw a black tip dividing the rushing waves. With a sinking feeling, I knew I'd spotted it too late.

"It's there!" I pointed.

We paddled backward as fast as we could, but it wasn't going to work. We weren't even slowing down. Boats never seem to be going very fast until you try to stop them. There was no way to avoid it. I squeezed my eyes shut.

The boat snagged, and we lurched forward. And then I was in the air.

Seconds seemed to pass as the mountains on either side of the canyon circled in my vision, the thin strip of blue sky swirling back and forth.

Then the water slammed into me.

FIFTEEN

NOW

My house, after the Shop-n-Go. Less than three months left.

When I got home that night, I took Cole's hair out of my pocket and put it in the drawer of my nightstand. Maybe someday I'd have the strength to use it.

Before I could think too much about what I saw at the Shop-n-Go, I heard a soft knock at my front door. When I opened it, there was Jules, standing on my porch, twisting the ends of her hair with her right hand. She was tired. Or stressed. The air around her tasted bitter and heavy.

"Hi, Becks." She hesitated. "Can we . . . talk for a little while?"

"Of course. Come in." She looked nervous, which made *me* nervous.

Jules followed me down the hall to my bedroom, and then sat on the corner of my bed. I turned my chair around so I was facing her.

"We used to do this all the time," she said. "I practically lived here."

I smiled. "I remember."

She looked past me to my desk, where a framed picture of the two of us stood propped against the wall. Her eyes met mine, and she said, "You've lost a lot of weight. And you were small to begin with."

"I know."

Jules folded her arms. "Look, Becks. I told myself I wasn't going to bug you with accusations or questions or any of that stuff, but after today . . . I don't know. I just can't stay quiet anymore. What's going on with you?"

I grabbed a pencil off my desk and turned it over and over in my hand a few times, trying to figure out what I could say. "I don't know what to tell you, Jules. I was away for a while, but now I'm back and I'm not trying to hurt anyone—"

"Then what are you trying to do?"

"I'm trying to get my life back," I blurted out, before I even thought about it. It was the truth, even though I hadn't let myself acknowledge it before. I took in a breath and leaned my head back against the chair. That niggling wish—the silent prayer that I could someday reclaim my life—was alive inside me even though I knew it was impossible. I shook my head, as if to chase away the rogue thought. "I can't talk about it anymore. I'm sorry."

She sighed and nodded. "Fine. I just think you should at least know about what happened here when you were gone."

"You mean with Jack?"

"Yeah."

I looked at the floor. "What about him?"

"It's tough to talk about, because it was so hard to watch. At first he went crazy trying to track you down. He was convinced you didn't run away, that somebody had taken you. He organized search parties. Dropped everything he cared about. Stopped eating." She paused and looked at me. "I'm sorry if this is hard to hear."

I hadn't realized I was clutching my stomach.

"Eventually, when it looked like you were never coming back, something in him just sorta died. He stopped talking, even to his friends."

I raised my gaze to see Jules shake her head. "This one time, in the cafeteria, Brent Paxton said something about you being a crackhead and Jack just flipped out. He threw Brent to the floor and started whaling on him. The principal had to pull him off. Jack got a two-week suspension. And Brent was his friend."

"I'm sorry."

"I know. You couldn't have known what it would do to him. But you know now."

Her words held an unspoken warning for me. *Don't hurt him again.* Jules was here as Jack's friend. Not mine.

"You were there for him," I said. It wasn't a question.

"Well, he kinda didn't give me a choice. I think he was clinging to anything that would bring him closer to you. He never gave up on you. And I was there to pick up the pieces." She leaned toward me. "He never got over you."

I craved those words, and yet dreaded them at the same time. Could he still love me, despite what he did in the past?

Jules walked over to my closet and started thumbing through my clothes. We always used to go through each other's closets, looking for new stuff to borrow. She paused at a purple T-shirt. "I thought that with you being back, things might turn around for him. At first, they did. But after that fight yesterday, and then the car accident . . . I'm not sure."

"I'll try to leave him alone. I'll stay away from him."

She turned toward me. "I'm not asking you to do that. You've already been doing that, and it's like he's chasing a ghost." She looked down at her hands. "I don't really know what I'm asking." She lifted her head. "If you could just talk to him and give him some sort of answer, maybe he'll stop running."

I looked at her helplessly. "Jules, I don't know what to say."

"Do you know what he wants?" Jules pleaded. "He's not being straight with me. I wouldn't ask if I didn't think it was important." The edge of her mouth pulled up in a rueful smile. "His car was wrecked, and I'm not sure how many more concussions he can get before brain damage sets in. I believe you that you don't want to hurt anyone, but you're hurting him. Can you think of anything that would help?"

I thought back to the fragments of conversations we'd had. What did Jack want?

Tell me you remember, Becks, he'd said.

"I'll try to think of something," I said. What I wanted to say was *Does Jack know you love him?*

I couldn't help thinking Jules was a hundred times better for Jack than I was. And I couldn't help hoping Jack would never realize it.

The next day, Jack didn't speak to me again in Mrs. Stone's class, probably because I'd ditched him one too many times. I thought about Jules's request. I ruled out talking directly to Jack; I wasn't exactly a model of composure when we were face-to-face.

He wanted to know if I remembered. So at lunchtime I took a small piece of paper out of my notebook and wrote two words on it.

I remember.

I slipped the piece of paper into his locker before I could think about it for too long. But during history class, all I was doing was thinking about it. I pictured him reading the note, and my fingertips started to sweat. I tried to get a better look at his face in my imagination. Was he smiling?

By calculus, I was second-guessing myself. Would he think this was just another confusing message? Would he be even more frustrated?

By the end of school, I still hadn't seen Jack. Why did I ever think two little words would make things better? So stupid. I walked past his locker on the off chance my note was sticking out of one of the slots and I could yank it away.

But it wasn't.

The note was small. Only two words on it. Maybe he

wouldn't find it, and if he did, maybe he wouldn't know who wrote it. There could be other girls out there who would write those words on a paper. And shove it in his locker.

By the end of school, I'd had no word from Jack. No sign that he'd read anything. He kept a messy locker, and I started to believe the note was lost, and maybe that was a good thing. I breathed a sigh of relief as I put away the last of my books and took my backpack out. When I slammed the door, I gasped.

Jack was behind it, waiting, with the corner of his lip pulled up in not quite a smile. "What?" he demanded.

"What what?" I asked.

He held my note up in front of my face. "What do you remember?"

Everything. But I couldn't tell him that. I shrugged and said, "Things." Then I made a move to leave, but Jack's strong arm blocked my way, his hand pressing against the locker behind my back.

"No you don't. You can't leave a note like this"—he waved the paper—"and then say 'things.' I want to know what, exactly, you remember."

People in the hallway stared and I could feel my face going red. Jack noticed, and put his other arm up against the lockers, blocking me in. My pulse went nuts. It had to be visible on my wrists.

Jack's face was inches from mine. His breath was minty, and I could smell the rustic scent of his aftershave, and whatever strong emotion he was feeling, it tasted sweet. I breathed it in, and the inhalation was embarrassingly loud.

His eyes searched mine. "This is the first opening you've given me, and I'm not letting you get out of it." He paused. "What do you remember?"

I looked behind him, at the curious spectators, and squinted my eyes shut, unable to bear the scrutiny anymore.

"Say something, Becks. Say anything."

"You," I said. "I remember you." I kept my eyes shut, and felt his hands drop. He didn't move back.

"What do you remember about me?" There was strong emotion behind his voice. Something he fought to control.

With my eyes closed, I could easily picture the other side of the century.

"I remember the way your hand could cover my entire shoulder. The way your lower lip stuck out when you were working out a problem in your head. And how you flick your ring finger with your thumb when you get impatient."

I opened my eyes, and the words no longer got stuck in my throat on their way out. They flowed. "And when something surprises you and you don't know what to say, you get a tiny wrinkle in between your eyebrows." I reached up to touch the divot, then hesitated and lowered my hand. "It showed on the day the coach told you you'd made first-string quarterback. And it's showing now."

For a moment the space between us held no tension, no questions, no accusations.

Finally he leaned back, a stunned expression on his face. "Where do we go from here?"

"Nowhere, really," I whispered. "It doesn't change anything."

Eyebrows still drawn together, he said, "We'll see." Then he turned and left.

I tucked this moment away.

In the dark, dank world of the Tunnels, I would call upon this memory. And there would be a flicker of candlelight. If only for a moment.

I closed my eyes, as if my eyelids were the levers of a printing press, etching the fibers into my mind. Memories were outside Cole's reach. As long as I held them, memories were mine and mine alone.

SIXTEEN

NOW
Home. Two and a half months left.

*T*ime was doing strange things to me. Sometimes a week felt like a day, and sometimes a minute felt like an eternity. It was like a clock that was running out of power, winding down except when it received an occasional jolt, and a week was suddenly gone.

Telling Jack the truth—that I *did* remember him—seemed to adjust things between us. Softened some of the tension. I could see it in the occasional glances he sent my way during class. And when I caught him staring now, there was no hostility in his gaze.

We had reached an equilibrium. A way to exist living in each other's world again.

I thought about my other efforts. I wasn't making any headway with Mary, since she'd missed the last couple of Saturdays at the soup kitchen. But things were getting better with my dad.

After school one day, he asked me to run the latest design change for his campaign flyers into town to give to Mr. Macy at the printing shop. His office had the latest technology, but when it came to my dad's campaign, it was strictly old-fashioned. He believed a handshake was the best social-networking tool, and a computer couldn't convince someone of the sincerity of a smile.

I grabbed the folder with the designs. As I opened the front door, my dad called from the kitchen, "The exercise will do you good."

Because exercise and service to others fix all problems. It was a good step, my dad giving me a task. We were approaching normal.

I made the trek into town and delivered the instructions to Mr. Macy, and when I came out of his shop I could hear music coming from somewhere near the center of town. I started wandering toward the sound. The song was soft enough that even though it sounded familiar, I couldn't quite place it.

I kept checking down side streets, looking for the source, so I wasn't paying attention when I turned the corner at the pharmacy and ran headfirst into someone's chest.

Jack's chest.

Several boxes he was carrying—all but one—fell to the ground. He froze, holding tightly to the last box.

"Oh," I said. "Sorry."

"Becks." He dropped the remaining box from his hand.

We both started to speak.

"What are—"

"I was—"

Neither of us finished.

Jack regained his composure. "You know, just once I'd like to run into you without *actually* running into you."

"You're the football player," I said. "Think about what it's doing to me."

I'd noticed a couple of these moments lately—the ones where things seemed so normal between us, if only for an instant.

"Are you working?" I asked.

"Yeah. Same job as always."

I panicked. I couldn't remember where he worked, and that moment of being normal was gone. His job wasn't one of the memories that had kept me alive, so technically it'd been a hundred years since I'd thought about it.

He bent down to pick up the packages. Each one had a name and address written on it.

"Delivery," I said with a start, suddenly remembering. "Of packages."

Of course, anyone with two eyes could've guessed that. He stood and gave me an amused look. "Yeah. I wish I shared your enthusiasm for it." He handed me the top two boxes. "Walk with me, Becks."

We strolled down the sidewalk. The air had a wintery bite to it, even though it'd been a record warm November. Winter came early in our town. Even the hottest summer days always held the threat of a rainstorm.

We passed a few tourist shops, Indian beads and jewelry places mostly, until we reached a window displaying turquoise artifacts.

"Wait here," Jack said, and he took two of the packages inside.

Now that I was still, I could hear faint music again coming from somewhere. It wasn't uncommon to find two or three street musicians near Main Street on any given night, playing for change. A breeze picked up, carrying the music with it, making the melody swell louder in my ears.

The door to the shop opened, and Jack came out just as I recognized with a sinking feeling the song that was playing.

Jack heard it too. "The Dead Elvises are in town again," he said. "They've been giving impromptu street concerts most nights."

Cole and his band, performing in town. Feeding on the audience, as they had done for centuries. They'd evolved from lyres and harps to sitars and lutes to guitars and basses. They played concerts until their lack of aging became obvious. Then they would disappear for a while, switch genres and locations, maybe even learn new instruments and start again. Starting over for them wasn't that big of a deal when they could manipulate the emotions of the people they played for.

I could feel Jack's gaze on my face, waiting for my reaction. Cole was somewhere nearby, with his band, but I made sure my face showed nothing. Holding the next box up, I said, "Where to next?"

Jack smiled. "This way. The Rusty Boot."

We had just finished delivering the last of the packages and had passed Mulligan's Saloon when a man called Jack's name from behind us. We turned around. Carson Smith, a bartender in the saloon, was waving us toward him. Jack looked at me and sighed, as if he knew what Carson wanted and he didn't like it.

"Sorry, Jack," Carson said, and he held the door to the bar open for us. "It's Will."

We paused at the door. "Will, your brother?" I asked. Last I knew, Jack's brother was serving in the war. I couldn't remember if it was Iraq or Afghanistan.

"Yeah. He's back. Wait here. Or if you need to go . . ."

"I'll wait."

Jack nodded and followed Carson into the bar. A few minutes later, the bar door flung back open, and Jack stumbled through, half carrying his brother. The last time I saw Will, he looked like a slightly shorter, slightly older version of Jack. But when he lifted his head, I barely knew him. He'd lost some weight, and a sheen of sweat covered his face; little tear droplets pooled in the corners of puffy eyes. His drinking had obviously only gotten worse.

"The other guy started it!" Will said to a couple of tourists walking by. They gave him a wide margin.

I rushed to Will's other side and put his arm around my shoulders.

"Thanks," Jack said. "My car's back at the store. If we can just make it there."

Will noticed me for the first time. "Hey. A girl." He studied my face for a moment, and then he gasped and stopped walking. "Nikki Beckett. You'd better get out of here before my brother sees you. He'd freak."

"And, we're walking," Jack said, heaving Will forward.

"Oh, hey, Jack. Didn't see you there." Will smiled again, undisturbed. His eyes glazed over and he seemed to have forgotten all about me.

Jack looked at me around the slumping head of his brother. "Will was wounded. And discharged."

Will swung his head around to face me. "They expected me to wear pants!" He sprayed the last word across my face, and I gagged at his foul breath. "Like, all the time . . . It was so hot." He stared at me again. "Hey, you look familiar. Hey, Jack, 'member that girl—?"

"Yes," Jack interrupted.

"You know, the one who totally messed you up—"

"Yes," Jack cut him off again. His eyes met mine, and he gave me an apologetic grin. I felt my own lips turning up.

Will pulled up short. "Uh-oh." He made a gurgled sound and Jack yanked him toward some bushes just in time for Will to empty the contents of his stomach.

I stepped aside as Jack patted Will's back. "It's okay, Will. It's okay."

Will straightened up, wobbled a bit, and then sank directly to the ground, barely missing the tainted bush. "I gotta rest."

"Just a little bit farther—up to that bench over there."

I didn't think Will would make it, but a few minutes later the three of us were sitting on the bench. Will closed his eyes and sank lower, leaning his head against the backrest.

"He'll probably be out for a while," Jack said.

"This has happened before?"

He grimaced. "Yeah. He got out of the hospital a couple months ago. My parents stopped coming for him after about the third or fourth time. Sometimes I come and get him. Sometimes he goes somewhere else to crash."

Will began snoring.

"It's been a rough year for you," I said.

A wide grin spread across Jack's face. "You could say that. My brother got shot. I crashed my car. Crashed my grades. Beat up my best friend and a few other random people"—he paused—"and lost you. All in all, not what I'd imagined for my senior year. Right now, I'm just in salvage mode."

"I understand." It was not an empty sentiment, and Jack knew it. He nodded.

Will snorted awake and gave me a bewildered look. His head swiveled back and forth from Jack to me. "Whoa. Is it last year?" Jack and I both laughed softly as Will raised his right arm over his head and rotated it. "Nope. Still hurts." He let his arm drop back down and his shoulders sagged. "I've been shot, haven't I?"

"Yeah, Will." Jack swung his arm over his shoulder. "You ready to walk again?"

"I think so."

I helped pull him up, although I doubted I was doing any of the actual work. Will was staring at me again. He turned away, toward Jack, and whisper-yelled, "I heard Nikki's back."

"Yep," Jack grunted as Will stumbled over the curb. "She is."

"How are you doin' with that news, little bro?"

Jack looked at me when he answered. "Better every day."

My bedroom.

That evening, I was riding a strange euphoria from my afternoon with Jack when my bedroom window rattled and Cole hiked himself up through the opening. Once inside, he shook his head from the downpour of icy rain, and as he came closer, the mark on my shoulder felt more like a burn, as if it were beginning to swell. Cole had said it would get stronger as my time ran out.

"Hello, Cole," I said without looking up.

He froze. "You seem happy."

"Not really. Just enjoying my homework." I tapped my open English lit book with my pencil. I kept my voice even. "What are you doing here?"

"I came to invite you to the Christmas Dance this weekend."

I grimaced. "No thanks. In fact, I'm pretty sure you're not invited."

"Oh, but I am. The Angels are playing at the dance, and they wanted a star appearance by yours truly." The Angels were a local indie rock band who would probably kill for the added publicity of having a Dead Elvis there too. What I couldn't understand was why Cole would agree.

I stared at him for a moment. "Why are you doing this? Why are you still here?"

"The whole band's here now. We're settling down."

"But you could go somewhere else."

"They know how much I need you. They're supporting me."

I turned back to my open book and listened as Cole strummed a few chords that didn't seem to belong to any song. "I'm not going to the dance."

Cole was suddenly at my side. "Come, Nik. I have to show you something there."

"Show me what?"

"Look at me." I turned toward him. "It has to do with what you are. I can't explain it, but it's something you have to see. I promise things will become clear."

I thought about it for a long time. Cole returned to my bed and strummed a classical piece I had only ever heard played on a piano.

"Will you leave me alone afterward?" I asked.

"I can't." He stopped playing and leaned forward. "But I promise to leave your house."

"And never come back?"

He nodded.

"Never come in through my window? And you'll stay away from my family?"

He nodded again.

"How do I know you're not lying?"

"Because I wouldn't lie to you."

I didn't know if that was true, but if he kept his word, he'd be that much farther away from Tommy and my dad. "Fine. I'll go to the dance. Not with you. But I'll be there."

"Deal."

He let a smile cross his face. "I heard Jack is taking the lovely Jules."

My face showed nothing, even though this was news to me. "Oh," I said softly.

He breathed in loudly. "Okay, then. Before I go, what color will you wear?"

I tilted my head. "What?"

"What color dress are you wearing that night? So I can dress to match."

I rolled my eyes and turned back to my book. "Black."

"Ah. Black. How daring," he said, his voice flat. "I'm sure I can find something in my closet that will do."

Cole only ever wore black. Despite myself, I couldn't help smiling. I leaned back over my book until I heard the window open and then shut.

SEVENTEEN

NOW

The Christmas Dance. Two months, one week left.

At the time, I would've agreed to anything that would get Cole out of my room and out of my house for good. But as the days passed, I started dreading our bargain. It snowed, which made everyone at school even more excited for the dance, and I realized how hard it was going to be showing up, alone, in that big farmhouse.

When the day arrived, my hands started shaking again, but this time it was mostly from nerves. Even after I'd gotten dressed for the dance, I wandered around my house trying to find the courage to leave.

My dad caught me midpace and handed me a mug of hot cocoa. "So you're really going to the dance?"

I nodded as I sipped from the mug.

"Alone?"

"Not technically. There should be other people there too."

He raised his eyebrows. "Did my sullen daughter just make

a joke?" I smiled as he gave a chuckle. "You always used to make jokes when you were nervous," he said. His smile disappeared and he put a hand on my arm. "Are you nervous?"

He knew me better than I thought. "A little."

"Then why are you going? I mean, won't most everyone there have dates?" He cleared his throat. "Because Tommy and I have a mean game of Uno planned."

I hugged him. "Thanks, Dad. Wish me luck."

I grabbed my keys from their hook and took off. Even though the Meier Farmhouse was partway up the mountainside, the Rabbit had no trouble navigating the curves, because the Meier family had hired armies of workers to plow the roads and keep them clear up until the night of the dance.

I parked down the road and pulled on my boots to walk the rest of the way.

As I got closer to the farmhouse, I could hear the music drifting through the doors, floating in the air, and gradually sinking to where it disappeared in the snow. It wasn't snowing tonight like it was last year. The slush on the ground was dirty and old. The air had a stale smell to it. We needed another storm to clear it away.

Last year, I had stood in this spot in a spaghetti-strap gown, next to Jack, thinking things couldn't get much better. Tonight I wore a short, simple black dress. I normally didn't like to show so much leg, but it was the only dress I could find with sleeves long enough to cover up the mark on my left arm.

I stood for a few long moments, my breath a tangible element suspended in the frigid air.

"Miss Beckett?"

I jumped and opened my eyes. Mrs. Stone stood in the doorway of the farmhouse. "Come inside. You'll catch your death out here." She met me halfway, then ushered me through the threshold. She didn't seem surprised I was alone.

The Angels were playing a slow song to the packed dance floor. I scanned the sea of faces. Near the middle of the crowd, Jules and Jack held each other, swaying back and forth to the music, her head resting on his shoulder. The familiar pain of jealousy started clawing at me, a pain I hadn't felt full strength for over a century.

Somehow it hurt more than I ever remembered.

Everyone was dancing. Everyone had someone. The only people standing along the sides were the chaperones, most of whom were focused on their smartphones.

I was so obviously alone.

A voice behind me startled me. "Hey, Nik."

I turned around to see Cole, dressed head to toe in black. Black suit, black shirt, black tie hanging loose around his neck.

He looked me up and down. His gaze paused briefly on my legs, and his mouth opened slightly. I folded my arms.

"Um . . . you . . . look beautiful," he said.

"You look black," I replied.

"Thank you. That's the look I was going for." He held a hand out. "C'mon. Let's dance."

I didn't move. "What were you going to show me?"

"Dance with me first."

I shook my head.

"Look, Nik, I know you don't like public scrutiny lately. If you stand off to the side, all mopey and such, without a date, you'll stick out like a nun at a strip club." He leaned in. "Trust me, I've seen one. A nun at a strip club, that is. Everyone was staring at her."

I rolled my eyes. "Fine. As long as we stay toward the back." Away from Jack and Jules.

Cole led me to the floor and took me in his arms with smooth, graceful movements. I don't know why I was taken aback. I'd seen him dance with surprising finesse during his concerts.

I couldn't look him in the face while we danced. It was hard enough being that close to him without remembering how we used to be. How separating from him in the Everneath felt like being torn in two.

This was a bad idea. "I shouldn't have come," I said.

"Of course you should've. Otherwise I'd be fending off advances from Mrs. Stone." He raised his eyebrows, but I didn't smile. "Fine. You need to be here to see the truth of the situation. You don't belong here."

I finally looked him in the eye. "*I* don't belong here? What about you? You're not human. You can't even survive in my world without stolen energy, and yet you won't go home. If one of us doesn't belong here, it's you."

He blinked a few times. "Wow, Nik. Going for the jugular, aren't you?" He used the arm around my back to pull me tight against him, his eyes fierce. "You know why I stay here. For you."

"You say that a lot."

"Maybe eventually you'll believe me."

"I don't know what to believe."

Frustrated, he took in a deep breath, and as he did, I stepped closer, knowing that unless he focused on *not* stealing my emotions, he would naturally incorporate my top layers of pain. I didn't plan to do it, but with his face so close, I couldn't help it. I didn't even know I'd done it until it was too late. I was weak for anything that would alleviate the pain of the Surface. As he breathed in, Cole unexpectedly took a tiny layer of it away.

The moment he noticed, his eyes narrowed, and he froze midbreath. "That's interesting. You say you hate me, and yet you use me to stop hurting."

I stared down at my feet. "I didn't think you'd care. You do it all the time. Besides, it's just a sign of how . . . messed up I am."

He put his hand beneath my chin and urged me to look at him. His face was earnest. "It's okay, Nik. If it makes you feel better, if it means you're close to me, I'll do anything for you."

"But it's not *real*."

"Of course it is. You feel it, don't you?"

"Yes," I whispered.

Right then Cole's name came over the speakers. The lead singer of the Angels was telling the crowd about their special guest star. It shook me out of my trance, and I broke apart from Cole and backed away from him. By the time most of the audience had spotted him, I was twenty feet away.

But he was still looking at me.

From the middle of the crowd, Jack turned and looked at Cole too. He hadn't seen us together. I wasn't sure he even realized I was there.

"Don't be shy, Cole!" the singer said. He gestured to the students. "Let's help him out, guys."

The cheers became thunderous as Cole slowly made his way to the stage, keeping his eyes on me. Just as he took the microphone in his hand, he mouthed a word.

Watch.

He adjusted his microphone and then tilted it toward his face, and instantly his rock star persona was back. "This one's for all you young lovers out there," he said.

The song he started playing was a departure from the usual Dead Elvises fare. It was soft and slow. Just Cole, his guitar, and a microphone. I glanced toward Jack and Jules, their arms around each other, their feet barely moving.

Cole's voice was smooth like velvet when he wanted it to be. He made sure I was looking and then pointed the end of his guitar toward the space above my head. I looked up. A strange purple fog had gathered there, almost like my own personal rain cloud. I glanced back toward the stage, at Cole.

He gave a tiny nod of encouragement and I frowned in confusion. I had no idea what was happening. He smiled and shook his head, as if he couldn't believe I wasn't getting whatever message he was trying to send. He pointed his guitar purposefully toward a dancing couple near the stage. Juniors, I think they were. As he focused in on them, a tiny pink cloud formed above their heads, which he then, using his guitar, directed through the air toward me.

He made his movements look like a simple stage act. Apparently no one else could see the colored clouds.

The pink cloud joined the larger purple one above my head. My mouth dropped open in horror. Cole was skimming the emotions from the students and putting them right in front of me. I closed my mouth and held my breath, determined not to taste any of it.

But I was a hypocrite. What was the difference between stealing from others and tricking Cole into stealing from me so I felt better? There was no higher ground here.

The purple cloud represented all the things I hated about myself now, and so I backed away slowly, holding my breath. Someone tapped my shoulder and I jumped. Will was at my side.

"Hey, Nikki," he said with a grin. "I didn't mean to scare you. I called your name. What are you looking at?"

I looked back at the cloud. It was gone. "Nothing. The decorations."

Will scanned the room. "Um, yeah. Lots of . . . tinsel."

I stole a glance at Cole, who had stopped singing. He

glanced at Will, his face tight, and then looked down at his fingers while he riffed on his guitar.

"You wanna dance?" Will asked.

"Sure," I said. Anything to get my mind off what had just happened. Will led me toward the dance floor. He looked lucid, compared to the last time I'd seen him.

"What are you doing here, Will?" I asked.

"I'm a chaperone, believe it or not." We snaked our way through the couples.

"Apparently they never found out it was me who spiked the punch here three years ago," he said with a shrug.

I noticed we were getting closer to Jack and Jules, and I tugged on Will's hand. "Here's good, right?"

But he didn't slow down until we were only a couple of feet away. Jack finally noticed me. He watched as his brother put his hand on my back and grabbed my other hand. I couldn't tell what he was thinking. Seeing Jack reminded me of all that was good and normal in this world, and it made the last ten minutes with Cole seem even more despicable.

Will kept a respectable space between us as we danced. I noticed his eyes. They weren't bloodshot tonight.

"You look good, Will," I said.

"Better than the last time you saw me, at least."

"I wasn't sure you'd remember."

"Remembering is easy. It's forgetting that's hard." His face had the sort of look that made me wonder what he'd been through the past year.

"I have the opposite problem," I said, trying not to be aware of how close Jack and Jules were. "I have to work to graft certain things into my mind. Otherwise I lose them." I thought about how much I had forgotten during the Feed, how it was a continual effort to hold on to Jack's face.

I kept my eyes on Will, but he seemed to know where my attention was, because he glanced over at Jack and then back at me. "You know, having a good memory is sort of a family trait with the Caputo brothers."

I felt the heat flood my cheeks.

"Jules," Will said loudly over Cole's song, releasing my hand and holding his out toward my friend. "May I?"

Jules looked at Jack before answering. I don't know if she was looking for permission or a reaction, but he didn't say or do anything.

"Sure, Will," she said. She didn't look at me as she took Will's hand.

I turned to watch them as Will led her farther toward the edge of the floor. I felt several pairs of eyes on me. Cole's gaze was almost physical. He was frowning, and when I caught his eye, he looked down at his hands forming chords and strumming.

I couldn't move. Then Jack's hand was on my shoulder, covering it like it used to. I turned around.

"How about it, Becks?" he said.

I nodded. He took me in his arms and we started dancing. His movements weren't as practiced as Cole's. But they were perfect.

"I didn't think you'd be here," Jack said.

"Neither did I."

He didn't squeeze me close like he did last year. In fact, at first he could hardly look at me. He kept his eyes focused on a bunch of streamers in a corner of the farmhouse. I peeked over his shoulder to where Jules and Will were dancing. Jules was watching us.

He took a deep breath and finally looked at my face, and his expression softened. "Jules and I agreed to come here together. Months ago."

"That's great," I said. "I think you two are a great couple."

He shook his head. "We're not together, Becks. We . . ." His voice trailed off, and he didn't finish the sentence.

Even if they weren't together, there was obviously a strong connection between them. "Whatever it is, I'm glad you have each other."

He leaned his forehead down, so it was almost touching my own. "What am I going to do about you, Becks? You've got me all twisted inside." He glanced down at my hand resting on his shoulder, and he seemed to get sidetracked. "We were here last year."

"I remember," I said.

He leaned closer and whispered, "Where will we be next year?"

I couldn't answer. I knew exactly where I'd be.

Right then something changed in the room. Cole's song had transformed from a soft lullaby to a harder, louder song.

The change was infinitesimal, but I was so familiar with Cole's music that I could pinpoint the fulcrum note upon which the two melodies balanced, just before the softer one gave way to the louder one.

Raised voices from right next to us made me turn. Claire White and Matt Despain, who had been dancing nearby, were having a heated discussion. They were still in each other's arms, but their angry voices carried over the music.

The mood on the dance floor had changed, and somehow, I knew Cole had something to do with it.

I turned back toward Jack, and his face was different. His lips pressed together in a tight line, and his back was ramrod straight. Whatever Cole was doing to the air, it was affecting Jack. "If you're gonna leave, I wish you'd just leave."

I flinched. "What?"

"Why do you keep coming back if you're not going to stay?" The hand that held mine tightened its grip, and my fingers turned white. "Because even when you're gone, you're never really gone."

I could feel his hot breath on my face.

"Whatever it is that's got a pull on you—and taking you away—it's strong. Stronger than any of us here. I can tell. And I won't get over it if you keep coming back."

I couldn't believe what he was saying. "Jack, I—"

"No. Losing you once was hard enough. And now you're here again and everything's coming back. I'm going to get screwed. And I can't do it again. And the people around me can't watch me do it again."

My eyes were burning, and I started blinking rapidly, so what happened next was a blur. A few feet away from us, Noah White, Claire's brother, struck Matt Despain, sending him flying into Jack and throwing all three of us to the ground.

Jack shoved Matt aside and helped me up, and that's when I noticed we weren't the only ones having a heated exchange.

Noah stood over Matt. "You're not getting near my sister again." He kicked Matt before he walked away. I'd never known Noah to be violent.

I wondered where the adult chaperones were, or any spectators for that matter, but the entire farmhouse was in an uproar. Couples yelling at each other. Girls stomping off the dance floor. The punch bowl crashed to the floor and red juice splashed everywhere, running along the grains in the hardwood.

And above all the racket, Cole's song continued, the strings of his guitar screeching.

I whipped to face him. Cole's face had drained of color, and his eyes were closed. He staggered for a moment before he sank to one knee, as if he were about to faint.

By then half the people had filed out of the farmhouse, some still yelling insults at each other. The others were gathering their things to go. Joy O'Leary walked by me, stunned, one sleeve of her dress torn and hanging off her shoulder.

I turned around. Jack was ushering Jules off the dance floor and out the door. I was alone in the middle of it all.

In a matter of minutes, the farmhouse was almost cleared out. A few of the chaperones were left, wandering the room and muttering questions about the strange turn of events. The dance floor, which had looked magical only minutes before, now looked trashed and broken.

Cole sat on the stage, his legs dangling over the side, his head in his hands. I stomped over to him, and in a loud whisper I said, "What the hell was that?"

He acted like he didn't hear me. His back was trembling.

I lowered my voice. "Answer me, Cole."

Nothing.

"Answer me!" I shoved his shoulder, and he toppled over onto his side, his head cracking down on the wooden stage floor. His eyes fluttered. He didn't look good.

"Cole!" I felt his forehead and cheek. I was expecting a fever, but instead his cheek felt cold. I slapped his cheek softly a few times, trying to rouse him.

"I'm sorry, Nik," he mumbled, his words slurring together as if he'd been drinking.

"What happened? What's wrong with you?"

He tried to turn his head away. "I don't want to talk about it."

I forced his head toward me. "You don't get off that easily. Somehow, I'm pretty sure you were at the center of that big brawl. Tell me what happened."

"Sometimes . . ." He paused and squeezed his eyes shut. "Sometimes our hearts . . . crack a little."

He went quiet again. A couple of sophomore girls had wandered back into the farmhouse and were hovering behind me. One of them had Cole's CD in her hands.

"Can we get an autograph?" the one with the CD asked

me tentatively, as if I were Cole's handler. Cole moaned softly, closing his eyes again. Were these girls blind?

I shifted so I was blocking their view of Cole. "Now's obviously not a good time."

"But—" The same girl started forward.

"You can go," I said more forcefully.

The girl frowned. "Fine," she said. She and her friend left in a huff.

I looked at Cole. "Your fans are idiots."

A weak smile played on his lips and quickly disappeared. I spotted a tub of bottled water, and I grabbed one for Cole and brought it to his mouth.

"Here. Drink."

He took a few sips, and it seemed to help. He opened his eyes, and some color came back to his face.

"Talk," I said.

He sniffed and rolled onto his back, staring at the lights above the stage. "It's not a big deal . . ." He paused and took a breath. "Sometimes, when something hurts us, our hearts break a little—in a slightly more . . . *literal* way than for humans. Our pain sort of spills out and onto anyone around us. We call it a cracked heart."

I sat next to him and used the sleeve of my dress to wipe away some of the sweat on his forehead. He was making it hard not to pity him. "Why did it happen to you?"

He looked at me. "Because you were dancing with Jack. And I know how that's going to end."

"How do you think it will end?" I said quietly.

He frowned. "You know how. Anyone can see this. When it comes to you and Jack, there is no happy ending. To expect otherwise is delusional."

He closed his eyes again, and I thought about leaving him here, but one of the chaperones came over to see if Cole needed medical attention.

"No, I'm pretty sure he's fine," I said.

Cole nodded in agreement.

The chaperone, one of the gym teachers, whose name I didn't know, asked, "You'll make sure he gets home okay?"

I took a deep breath and looked at Cole. He was the cause of all my pain. But maybe that wasn't exactly true.

Despite all the other factors that had contributed to my fate, in the end it was my decision that destroyed my life. And all the hurt I was enduring now was my doing.

The blame rested solely with me.

"Yes, I'll make sure."

When I dropped him off at his condo, I reminded him of the deal we'd made—that he would never come to my house again.

He said he'd keep his word.

As I drove home, I thought about what had happened, and came up with two conclusions. First, Cole was clearly trying to convince me he had feelings for me. Whether or not it was true, I didn't know. But it was vital to him that I believe it.

Second, even in total exhaustion, Cole was telling me to

stay away from Jack. He'd caused the disaster at the dance just because I was dancing with Jack. But why?

Why was Cole so freaked out about me being close to Jack? Did he really think Jack could ever fall for me again? And so what if he did? That wouldn't change my fate. I'd still be stuck in the Tunnels. It would just make it harder for me. Not Cole. If it were anyone else, I'd say he was jealous. But that would mean Cole had real feelings for me, and that was impossible.

I didn't know how to find out the truth to conclusion number one, but I had a plan for the second, and that was to do the one thing Cole feared the most.

I parked the car in my driveway, went inside, said a quick good night to my dad so he wouldn't be worried, and then sneaked out through my bedroom window.

I'd go to Jack. Maybe I wouldn't tell him everything, but I'd tell him enough for him to understand what was going on. It would be a gamble, and it might drive Jack further away, but I had to take the chance so I could incite a reaction out of Cole by doing the one thing he'd never expect.

EIGHTEEN

NOW
Walking. Two months, one week left.

The freezing-cold air didn't make a dent in my resolve—my anxiety over what I was about to do was enough to keep me warm through and through. Jack's house was only a few blocks away. The white picket fence at the Boltons' house marked the exact middle point between our houses. We knew because we'd measured the distance one time when I was about eleven years old. We both left our houses at the same time, and walked until we met up.

I ran my fingertips along the fence as I passed the halfway point. Jack always said it wasn't perfectly halfway. He claimed he walked faster, and so it was a longer distance from the Bolton home to the Caputos'.

But when I reached Jack's house, it felt like no time had passed at all. Jack's house, like most of the homes in our development, had a similar floor plan to mine—three bedrooms and two bathrooms on the main floor. Jack had the room on the corner, facing the street. I hoped he hadn't changed it since I'd left.

I tiptoed through the bushes and put my hand up to the glass as I peeked in. I caught just a glimpse before my breath fogged the view, but that was all I needed. Jack's backpack was hanging on the doorknob of the closet.

He was in bed, asleep. For a moment, I thought about turning back, but I didn't.

I held my breath as I tugged on the window. It gave. Jack had one of those older windows that opened outward like a door. The latch had been broken for years.

I slipped through. Jack shifted in his bed in the corner of the room, but he didn't wake. I watched him sleeping for a minute. I focused on his breathing. The air leaving his body. The soft fluttering of his eyelids as he dreamed. His legs jerked a couple of times.

Running. I was pretty sure he was dreaming of running. Escaping something. The panic rolled off his skin in waves. I could taste it.

Maybe I was just imagining his fear. Maybe I needed it to give me the okay to wake him. I stayed as far away from his bed as his small room allowed. If he didn't move when I said his name once, I'd leave.

"Jack," I whispered.

He stirred and then rolled over, shaking off the sleep.

"Jack." This time he shot into a sitting position, his hands flying to the nightstand where he kept his glasses. He didn't turn the light on.

"Becks?" he said. "That you?"

"Yeah."

"I'm dreaming."

I couldn't help but smile. "No."

For a person who'd just discovered an intruder, Jack didn't seem as surprised as he should have been.

He tilted his head. "I used to dream of you like this. After you disappeared, it was like you came to my room every night . . ." His voice faded as he lowered his head and ran a hand through his hair. "Stupid," he muttered, so quietly I couldn't be sure he'd said it. Then he reached over to his nightstand again and turned the clock to get a glance. "Two thirty," he said.

"Yeah."

"You okay?"

"Yeah."

We were quiet for a few moments after that. He didn't ask what I was doing there. He didn't look upset. He just waited.

If I was going to tell him anything, it would be in this room. But now that I was here, I had no idea where to start. How to begin.

I glanced around the room I used to know so well. I recognized his clutter. The picture on top of his dresser of Jack as a ten-year-old, standing next to his grandpa. Behind them, a ranch house. His grandpa had been one of the last of the old-West cowboys, a relic of the history of our town.

Next to the picture was a painted rock from a grade-school art project. Jack had a real problem with throwing things away. Next to the rock sat a folded picture that looked like it had been crumpled up and refolded several times.

I pointed at it. "Is that—"

"Your picture," he finished for me. "I showed it around when I used to look for you."

"Oh."

Above the desktop, on a shelf, were several books, most of which had *Zen* in the title. The one that didn't was called *What the Buddha Taught.* I'd never seen any of them before.

Jack answered my unasked question. "They helped. When things got really bad."

"Oh."

He rubbed his eyes under his glasses, and then he opened the drawer in the nightstand and took something out, but I couldn't tell what.

"You deal," he said. He tossed me the deck of cards. They landed in my lap. "Then when you're ready to talk, talk."

Jack slid out of his bed and walked over to the closet to get a sweatshirt. His black T-shirt clung to his body and he was wearing cotton pants with the San Francisco Giants logo. His favorite team. Once he'd put the sweatshirt on, he sat on the floor across from me.

I'd been watching him, holding my breath, so I hadn't even taken the cards out of the box.

"Do I need to review how to shuffle?" he asked.

I didn't answer. I shook the cards out of their box, cut the deck, and then shuffled them back together. He cut the deck again and I dealt.

I couldn't count all the times we'd done this before, from

the time we were kids and my dad caught me in my backyard playing poker with Jack and Will under my trampoline.

Jack had told him the losers would volunteer at the home for the elderly. He knew my dad would go for that. Jack and I lost that day, and we kept our word. It was the one game I remember him losing.

Jack pulled a tin box full of old poker chips out from under his bed and gave us each a handful. The same poker chips we'd always played with. Red and black ones, from a casino in Wendover.

He put a toothpick in his mouth to chew. So Jack.

"Do you remember—" I started to say.

He watched me. Didn't say anything. I wondered why he didn't press, then I realized he was waiting for me. Everything out of my mouth tonight would be offered on my own.

I fanned my cards out in my hand and put them in front of my face, grateful for the barrier to Jack's searching eyes. I could do this. I could do this. "I've been gone a long time," I said. "Longer than anyone knows."

I didn't know if it was the draft that made me shudder, or the sudden release of a burden of secrecy, even though Jack couldn't possibly guess the full meaning behind my admission.

He studied his cards, arranging their order. "How long?" he asked.

My answer came out in a sigh. "Years and years. I know how it sounds."

But he didn't question me on the time discrepancy. Instead he asked, "Were you hurt?"

The sheer innocence of the question made me sad. "A little."

"Have you told anyone else?"

"No. I . . . don't know how . . . really." My voice started to waver, and I buried my face in my hands. I shivered again, and he reached behind him to pull the top quilt off his bed. The quilt his mother had made for him when he turned twelve. He sat beside me and put the quilt over me.

"Shh. It's okay. You're okay now. You don't have to talk anymore. Just close your eyes." I curled up on the floor, and he lay down next to me, staying on top of the quilt while I was under it. He rubbed the back of my hand. "I'm here, Becks. Whatever it is you're scared of, I'm here."

I lost the ability to dream long ago. Dreams can't exist where so much energy has been taken away.

I had dreamed during my first few years—or maybe decades—in the Everneath. But as my own supply of energy dwindled, the dreams became shorter and shorter, until they disappeared completely. Along with all of my memories.

But that night with Jack, I dreamed.

Senseless dreams at first, as if my brain had been kick-started after a long winter in the garage. No defined shapes, no awareness of location.

But then my dreams held meaning. I dreamed I was thrown into a shallow grave, with layer upon layer of dirt piled on top of me, crushing my chest until my heart exploded.

But I *couldn't* dream. It was supposed to be impossible.

I jerked awake.

My face was so close to Jack's. Almost touching.

Still asleep, Jack tilted his head toward me, and his lips brushed against mine. At that moment, I felt something rush through me, like a surge of power. Jack's eyes opened wide. I leaped back and we both froze.

"Whoa," he said. "Were we . . . ?"

"About to," I answered. Then I thought about how I was dreaming, even though I wasn't supposed to be able to, and it hit me.

I'd stolen energy from him.

When our lips were so close, I stole enough energy to Feed, and that put me over the dream threshold.

I shot up and backed away until I was in the far corner of the room. "I'm so sorry. I never should have . . . I should go."

"No. No more running away, Becks." He held his hands out in front of him, palms down. His calm voice couldn't mask his confusion. "What was that?"

"Um . . . I'm so sorry."

"Stop apologizing. Just talk."

"Okay, but you stay over there."

He nodded, as if he weren't even considering coming any closer to me.

"I don't know where to start." I hugged my knees into my chest and rested my chin on top. "I think of the words I would have to use to explain everything, and I don't believe them myself."

"I'll be straight with you. Up until that kiss, I thought it was drugs. Now I don't know. So try me."

I took a deep breath. "That kiss felt different?"

"Yeah."

"Good different?"

He paused. "Yeah."

"I'm sorry, Jack. I know exactly how you feel, because I felt it too my first time." When Cole fed off me. I couldn't believe I'd just done the same thing to Jack. How did I let it come to this?

"Your first time?" He grabbed his glasses off the nightstand and wiped them with the sleeve of his shirt. "Then start there. Tell me what happened."

"I'll try. You remember leaving for football camp?"

"Yeah." Jack rubbed his eyes with the palms of his hands and put his glasses on. "It was the last time I talked to you. You were standing with Cole. Is that when you started to hang out with him?"

"Yes. Going to concerts. Stuff like that." I bit my lip. "Look, I'm just going to try to keep talking, and it may not make sense at first, but if I stop, I won't be able to start again." Jack nodded. "Cole took me rafting one day, with the rest of the band. They wanted to shoot the Tube, and they invited me."

Jack shook his head. "Shooting the Tube after the spring runoff?"

"I know. Not the smartest move." I squeezed my eyes shut for a moment. "We hit a rock and I fell out."

He drew in a sharp breath. "He never should have taken you. You're not big enough. Were you hurt?"

"The current dragged me under, and as I kicked to the surface, my leg caught on a branch or rock or something. I couldn't get it free. I practically had to rip my leg off to get to the surface again, and when I did I was bleeding. A lot."

I closed my eyes, remembering strong hands pulling me to the bank of the river. *"Hang on, Nik. You'll be okay," Cole said.*

"Keep talking. What happened next?" Jack said.

I opened my eyes. "I was lying on the bank. Pressing on the gash." Red liquid had seeped between my fingers.

"I can make it go away," Cole said. "Do you want me to take the pain away?"

Jack placed his hand on my ankle and urged my leg straight. He pushed the hem of my jeans up. The raised skin of my scar twisted from my shin around to the back of my calf in a jagged line.

"Oh," Jack said. He lightly touched the scar and traced the line. "It's deep."

I nodded and watched his hand on my leg, his callused fingers on my skin. Goose bumps appeared and I shivered.

"Are you cold?"

I shook my head and tucked my leg back in, pulling my jeans leg down in the process.

"What happened next?"

"Cole said he could make it feel better. And I let him."

LAST YEAR

The shore of the rapids. One week before the Feed.

The shivers were violent enough that my teeth bit into my tongue several times. I could taste blood. But I didn't care, because all I could think about was the pain in my leg. It was so bad, I wondered if the leg was still attached, or if it had been ripped off and was floating down the river somewhere.

"She's in shock," a voice said above me.

"My leg," I said. Speaking made me choke. There had to be some river water down my throat. I coughed, throwing up water.

Strong hands helped turn me over, so I wouldn't puke lying on my back.

"You're okay, Nik." Cole's voice.

I needed someone to tell me if I still had my leg. I tried to point to my leg, but my arms flailed about.

"Whoa. Settle down." His voice was soothing. "You're fine."

"Dude, it's gushing blood."

"Shut it, Gavin," Cole growled. "Take off your jacket."

I heard fabric tearing and felt pressure on my leg. "This might hurt a little," Cole said.

Then the real pain hit. Like a hot poker jabbing through the skin and muscle of my leg, burning as it tore its way to my bone.

I screamed. I had to get away from the poker. I thrashed and twisted, trying to free myself.

"Nik! Stay still."

I screamed again and shook my head. Two hands clenched my shoulders, and I heard Cole's voice.

"Nik. Open your eyes." I did. Cole's face was inches from mine. "Do you want me to take the pain away?"

"Cole!" Maxwell said from somewhere behind him.

Cole kept his eyes on me, but he shook his head. "It's not your decision, Max."

"But the exposure," Max said.

"Enough!" Cole growled. "It'll work out."

Maxwell didn't say anything else. I could barely keep my eyes open; the pain in my leg was making everything else blurry, but Cole wouldn't let me move.

"Do you, Nik? Do you want me to help with the pain?"

I nodded, keeping my mouth shut so I wouldn't scream again.

"Tell me. Tell me what you want."

"Please," I said, and then I gasped and tried to grab my leg, but Cole had me pinned. "Make it go away."

Cole leaned even closer, and for a moment I thought he was going to kiss me, but I didn't have the presence of mind to turn away. His lips didn't touch me, though. He closed his eyes and sucked in a deep breath, and with that, the sharpest edges of the pain in my leg dissipated.

He took in several more deep breaths, and each one made the pain less and less, as if I'd been bitten by a snake and he was sucking the venom out. I could finally breathe without wincing, and when Cole asked me if I was okay, all I could answer was, "Keep going."

NOW
Jack's bedroom.

"So, what, he had drugs or something?"

I shook my head. "The drugs were just a rumor. He . . ." I couldn't finish. Putting it into words was harder than I thought it would be, and it was only a fraction of the whole story. I wanted to give up.

"Tell me, Becks. Just keep going."

"He sort of kissed me, and he was right. He took the pain away." I skipped the part about the century underground. I had to see how Jack would react to this small piece of the puzzle. "And now I can sort of do the same thing. But I don't need to. I can survive without it."

We sat in silence for a few minutes. I couldn't look Jack in the face, even though it was dark in his room, so I looked out the window. There were no stars tonight, or maybe the clouds were blocking all of them.

"Is this some sort of metaphor? Are you messing with me?"

"No."

"Show me," Jack said.

I jerked my head around to look at him. "Show you what?"

"Kiss me."

"No." I didn't realize I'd been holding my breath until I let it out. "I can't."

"You have to."

"Why?"

He shrugged. "I don't know. Maybe it will help me understand. If I hadn't felt it before, I wouldn't have believed a word. Do it again, so I know it wasn't all some weird dream."

I shook my head, but I could feel myself giving in. I wanted to give in. "I won't kiss you."

"But—"

I held my hand up. "I can show you without kissing you. I think."

This seemed to satisfy him. "Okay."

I thought about how much time I'd been back. How much I had replenished my soul. It was nowhere near full, but there had to be enough that when I sampled Jack, I wouldn't lose control. Jack made a move to close the distance between us.

"Don't," I said. He froze. "Just stay still."

"Why are you so worried, Becks?"

"Because we need to be able to stop. It will feel good to you. It'll feel like suddenly everything you're worried about disappears."

"What will it feel like to you?"

Like a starving person eating a feast. But I didn't tell him that. "Close your eyes and hold still."

"Okay."

I scooted toward him and leaned forward, moving as slowly

as possible. Jack remained perfectly still. When my lips were a couple of inches away from his mouth, I breathed in. And focused on taking the energy that was in front of me and pulling it inside. It was as if warm, charged air were coating my throat, replacing the cold emptiness inside me.

His eyes popped open. We watched each other for a few long seconds as I continued to taste his emotions. Residual pain, mostly. Heartache at first. These were at the surface. The negative ones always were. That's why Forfeits kept coming back for more. In the beginning, it felt like a release.

The well inside me received its first drops of moisture from someone else. Jack leaned in even closer, and I scrambled back until I was against the wall once more.

"Did you feel it?" I asked.

Jack pressed his lips together and nodded once.

"I'm sorry," I said. "I know this can't possibly make any sense to you."

He looked at the floor. "What are you, Nikki?"

Nikki? He hadn't called me that for so long. "I don't know." I winced. Being truthful with Jack wasn't working. I could feel it in the space between us. I was losing him.

Still looking down, he said, "I think you should go now."

Jack was scared of me.

I walked over to the window and climbed out.

NINETEEN

NOW
Home. Two months, one week left.

When I got into my own bed, I dreamed I was standing in the aisle of the Shop-n-Go and my feet started to sink into the ground. I tried to step out, but the floor was like quicksand. I grabbed the stand with the chocolate doughnuts and it toppled onto me, pushing me even farther under. And when I opened my mouth to scream, several arms came out of the floor, covered my mouth, and dragged me the rest of the way under.

The ability to dream again was highly overrated.

Frantic knocking on my bedroom door woke me up after what seemed like only moments. "Nikki?" It was Tommy's voice. "Nikki? Are you awake?"

"Yeah, bud. C'mon in."

Tommy poked his head in, his brown hair scruffy with sleep. "You're in the paper."

"What?" I sat up in bed.

"Dad says you're in the paper. He's kinda mad."

I threw the covers back and grabbed my robe on the way out of my room. How in the world was I in the paper?

My dad was sitting at the kitchen table, forking a breakfast ham. He didn't look up.

"Dad? What's going on?"

He pushed the paper over toward the empty chair across from him. I sat down and scanned the headlines. At the bottom of the front page, I found it. MAYOR'S DAUGHTER AT CENTER OF CHRISTMAS DANCE BRAWL. Beneath the headline was a fuzzy picture of me just after Jack and I had been knocked down. It looked like it'd been taken by a camera phone, and it looked ten times worse than it was.

I shoved the paper aside without reading further. "I didn't start it, Dad."

He took a long sip from his mug of coffee, his eyes still focused on the paper. "It doesn't matter, Nikki. What matters is how it looks."

"But it's not the truth."

"Haven't you learned anything? It's not necessarily about the truth. It's about how people perceive a thing that makes it damaging. What does it really matter where you were for six months, when people are going to think what they want to think? In the absence of proof, all that matters is perception." He picked up the paper, and I realized this was about more than just the photo. "I can't fight this. The article says I have no comment, because the only choice you've given me is to hope that it goes away. And in an election, nothing goes away."

"But what I do shouldn't make a difference," I mumbled.

"You know better than that. Tomorrow's headlines will read something like, 'How Can the Mayor Run the City When He Can't Even Run His Household?' What am I supposed to do with you? Do I have to hire a nanny for my seventeen-year-old daughter? Do I have to stay home from the office? Send you to a private school? Tell me."

"No, Dad. It won't happen again." I got up to leave. "But it wasn't my fault."

"That may be true. But pictures"—he held up the paper— "drown out everything else. My denials will be like . . . a whisper at a rock concert. No one will hear it."

"So you're not mad about what really happened." I smacked the paper on the table. "You're just mad about the picture."

He stared at me and breathed through his nose. "You may have cost me the election." He cut off a large chunk of ham and shoved it in his mouth. "Maybe I should've sent you to live with Aunt Grace. Or even to a boarding school."

I looked away.

"Mrs. Ellingson is on her way over."

"Okay." Time to pee in a cup. At least I knew I couldn't mess that up.

The next week passed in the flap of a bird's wing. Jack was avoiding me, I still hadn't seen Mary, and I'd damaged my dad's bid for reelection. All in all, not what I'd intended for my Return.

The chance to make things right with my dad came the last week of Christmas vacation, when his latest campaign flyers arrived. I promised him I would help distribute them. The volunteers were to meet at campaign headquarters on Apple Blossom Road.

Today the sun was reflecting off the latest layer of snow in the town, making it seem a lot warmer than it actually was. When I got to the office, my dad was at a desk near the back, talking to a tall man with thick dark hair. He motioned me back.

I walked toward them and stood awkwardly while my dad finished his conversation. The man was talking about labor unions. He had an accent. I hoped my dad wouldn't include me in the conversation, because he had a tendency to provide English-to-English translation for me. As if I were too young to understand someone with an accent. It was always embarrassing.

Before my dad could speak to me, however, the front door rattled, and Jack and Jules walked in. Jack shoved his hands deep in his jacket pockets, as if to warm them. He kept his eyes down. My breath stopped in my chest. We hadn't spoken since that night in his room.

What are you, Nikki?

I shook my head, trying to clear the memory. Jules spotted me and waved.

I'd started to walk toward them when Percy Jones, my dad's

campaign manager, called everyone to attention near the front door to organize the distribution of flyers and maps.

Jack grabbed a stack and Jules picked a route map, and then they came to me in the back.

"Hey," Jules said.

Jack kept his gaze on the wall with the posters and didn't look up when I said hi. "Percy called me," Jules said. "I guess I signed the volunteer list . . . a while ago."

"Oh. That's nice of you."

We stood silent for a moment before Jules held up the map she had gotten from Percy. "We have the block north of Maplehurst. It's big. You want to come with us?"

I glanced at my dad, who was still talking to the man with the accent. He caught my eye and waved me away.

"Sure," I said, turning back to them.

Jules tilted her head toward the exit. "Great. Let's go. Jack, give us a few of those."

Jack divvied up the pile. His fingers brushed mine as he handed me several flyers, and then he handed Jules the rest and shoved his hands in his pockets again.

We walked out into the cold, and I remembered something in my bag. I reached inside and pulled out a pair of gloves I had knitted—with Jack's hands in mind—days ago, and held them out to him without a word.

Jack stopped. He looked at the gloves in my hand, then at my face, and his lips twitched a little bit before he reached out to take them. He put them on. They were a little big. The fingertips of the one on his left hand flopped around a bit. He looked like he was wearing two doilies.

I shrugged.

Jules turned away and pretended to study the map. She pointed up a hill. "We're supposed to start this way."

The three of us started walking the map, Jules in the middle. After a few failed attempts at conversation, we stopped trying to talk altogether. Our route took us near the soup kitchen, and as we went by, the side door opened and Christopher appeared. He spotted me and waved, and I stopped.

"Hey, Nikki. How's it going?" He turned a key in the door to lock it, and then walked toward us.

Jules and Jack stopped too.

"Hi," I said. "We're just delivering stuff. For my dad."

Christopher glanced at Jules and Jack and stuck his hand out toward Jack. "I'm Christopher. I work with Nikki at the kitchen."

Jack took his hand. Christopher stared at the homemade glove.

"I'm Jack. I didn't know she worked there."

Christopher shook Jules's hand next. "Yeah. Every Saturday. You know, we're always looking for more help if either of you would like to do some good."

I smiled. "Always recruiting."

"Always," Christopher said. "I have openings Saturdays—"

I interrupted Christopher before he could go on. "Oh, these guys have . . ." I stopped, not sure how to finish that sentence or why I'd interrupted in the first place.

Jules broke the silence. "Thanks, Christopher, but I work at the mall Saturdays."

"I'd be happy to help," Jack blurted out.

We all turned to look at Jack.

"Wonderful," Christopher said. "Jack . . . ?" He waited for Jack to fill in the blank.

"Caputo. Jack Caputo."

"Caputo? The quarterback?"

"Yeah."

"Great. When can you start?"

Jack's eyes flicked to me for a moment. "I'll have to work out my schedule."

After we said good-bye to Christopher, we walked for a long time in silence.

Being together used to be as easy as breathing, but of course, everything changed when I got back, and it was never more evident than when all three of us were together.

For a moment, I mourned the loss of our simple friendship, and in that moment of grieving, I realized that Jules and Jack would be okay if I were gone for good. They would probably be better than they were now.

TWENTY

NOW

Mrs. Stone's class. Less than two months left.

*T*he day with the flyers was excruciating, and I had no idea where it left me with Jack.

When we returned to school after the holiday break, we were in a strange limbo. He wasn't avoiding me, but he wasn't really talking to me, either. Finally, on Friday I thought I could feel Jack watching me from the adjacent seat, but I never turned to look. Mrs. Stone lectured on Euripides's use of the Greek chorus, and I let my mind wander until a small piece of paper landed on the corner of my desk. It could only be from Jack. I grabbed it and brought it near my lap to unfold it.

Becks—I'm ready to know more. Meet you for lunch.

I kept my eyes on my paper and nodded. Maybe Jack wasn't ready to give up on me just yet.

When the hour finally came, I jogged down the hall toward my nook. I turned the corner with a smile on my face, but it wasn't Jack waiting for me. It was Cole in his black-haired disguise. When he saw me, he smiled.

"Hey, Nik. Can we talk?"

I stood, frozen in place, staring at him. My lunch sack fell to the floor, the yogurt inside making a *splat.*

"Here, let me get that." He stooped and gathered up the mess, then lazily threw it across the hallway, where it arced perfectly into the garbage can.

"No." I answered finally. "We can't talk." I looked behind me, wondering how soon Jack would show up. "What are you doing here?"

"Today's my first day." Cole smiled at my confused expression. "I told you I was starting school here. Everyone has a right to a public education."

A couple of sophomore girls walked past our nook, and as they caught sight of "Neal," they smiled and waved. He winked in return, and the girls giggled as they walked off. One of them looked at me over her shoulder and flipped her hair.

I rolled my eyes. It didn't matter what form Cole took; he was still a magnet for girls. He gave me a playful shrug. "Sophomores. They can't help it."

I folded my arms. "What do you want, Cole?" He patted the space next to him. I didn't want to make a scene, so I sank to the ground and spoke softly. "Please make it fast. I don't want Jack to see you."

"It doesn't matter if Jack sees me."

"It matters to me."

He scoffed. "But it *shouldn't*. Why can't you see that nothing that happens on the Surface means anything to you anymore? School, homework, friends, family . . . The truth is, your stop here is as unimportant as an airport layover." He let his finger trace a line over my shoulder, where my mark was hidden beneath my shirt, then drew a series of concentric circles, each one bigger than the last. As he did, I could feel the Shade bumping against my skin to meet his fingers. "It's like one last dream before you're forever awake. Because that's all the Surface life is, Nik. It's just a dream for you. It's not real anymore."

Just then a voice cut through the tension. "Becks?"

I whipped my head up to see Jack standing in the hallway, staring at Cole and me. I scrambled to my feet, at a loss for words. Jack had no way of knowing the boy next to me, the one he'd fought on the field, was Cole. He just knew he was an old friend of mine. Jack looked from me to Cole and back again, and seemed to make a conclusion, then a decision. Then he did the last thing I ever would have anticipated.

He took a deep breath and held out his hand. "We got off to a bad start, but you're obviously a friend of Becks's."

Cole stared at his hand, stumped. He looked at me like, *What the hell am I supposed to do with* this*?* I'd never seen him so baffled. It was almost comical.

Then the second-to-last thing that I ever would have anticipated happened. Cole took Jack's hand and shook it. "I'm Neal."

"Jack." Jack briefly glanced sideways at me. "I'll try not to hit you again."

Cole and Jack, shaking hands. I covered my eyes with my fingers, wondering when the world had officially tipped over onto its side. When I lowered my hand, they were both looking at me. I'd had enough awkward.

"Let's go," I said, tugging on Jack's arm.

Cole frowned and looked away. "Take care of *our* girl," he muttered sarcastically.

Jack let me pull him away, keeping his eyes on "Neal" until we had turned the corner. He didn't say a word as we walked out of the school. When we reached the front lawn, Jack stopped. He stood there for a moment looking straight ahead at nothing. I stayed next to him and waited. We were on shaky ground, and I didn't want to scare him again.

"Becks, are you . . ." His intake of breath was audible. "Are you with that guy?"

"No," I said firmly.

He turned toward me. "He's been following you everywhere. I saw the way he looked at you—"

"No."

His face seemed to relax a little, which made him look tired. "Then who is he?"

I hesitated. This was not the conversation to have while standing in the doorway of our high school.

Jack misread the pause. "Becks, it's okay if you're with someone else. I know we're not together anymore. But we can't be friends if you're going to keep secrets from me."

"I'll tell you. But not here."

A hint of a smile showed on his mouth. "Name the place."

"Somewhere no one can hear."

He grabbed my hand and started pulling me. "How about that place by that tree where we went that one time?"

I smiled because I knew exactly where he was talking about. A little shack of a coffee hut, hidden behind this giant oak tree that sat on the border of the city park. Somewhere only we knew. "Now? But school. Classes."

"School will be here tomorrow. I'm not as sure about you."

I followed Jack to his car, and then he drove toward the coffee hut. Once in the car, I brought my feet up and hugged my knees, facing the window, aware of the pit in my stomach. I was going to tell Jack more of the story, but would he believe me?

He'd believed me the night of the dance. But it had taken a kiss.

Before we got there, Jack's phone vibrated with a text. He flipped it open and shut it with a sigh, then turned the car around.

"Where are we going?" I asked.

"Just a quick stop." Jack pulled up in front of Mulligan's and put the car in park. "Be right back." He went inside, and a few moments later he came through the door with a staggering Will. He shoved his older brother into the backseat. "And we're off," Jack said.

He turned the car around again and drove straight to the coffee shop—the Kona—and the three of us went inside, taking one of the four tiny booths. Will sat in the corner, facedown on the table, passed out, or maybe just in a deep sleep. Jack sat next to him. I sat on the other side.

Except for two guys at the small bar by the ordering window, the place was empty. We didn't talk until the coffees came. Then Jack said, "So who was that guy?"

I glanced nervously at Will.

"It's okay," Jack said. "He won't hear a thing. Who was that guy?"

"Cole." I let out a deep breath.

"Cole?"

I nodded. "He can, um, change his appearance."

"What? How?"

"I don't know. I just know that he can alter his appearance. He can switch back and forth between what he looked like when he first came to town and this new disguise—Neal. Everlivings don't like to do it a lot because it takes up too much energy, and they don't like to waste it, considering they have to steal it. So they try not to use it. But Cole wanted to go to high school, and he can't do it as . . . Cole." I buried my face in my hands. "I knew this would sound crazy."

"Just talk. I'll listen."

"Okay."

I pushed my coffee aside, put my elbows on the table, and told him everything. How the Everlivings had found the secret to everlasting life by stealing human energy. How every hundred years on the Surface, they needed to go to the Everneath and Feed. Drain one human of energy almost completely. One

Forfeit. How I followed him down and stayed for a hundred years, even though only a few months had passed on the Surface. Jack winced at this, and he looked like he was about to say something, but he remained quiet.

I told him about how Cole wanted me to return with him.

I told him almost everything. I didn't talk about what had happened just before I left with Cole and I didn't tell him that the Tunnels of the Everneath were coming for me soon. Jack would freak out if he knew I was leaving again, and I didn't want to waste time trying to convince him it was hopeless.

I didn't tell him I'd thought of him every day. That even when every other memory had faded, he never left.

My chest relaxed, as if a band had snapped upon my telling the truth to someone. Eventually I had finished my coffee and my bizarre story, and someone else knew about the Everneath, yet the world didn't implode.

"You said Cole steals energy," Jack said.

I nodded. "He explained it to me once. All of us are alive because of what amounts to a series of electrical impulses inside our bodies. He steals the electricity. But to the people he steals from, it feels like he's draining them of emotions."

"Then why does it feel good?"

"It only feels good at first. Because the top layer of electricity is made up of our negative emotions. Pain. Heartache. Suffering." I looked down. "Those are the first to go."

"And then after—"

"It takes a long time, but after that, the positive ones go. Joy. Contentment. And then it just feels empty."

Jack stirred his untouched coffee. "What about the mark?"

"What?"

"The mark that Cole, or whatever his new name is, talked about that day he came to Mrs. Stone's classroom."

Jack had remembered. *Great little tattoo on her shoulder that tastes faintly of charcoal*, Cole had said. I reached up to the collar of my shirt and pulled it aside, exposing part of the black mark on my shoulder.

"What does it mean?" he asked.

It means there's a Shade inside me. It means the clock is counting down. I shrugged. "I don't know. It was there when I Returned."

"You don't remember getting it?"

"I don't remember a lot of what happened in the Everneath. It feels like a dream, where you wake up and it all seems fuzzy. But bits and pieces come to me at different times. I was sort of semiconscious the whole time."

"Were there other people with you?"

I hadn't thought about it until then. "I don't remember anyone else specifically. Cole and I were in our own . . . little cocoon, sort of. But there were hundreds, maybe thousands, of other cocoons like ours. And they all Feed at the same time. It's an entire world under there. A world of the Everliving. Like an alternate universe, where they've found the secret to living forever, but they have to steal from our universe to make it happen. In fact, they have to make regular offerings to the other side."

I told him about the doorway I'd discovered at the Shop-n-Go. I didn't tell him about the hair Cole had given me.

"That night. In my room . . ." Jack began. My cheeks went red as I remembered. He took a breath and went on. "You could steal energy too. Does that mean you're . . . ?"

"An Everliving? No. Every human takes a little and gives a little each day. Like how someone's smile feels contagious? It really can be just on microscopic levels. I happen to be . . . more empty, I guess, than everyone else, so there's a stronger vacuum in me. When I recover all my emotions, it won't be so strong. It'll be like everyone else's, and I won't have to do it anymore."

"But part of you wants to?"

I smiled. Jack could always read me so well. "Right now, yes. I think that's why Cole is trying so hard to make me give up. Because I guess I'm still weak. But the longer I stay here, the stronger I get."

Jack nodded and leaned back. "How come I've never heard of anything like this before? I mean, how could they stay hidden? Without anyone knowing?"

"They haven't, exactly." When Jack tilted his head, I went on. "Half truths have been told for centuries. Myths about the Underworld."

"The Underworld. Like hell? Like Hades?"

I nodded. "Only Cole calls him Osiris. And it has nothing

to do with hell, or the afterlife. The Everneath is for the Ever-living."

I paused and ran my finger along the rim of my coffee cup. Will twitched a bit from his position of head-on-table. "I've been to hell," he mumbled, releasing a little string of drool from the corner of his mouth to the table. "I totally know what you mean." He turned his head so he was facing the wall, sighed loudly, and seemed to be asleep again.

Jack shook his head. "I can't believe we're having this conversation." He ran his hand through his hair, and a part of it stuck straight up. I wanted to reach over and fix it. "I mean, I thought you were getting high."

"I know. Everyone did. They still do."

"But I should've known better." The owner dropped off two more full mugs of coffee, and this time Jack started sipping. After a moment, he said, "What do we do about Cole? Can't we . . . expose him or something?" Immediately after he asked the question, he shook his head. "They'd never believe us."

"Jack, I've messed up enough of your life. There's nothing you can do about Cole. I'll handle him. You don't have to—"

"Enough, Becks. This is what friends do. Before we got together, we were friends, remember? The friendship is still there, isn't it?"

I didn't say anything for a moment. It was so much more than friendship on my side. Despite everything, I'd never stopped loving him.

"Isn't it, Becks? I mean, you didn't completely forget about me in the Everneath, did you?"

"No." Wasn't it obvious on my face? That he was the only thing I remembered? My memories of Jack should've been etched on my skin by now, for all the world to see.

"Okay. Friends talk. Friends help each other."

I nodded.

"Friends don't eat friends' souls."

I smiled. "Got it."

"Can I ask you something else?"

"Of course."

"Why did you finally decide to tell me the truth?"

I traced my finger along the lip of my coffee mug. "It's probably nothing, but Cole seems anxious to keep me away from you in particular. I wanted to see how he'd react, and maybe that would give me an idea as to why."

He grimaced. "I have an idea."

"What?"

"He's in love with you."

I wrinkled my forehead. "No he's not. He's not capable."

Jack leaned forward. "Trust me, Becks. I know exactly what loving you looks like on a person. And he loves you."

My face went warm and I looked away. If only Jack were talking about now, and not before. I shook my head. "There has to be something more to it."

Jack put his chin on the palm of his hand. "Well, let's find out."

"How?"

He raised his eyes to meet mine, a shy little smile on his face, so different from his usual confident grin. "We'll spend time together. And let Cole know it."

I lowered my eyes as butterflies swirled all around in my stomach. He pulled out his wallet and put a five-dollar bill on the table. "C'mon. We can make it back for seventh if we leave now. I've got calculus."

TWENTY-ONE

NOW
School. One month, three weeks left.

The silence on the ride back to school felt like a warm blanket, now that so many secrets had been shared between the two of us. We got to school in time for last period. When I walked into the art studio, Cole—wearing his Neal disguise—was standing in front of the easel next to mine.

"Cole," I said, stopping a few feet away.

Cole gave me a smile and raised his eyebrows. "It's Neal, actually. Nikki, right?"

I didn't answer, and turned to my canvas. Mr. Tanner told the class to quiet down and start sketching. I put my pencil up to the canvas, but I couldn't concentrate on anything except the fact that Cole was suddenly in my art class.

A couple of girls on the other side of Cole whispered back and forth, shooting him curious stares. He had a smirk on his face that told me he knew he was the center of attention.

"Boy, drawing is so hard," he muttered loudly.

One of the girls leaned toward him and said, "I could help you with that, Neal."

I rolled my eyes and watched the clock anxiously for the rest of the hour. My canvas remained empty. As soon as the bell rang, I shot out the door. Cole trailed after me, whistling one of the Dead Elvises' songs.

As we approached my locker, I could see Jack waiting, leaning against the locker next to mine, his thumbs hooked in his pockets. Cole put his arm around my shoulders. I let him.

"Afternoon, Caputo," Cole said.

Jack's face remained a cool mask. "Hello, Cole. Becks."

Cole froze at Jack's casual use of his real name. His arm dropped from my shoulders. I couldn't help but smile.

Jack looked at me. "I'll see you in Mrs. Stone's room, Becks. You're coming, right? Mythology paper?"

I nodded. Just before he sauntered away, Jack winked at me and slapped Cole hard on the shoulder. "See you around, *Neal*."

I didn't look at Cole as I shifted my bag higher up on my shoulder. I was having a hard time acting as casual as Jack. I said, "Well, see you later."

He grabbed my elbow. "You told him?" The anger in his voice was evident.

"Yes."

"And he believed you?"

I looked up. "Yes."

Cole narrowed his eyes. "You told him *everything*?"

Uh-oh. "Yes," I lied. Cole studied my face for a moment, and I yanked my arm free. "I have to go."

I turned and started to walk away, but before I took three steps Cole called out from behind me. "He doesn't know about you leaving, does he." It was a statement, not a question.

I tried not to falter as I ignored him and continued down the hall.

"I'm right, aren't I?" he said. "You don't want him to know!"

I couldn't shake the chill as I rounded the corner. There was no way I was ready for Jack to know the truth about the Tunnels coming for me.

I heard loud footsteps behind me as Cole ran to catch up.

"Wait, Nik. Please hear me out."

I turned to face him.

"How can you trust Jack?"

He had to be kidding. I sighed and turned, but he grabbed my shoulder.

"Nik, you know what he did to you," Cole said softly. "You know what you saw at the dorm. The night you decided to go under with me." I closed my eyes. "Are you sure you're betting on the right guy? I would never hurt you like that."

I shook his hand off my shoulder, realizing for the first time just how much Cole may have contributed to my fall. I'd seen at the Christmas Dance how Cole could influence people's moods.

"Stop pretending you had nothing to do with my decision. I know what you can do." I remembered how Cole's breath had washed over me on my front porch right before I'd left for Jack's dorm. I was sure now he had the ability to influence my emotions. "You made me doubt him."

LAST YEAR
Two days before the Feed.

I never thought I would care whether or not the man who was driving the car that struck and killed my mother was convicted of manslaughter. My mother was still dead. Verdict or no verdict.

But the day the jury came back with their decision, I realized how wrong I'd been.

I heard the news at school. Kevin Reid was going free. Case dismissed on a technicality. The blood-alcohol test had been tampered with.

I left school early, and when I got home, I could hear my father's voice coming from the bedroom. He was on the phone. I was about to call his name, but then I heard what he was saying.

". . . Our official response is that we have faith in the legal system we have been given and will accept the outcome our system produces."

He was quiet for a minute.

I didn't realize I was frozen in place in the hallway. His bedroom door was open a crack, and so I pushed it open further. My dad turned to look at me, smiled, blinked his eyes, and nodded his head. I knew that look. It was the practiced look of sympathy he would pull when questioning a victim in front of a jury.

He held up a finger as he continued his end of the conversation. "We have no plans to appeal. At this point, the only way my family will move forward is if we forgive—"

I threw my backpack at him. Without warning. It hit him in the face before I even realized it'd left my hands. He looked at me with a stunned expression, and for a moment the only sound in the room came from my heavy breathing. How could he talk about forgiveness?

"Lemme call you back, Phil. 'Kay?" He didn't wait for Phil's response; he just snapped his phone shut. "Nikki? What the hell was that all about?"

"Reid!" I couldn't think of anything else to say.

"He got off, Nikki. You knew this was a possibility."

I knew it. But nobody believed it would actually happen. "There's got to be something we can do. He can't get away with it."

My dad sighed and sat on the edge of his bed, patting the spot beside him. "Sit down, Nikki."

"I'm fine," I said. "Who were you talking to on the phone just now?"

"Phil at the *Trib*."

"He's going to run it in the paper? That we forgive him?"

He nodded. "Nikki, the entire town has been affected by

this whole thing because of my position as mayor. It needs to be known that we trust in the legal system. And with the election coming up . . ." His voice trailed off.

I couldn't believe what he was saying. "I get it. You look good if you lie."

He stood up and walked toward me, his hand outstretched. "Nikki. Your mother would've wanted us to stand together. We'll never heal until we forgive."

I slapped his hand away. "You don't know what she would've wanted. You'd have to actually be here to know her." He winced, but I couldn't stop myself. "Good luck sleeping tonight."

I left him standing there, looking at the hand I'd slapped. He didn't call after me.

I didn't know where to go. Jules was in Vancouver with her family for spring break. Besides, Jack was really the only person who would understand.

I didn't give myself a chance to change my mind. I grabbed my keys and headed out the door, almost running into Cole on the porch.

"Whoa, Nik. You okay?" His brow creased in concern.

"Cole." I brushed the tears off my cheeks. "What are you doing here?"

He held up the T-shirt he'd been carrying. "Wanted to show you the latest design, but it looks like now's not a good time."

"I'm sorry, but I have to go. I have to see Jack."

I started past him, but he grabbed my arm. "Wait. Can I do anything?"

"No. Thanks. But I need to go."

"Of course." He put both hands on my shoulders and pulled me toward him so we were face-to-face. "Drive safely, okay?"

I nodded, unable to think clearly with him so close. "Umm . . . thanks. I'll see you later, okay?"

He released my arms and then I jumped in my car, trying to ignore the sudden niggling feeling in the back of my mind that it might not be a good idea to crash Jack's football camp unannounced. I pushed the thought aside. Once the engine started, I blasted music and began the hour-long drive to the dorms at Utah State University.

By the time I got to Logan, my ears were ringing. I had to admit my resolve was shaken a little, but not enough to convince me to turn around and go back.

I wasn't sure what Jack would tell me. Who he would side with. He'd been the one who always tried to talk to me about Reid's trial, but I never wanted to. Now that I knew Reid was free to go home to his wife and kids and heal his fractured family, while we were all left broken . . . I couldn't take it.

I drove to Henley Hall. I didn't know where Jack was staying, beyond the name of the dormitory that housed the team year after year.

The thought of burying my head in Jack's chest, his arms wrapped around my waist, kept me from searching for a legal parking space. I pulled into the handicapped spot closest to the building. Who cared if I got a ticket? It would go on my dad's insurance.

A storm was brewing, and tiny little ice flakes danced in the bitter wind. My long-sleeved tee offered no protection, and the ten seconds it took me to sprint to the bottom doors were painful with the cold.

I threw the door open and darted inside, running into the broad shoulders of Brent Paxton. Linebacker. In charge of protecting his quarterback.

"Hey! Nikki? What are you doing here?" He seemed anxious about my being there, and I remembered this was a boys-only dorm. But I didn't care.

"Where's Jack?" I started for the stairs behind Brent, ready to search the building. Brent stepped in front of me.

"You're not supposed to be here."

"Look, I know I'm breaking rules." My voice cracked and I could feel my eyes getting wetter. "But I need Jack. Where is he?"

"I don't know." He wasn't looking me in the eye.

Ky Wilson came bounding down the stairs at that moment. "Did I hear someone of the female persuasion . . . Oh, hey, Nikki."

I didn't bother with pleasantries. "Where's Jack?"

"Offense up. Defense down." He thumbed in the direction behind him. Brent cleared his throat behind me and caught Ky's eye. "What?" Ky asked.

I didn't stick around to hear Ky get in trouble for helping the girlfriend. I took the steps two at a time. On the second floor, a couple of players were hanging out in the hallway. And a few cheerleaders. Most of the doors were open.

I asked the first person I saw. A freshman. I didn't know his name. "Jack Caputo's room. Where is it?"

"There," he said, pointing down the hall. "Two thirty-seven."

"Thanks."

So close. So close. I walked as fast as I could, ignoring the many stares. *Settle down, everyone.* I wasn't trying to crash the cool kids' party. I just wanted my boyfriend.

I stopped outside 237, and suddenly I didn't know what to do. Knock? Throw the door open? That same uneasy feeling gnawed at my insides. I decided to knock. There were probably two to a room, and I didn't want to walk in on a half-naked player.

I raised my fist to knock, but then I saw the handle turn. The door slowly creaked open. It was dark inside the room. A figure appeared, with her back to the hallway, her long dark hair reaching almost to the waistband of her silk shorts. I knew that hair. It belonged to Lacey Greene. She tiptoed backward out of the room, as if she were trying not to disturb whoever was inside. I had to step aside so she wouldn't back into me. She turned the handle as she closed the door, so it wouldn't make a click.

The hallway had gotten very quiet. Lacey turned around, and when she saw me right in front of her, she let out a tiny yelp. Then she smiled. How was it that girls like Lacey could recover their composure so quickly?

"Jack's room?" I whispered.

Her smile grew wider. Things in the hallway stopped making sense. The walls became distorted and Lacey seemed very tall at that moment. Taller than I ever remembered, even though she was barefoot.

I looked down at her perfectly manicured toes. "The carpet's dirty."

She giggled as if I had lost it. "Well, isn't this awkward?" she whispered.

I'd felt humiliation and rage in my life before, but never at the levels I was feeling now. All I knew was that there was this awful secret everyone was in on. Everyone but me. I should've seen it coming. I did see it coming.

I ran out of the building as fast as I could and fumbled with the keys. I was in such a hurry that I slipped on a patch of black ice just in front of my car and went careening into the front bumper, smacking my arm hard. That was all I needed to squeeze the first tears out.

I scrambled inside the car. The ignition coughed and sputtered momentarily, and I thought it would be just my luck to be stranded here, but it finally started. The windshield wipers swiped back and forth, carrying a small red envelope across my windshield. A parking ticket, I was sure.

I leaned my forehead against the steering wheel and sobbed. I hated everyone. I had nothing. No one anymore.

A flickering light from the building caught my eye, and I glanced up at the source. It was coming from the second floor, where a light was turning off and on. Jack was standing in front of the window, shirtless, waving both arms at me, and when he saw I had looked up, he held his hands out, palms toward the outside, and mouthed the words *Don't go. Stay.*

He didn't move. He was waiting for me to answer. I nodded and he disappeared.

There was a chance talking to Jack would make me feel better. But there was a better chance whatever he had to say would make everything worse. Crush me. I threw the car into reverse and peeled out of the parking lot. I didn't check my rearview mirror.

There was one person who I knew could make me feel better. All I had to do was find him and ask.

Cole would take the pain away.

As I climbed the outside stairs to the second floor, I could hear music coming from Cole's condo. It was so loud, I almost expected the door to vibrate with the beat.

I didn't have to knock. The door swung open and Meredith Jenkins looked out at me. Apparently, she was back early from cheerleading camp. "Nikki. What are you doing here?"

"I'm looking for Cole," I said, but I couldn't hear my voice above the music.

She leaned closer. "What?"

"I said I'm looking for Cole."

She shifted in the doorway. "It's not a good time, Nikki. Why don't you go home and I'll give him a message?" She started to close the door, not waiting for an answer.

At that point, I wasn't sure I could see straight enough to even drive my car. I put my hand on the door. "It won't take long."

She looked at my hand. "I don't know if he's still here."

"Could you please check?" I let go of the door and hugged

my arms into my chest, rubbing them. "Please?"

"Wait here," she said, and she closed the door.

I thought about turning around and walking away. There was a party going on and it was obvious I wasn't welcome. But what would I be going home to? The pain in my chest would only get worse. Even now it was scraping at my lungs, threatening to tear apart my insides.

I turned around and clutched my stomach.

"Nik?" Cole's voice came from behind me.

I composed my face and turned toward him.

"What are you doing here?" he asked, and then he looked closer at my face. "What's wrong?"

"Nothing, I just . . ." My voice caught, and I knew another word would bring on the tears.

He watched me as I tried to calm myself.

"I just needed . . . someone."

He glanced over his shoulder at the party and then faced me again. "Where's Jules?"

"Never mind. I've obviously interrupted something." I turned around to leave, but he grabbed my arm.

"Wait." He sighed. "Tell me what's going on."

I looked at the wooden slats.

He was quiet for a moment, and I started picking at the sleeve of my T-shirt.

"You're hurting," he finally said. I nodded without looking up. "And you want me to take the pain away."

I raised my head. "I can't breathe, it hurts so much. Can

you do that thing that you did on the river? Whatever it was?"

"It's dangerous, Nik."

"I don't care."

"You won't be able to stop me, and eventually you won't feel anything anymore."

"I'm tired of feeling."

He was quiet for a moment. He raised a hand to my cheek. "You have so much raw emotion in you. You're young. Everything is so fresh."

"What does that mean?"

"It means you don't know what you're doing." He looked away from me, out toward the night sky, and it seemed like he wasn't talking to me anymore. He wasn't talking to anybody. "It was an experiment. It wasn't supposed to work."

"What are you talking about?"

He put his elbows on the balcony and dropped his head down. He was quiet for a long moment. The only sounds came from his deep breaths in and out. Something big seemed to be happening for him. Finally, he spoke. "You should go home."

I sniffed. Home. Where my mother was gone. Where I couldn't look at my father. Where Jack could find me and tell me in person that he'd found someone else. "I can't go home."

I don't know if it was something in my voice, but he finally looked at me. "Nik, you're killing me."

I sensed he was close to caving in. I put my hand on his arm and he let me turn him toward me. "Please."

He grimaced. "I can't say no to you. And that's going to be a problem."

"But you'll help me?"

"I'll take the pain away," he corrected. "If you want me to. But once I do, there's no going back. Do you understand?"

I nodded. He took my hand and pulled me into his apartment. The place was filled with the strangest assortment of people I'd ever seen.

Meredith, who'd been oddly cold, watched me and called out to Cole, "Feeding off naïveté now?"

"Go find Max, Meredith. He'll take care of you," Cole said.

"You're not going to find the answer with her."

"The other way isn't working either."

She shrugged, then we snaked through the crowd as Cole led me down a hallway to one of the bedrooms and shut the door behind us.

When he turned to face me, I could already feel the thinnest layer of pressure slipping away, and that overwhelming feeling of paranoia and rage and insecurity—the three strangers that had taken residence inside me—whooshed out of me like a deflating balloon, and instantly I realized I should've stayed and heard Jack out. I knew him. I'd memorized the architecture of his soul, and right then I knew he'd never do anything to hurt me.

"I have to go back." I tried to move, but my muscles wouldn't obey my mind.

"There's no going back," Cole said.

I'd come here because Cole had the bizarre ability to take away pain, but now that I was thinking more clearly, I wondered if he also had the ability to force other emotions on me. Cole had been there every time I'd felt most insecure about Jack. The day he was leaving for football camp. The night of Cole's concert at the Dead Goat Saloon, when I couldn't stop thinking about Lacey.

"Did you do this?" I asked him.

"Do what?"

"Make this whole thing happen?"

"I can't force people to do something they don't want to do." He looked down for a moment. "You just tasted a little bit of my own doubts about Jack."

He looked back up, and started draining my pain away at an alarming rate, and I felt woozy and lightheaded. "I have to go back. I have to talk to Jack. . . ."

"Relax, Nik. Soon you won't even remember his name."

TWENTY-TWO

NOW

Home, at night. One month left.

My dreams of the Tunnels became more frequent, and more intense. One night, I dreamed Jack and I were at opposite ends of a hallway at school. I walked toward him, reaching out, but my feet became heavier and heavier with each step. The floor transformed into tar, and before I could call out to Jack, it engulfed me in darkness.

I woke up with a start. Why had I ever missed being able to dream?

My clock said it was just after two in the morning. I was about to turn back over when I heard a noise. I froze, listening. A soft voice was coming from outside my room, so I got out of bed and followed the sound out to the hallway and toward my father's room.

His door was closed, but I could hear his voice inside, talking to someone. I tiptoed closer and leaned my ear against the door.

"... you would know. It's just not working. Do I try to be

harder on her, and risk losing her again? Or do I go soft? Treat her like an adult . . . and risk losing her again."

He was quiet for a moment. Who on earth would he be talking to at two a.m.? About *me*?

"You would know what to do . . ." he said. "You always did. You could talk to her about everything and she would actually talk to you, too."

I held my breath.

"Anyway, I wanted to catch you up on everything. . . . I miss you."

Then he was quiet. There was no beep of the phone disconnecting. No slamming of the receiver.

My dad wasn't on the phone. He was talking to my mom, searching for guidance about me. He really did believe she was above us, watching and listening.

I crept back to my room. I wished I believed my mom were out there somewhere, and that I could talk to her like my dad did. I wished I could talk to my dad like I had talked to my mom, but we never had that kind of relationship. Not because of anything either of us was doing. Sometimes the closeness isn't there.

It didn't mean I loved him any less. Or he, me.

I had been so horrible to him when I'd left with Cole. If I couldn't get out of the Tunnels, at least this time I would leave him in a good place, without any doubt that I loved him.

The days were slipping through my fingers. I knew I needed to tell Jack the truth about me leaving again, if only to take away that little bit of power Cole held.

But it had to be the right time.

After Cole realized Jack knew who he really was, he started showing up in more and more places, shadowing us in the halls of the school, always in the parking lot when I was pulling out. The band played concerts almost every night, and they were hard to avoid. Even when Cole wasn't around, traces of him followed me everywhere. He was angry I'd confided in Jack. It was obvious. But I still didn't know why.

True to his word, Jack arranged his schedule so he could volunteer at the soup kitchen. When he showed up, Christopher put him to work in the serving line. He wore a plastic glove and grabbed handfuls of lettuce for the salad.

"You're here," I said.

"Where else would I be?"

I smiled. Except for a little small talk, we worked side by side in silence. I was aware of how close he stood by me, his arm almost touching mine. Occasionally I glanced at him in the side of my vision. I studied the length of his eyelashes, the curve of his lips, and I would forget to ladle the soup. I think he was just as aware of me, too. When I wasn't looking at him, I felt him looking at me.

We went on like this until Mary showed up at my serving station. She nodded at me and stared at Jack.

"Mary, this is Jack." I ladled a bowl of steaming vegetable soup. "He's a new volunteer."

She didn't take the bowl, so I leaned over the counter to put it on her tray for her. Jack smiled at her and held out a fistful of lettuce. "Salad?"

Mary shook her head, still looking at Jack quizzically. "Did you forgive her?"

I looked at her with a start.

Jack dropped his salad back in the bucket. "What?"

"Did you forgive Nikki?"

"Umm, Mary, I don't think you—" I started, but Jack interrupted me.

"No, it's okay. What do you mean, Mary?" He spoke slowly. "Did I forgive Nikki for what?"

Mary frowned and reached under the separation glass and touched Jack's gloved hand. "Did you forgive her for leaving you?"

Jack's lower lip sank, and his eyebrows lifted. He looked like he was about to speak, but no words came out of his open mouth.

Mary leaned even closer and whispered, "I have a theory. A theory about anchors."

"Oh," Jack finally said, his forehead now creased with confusion. "Anchors."

The people in line behind Mary shifted impatiently.

"Um, Mary, you're holding up the line," I said. Mary looked at me as I continued. "Why don't you go grab a table, and I'll eat with you."

The tension slipped from her face. "Okay. But hurry. My tee time's at one."

She started down the line again. Jack's hand still rested in the lettuce, so I nudged him with my elbow, and he seemed to restart. "Don't worry about her," I said. "She gets confused easily."

"That wasn't confusion." Jack kept his eyes on my face as he served the salad. "It was like she knew me. Knew us. Did you talk to her about us?"

"Of course not. She also knows about anchors, apparently. And she's late for her tee time. None of it makes sense."

We didn't talk much for the rest of the lunch rush. When enough people had cleared out, I said to Jack, "Do you want to help me clean up?"

Jack looked at me and smiled as if nothing sounded better. "Yep."

"Okay, so the brooms are this way." I pointed toward the closet near the bathrooms.

Jack nodded and followed me to the broom closet. He grabbed a mop and bucket. I slammed the closet door behind me, but the cuff of my shirt caught on the doorknob and yanked the sleeve. "Whoops." I unhooked the snag and pulled my shirt back into place. "Once a klutz . . ." I held my broom with one hand, the dustpan with the other. "We'll start in the corner over there and work our way back. Okay?"

But Jack just looked at me, puzzled.

"Jack? What's wrong?"

He wasn't looking at my face. He was staring at my shoulder. When my shirt had gotten caught, it had slipped out of place, revealing part of my mark for a split second. It now reached from my collarbone to the edge of my shoulder.

"It's getting bigger."

I shoved my shirt even farther up to the base of my neck and tried to keep my voice calm. "What are you talking about?"

Before he could answer, I turned and started clearing off a table, but then Jack's hand clamped on my shoulder and he yanked me around. "Don't tell me you haven't noticed."

I shrugged his hand off. "Okay, yeah, it's growing a little."

"That's not a little, Becks. It's covering your entire shoulder. What is it?"

I sighed. "I told you. It's just something that appeared when I was . . . gone. It's nothing. I can't even feel it."

"Why is it growing? Regular tattoos don't grow."

"I don't know. Maybe it will go back down, or go away someday."

He paused. "Shouldn't you see a doctor . . . ? Don't give me that look, Becks."

"I think you know a doctor can't help."

He took two tentative steps toward me, closing the distance between us. He took the broom out of my hand and leaned it against the wall, then he reached up and pushed my shirt aside, exposing the mark all the way to the end of my shoulder.

His fingers were rough and callused against my neck and shoulders, but they were soft, too.

"Up close, it doesn't look quite like a tattoo."

"How would you know?"

One corner of his lip pulled up into a sort of smile and he pushed his own sleeve back, exposing his right forearm.

Black markings covered the inside, just underneath the crease of his elbow.

"What is it?"

He ignored my question. "My tattoo looks like ink on skin, whereas yours"—he focused once again on my own mark—"doesn't. Your skin doesn't feel different," he said, looking closer, tracing the edge of the mark. I could feel his breath. I smelled the sweet and rustic scent of his aftershave. "It's almost like the black color is coming from beneath your skin, not from the skin itself. And it can't be a burn, because the skin isn't distorted in any way."

"No. It's not," I whispered.

"And it's not raised, like a scar would be. . . . Becks? Are you okay? Did I say something wrong?"

I realized I was straining my head away from him and squeezing my eyes shut. I opened them and found Jack studying my face. I wanted him more than anything. "No. I'm fine. I was just . . . thinking."

He cracked a smile. "Does thinking hurt you these days?"

"No." I took a step back. He couldn't possibly guess what the mark meant, but I wasn't going to take the chance.

Jack watched me carefully. I kept backing up, dragging my hand along the wall as I did.

"Where are you going?"

He can't know. I can't do this to him. "I have somewhere . . . something to do. Christopher can clean up by himself."

"Becks?" He held his hands out, palms down.

"You can leave too, I'm sure. You've already done so much. And thanks . . . for helping out today, okay?"

"You're running."

I shook my head. I had reached the swinging doors that led to the hallway and out to the parking lot. "It's late. I have to go. I'll see you later."

Before he could protest, I slipped out the door and started a slow jog toward my car. But I stopped when I saw that Cole, as his blond self, was leaning against the side of the Rabbit, like he knew the exact moment I would be rushing out to the car.

"Hi, honey. How was work?" He grinned.

I ignored him and dug around for the car keys in my purse, keeping my eyes on him. When I had them in my hand, I started walking toward the car again.

I held the car key out, pointed and ready.

Cole eyed the key. "Uh-oh. Is that key loaded?"

"I'm in a hurry." I made it to the car, but Cole held his ground in front of the driver's-side door.

"That's nice that Jack wants to feed the dregs of society. He's here now, isn't he?"

"How did you know?"

His eyes narrowed in a sly way. "Jules came to me. Crying. She said Jack couldn't stay away from you. She asked me to take the pain away. Begged me to take the pain away. Said she wants to stop feeling."

For the just briefest moment, I believed him, and I hated myself for hurting someone else, especially Jules. He knew I was vulnerable where she was concerned. She was my friend, and Cole knew I had come back for my friends and family. "Jules doesn't even know you."

"Maybe not formally. But she is hurting. All I needed to do was taste her pain at the little scented-candle stand at the mall today to know that Jack was with you. You know she works at the Scentsy candle shop on Saturdays."

"They're not together. Jack doesn't feel that way about her."

"But he could." He tilted his head. "Maybe if you hadn't Returned, they'd be a couple. Can you really do this to your best friend?"

It wasn't my fault they weren't together. At least, that's what I tried to believe. "I can't help it if Jack still has feelings for me," I said. It was the first blatant lie I'd told Cole in reference to Jack. I had no idea how Jack felt about me anymore.

Cole looked at the soup kitchen, then back at me. "If that's true, why isn't he with you? Leaving with you?"

"Because . . ." My voice dropped off. "He had to clean up."

Cole's lip pulled up. "He'd rather clean for free than be with you? Ouch."

"Just move," I said.

"Becks!" Jack jogged casually until he reached me, not even sparing one glance at Cole. He put both hands on my arms and pulled me toward him. "Sorry I took so long in there. I couldn't remember where you told me to put the mops."

He put an arm around me protectively and drew me close, away from Cole.

"Wow. You two seem to be right as rain again," Cole said from beside us. I could hear the undercurrent of rage beneath his voice. "I hate to interrupt this sudden case of the touchy-feelies, but with the three of us standing here, it almost feels like that spring day so long ago. Almost as if Jack hadn't left for camp. Almost as if Jack had nothing to do with you going under, Nik."

Jack winced, but he kept his eyes on me.

"You should've seen her. Did you know that when she left your dorm that night, she came straight to me? Begged to go with me. Barely able to breathe for the pain." He enunciated each word.

I studied Jack's face and shook my head. Jack dropped his arm from my shoulders. "You never let me explain. I ran to you, but you drove off. You didn't trust me."

There was silence for a few long moments.

"Would either of you care to know my opinion?" Cole said.

"Shut up," we replied at the same time.

Cole shrugged. "You know where to find me." He turned and walked across the parking lot to the sidewalk that led around the corner of the post office. I watched him until he disappeared, then I faced Jack again.

Jack roughly ran both of his hands through his hair. "This is a mess." It sounded like he was talking to himself, not to me. "I know how it looked, but you should've let me explain. I hated you for leaving." He looked up at the sky. "I hated you."

Jack took a step backward, away from me, and as he did, a voice called out to us. "Don't let him drive you apart!"

We both turned toward the sound. Mary was sitting on a bench under the shelter of the bus stop. I hadn't noticed her before. She'd been watching us.

She stood and came over. "That's what he wants. He's scared of anchors. I told you I have a theory about anchors."

Anchors again. I sighed. "Okay, Mary. Are you waiting for a bus? Do you need me to give you a ride somewhere?"

Jack hadn't moved beside me. He seemed to be taking her way more seriously than I was. Mary spoke to Jack. "It's happened before. And he doesn't want it to happen again."

"Who doesn't?" Jack asked.

I put my hand on his arm. "Jack, she doesn't know what she's—"

"Cole," Mary interrupted.

My breath caught in my throat. She knew his name. "What?"

She didn't answer me. She shook her head. "I've said too much."

One of the free city buses rounded the corner, its brakes squeaking as it headed for the bus stop.

"I have to go." Mary turned toward the bus and waved to the driver.

"Wait, Mary. You can't go," I said. "How do you know Cole?" I grabbed her arm, but she yanked it free and ran for the bus with the energy of a twenty-year-old, not an eighty-year-old.

"Mary, please!" I called after her, but it was too late. Mary stepped onto the bus, and gave us a small wave and a crazy smile as the doors closed.

"What was that?" Jack asked with a stunned expression.

"I don't know," I said, dazed. "She seems to know Cole."

"Then we can't let her go."

"But the bus—"

"It's the free shuttle. It goes to Prospector Square next." He took my keys out of my hand. "We might beat it if I drive."

Jack drove like a madman, navigating the back roads and running stop signs. We pulled to a stop right in front of the shuttle sign.

"Did we pass it?"

We watched in the rearview mirror, waiting . . . hoping the bus would appear. If Mary was spooked, there was a chance she wouldn't return to the soup kitchen. We had to find her now.

"Please," I said under my breath.

Jack grabbed my hand. Finally, the white shuttle rounded the corner. Jack cut the ignition, and we waited by the stop. When we got on, Mary popped out of her seat and started to back up to the end of the bus.

We followed her and kept our voices low.

"It's okay, Mary," Jack said. "We just want to talk."

Mary sat in the last row. We'd physically cornered her.

Her hands were shaking, so I sat next to her and took one of her hands and held it in my lap. "Please, Mary. You said you knew Cole."

Mary's lower lip trembled. "It's because you weren't a

daughter. That's why he wanted you. You were an experiment."

"What do you mean, I wasn't a daughter?" Then it hit me. "Wait. You're talking about the Daughters of Persephone, aren't you? You really *did* ask that girl about finding the Daughters of Persephone."

She nodded. "I was lost when I Returned. I thought they could help me find my mom." She started rocking back and forth. Jack was sitting in the row in front of us, listening intently.

"It's going to be okay, Mary. Who are the Daughters of Persephone?"

The rocking continued. "We're raised to be Forfeits. To have no attachments. To have nothing to leave behind. We prepare our daughters to be chosen for the Feed."

At this, she put her head in her hands and started moaning. Some of the passengers in the back started to look.

"Shh, Mary." I squeezed her hand and wondered how much more information we'd get out of her. "Please keep going."

She took a few deep breaths. "For thousands of years, they've chosen Forfeits from the Daughters. But none of them survived. That's why Cole tried someone else. Someone who wasn't a Daughter."

"Me," I whispered. She nodded. "Mary, was your daughter a Forfeit?"

She shook her head slowly, and let go of my hand to pull aside the collar of her shirt. There, on her neck, was a black mark. Exactly like mine.

My mouth dropped open.

"You were there?" I could barely get the words out. "But you're . . . older. Cole said they only take young Forfeits." Mary watched as I tried to put the pieces together. "You must've found a way to escape. But the last Feed was a hundred Surface years ago. How old are you?"

"I told you, Nikki. You weren't listening. Nobody listens to me." Her hands were shaking again, but this time I didn't think I was in any position to comfort her.

I thought back to that first day I met Mary—the day she threw her plate to the floor. "You're seventeen. You're my age."

She looked at me with an expression that was lucid for a moment as she waited for me to figure it out.

"You were there, in the Feed, at the same time as me," I said. My age. From Park City. Could she be the same girl who'd introduced me to Cole in the first place? "You're Meredith."

Her face crumbled, and she started rocking and moaning again. "Don't say that name. Meredith's gone. Look at me. Brittle bones. Skin like paper. I don't know who or where I am. *Meredith* didn't survive. Not like you did."

I put my hand on her back to comfort her, but she threw herself against the wall as if I'd hit her.

"Leave me alone!" she screamed.

Now everyone, including the bus driver, was looking at us.

"Everything okay back there?" he said over the speaker.

Jack answered. "We're fine. We're getting off at the next stop."

Mary's cries were getting louder and louder, and so Jack

and I made our way to the back exit of the bus to show her we weren't going to hurt her anymore.

When the bus pulled over and the doors opened, I gave one last look at Mary. She suddenly had a peaceful expression on her face, and right before I stepped down, she called out, "Remember Orpheus, Jack! He was strong!"

Through the open door, she tossed me an object, which I reflexively caught. The door started to close and the bus pulled away.

I looked at the object. It was her silver bracelet.

TWENTY-THREE

NOW

The side of the street. One month left.

$\mathcal{I}$held the bracelet out to Jack. "She wore it a couple of times to the shelter. She said it was a family heirloom or something." He fingered the bracelet in my palm, turning it over a few times before shaking his head in confusion.

"I don't get it. That was Meredith Jenkins?"

I shrugged.

"How is it possible? She's old. And crazy. I thought Meredith Jenkins moved away with her dad."

It hit me that Jack wouldn't have known Meredith was Maxwell's Forfeit. The move was probably the story her mom told people to explain Meredith's absence. I filled Jack in.

"I guess I know what Cole means when he says I survived like no one else." The bus made its climb up the street and then turned right at the top. "Poor Meredith."

I shoved the bracelet in my jacket pocket, unsure if Mary—Meredith—had even meant to give it to me. She'd seemed so protective of it at the soup kitchen.

"They all end up like that?" Jack said. "All the Forfeits?"

"The ones who don't survive do."

"Why didn't you?"

I shook my head slowly. "That's the question, isn't it?"

"That's why Cole wants you," Jack said. I didn't reply, but the same thought had crossed my mind. "Mary said something about you having an anchor."

Oh yeah. I hadn't been paying attention because I'd thought they were the ramblings of a senile old woman. "I don't know what that means."

I thought about all the things I didn't know. All the unanswered questions. And I started to tremble.

Jack held me tight against him. "It's okay, Becks. We'll find out. Starting with that Orpheus story."

"I know the story."

The bus had dropped us off at least a couple of miles from where we'd picked it up, and so we began the walk home, and on the way I told Jack what I knew about Orpheus and Eurydice.

My car. The parking lot.

We ended up back in the parking lot of the soup kitchen, sitting in my car and trying to make sense of everything.

I'd told him the same story about Orpheus that Mrs. Stone had told me. How Orpheus had saved Eurydice, but she still got sucked back under. "But sometimes the myths get parts wrong."

"So, this Eurydice went to the Underworld, and then, what, Orpheus went there too and rescued her? What is that supposed to mean?"

I tried to lay the story out in my head. Eurydice went to the Everneath, as I had. Like me, she didn't age. Maybe her Everliving wanted her to go back to the High Court too, but instead Eurydice chose the Tunnels. She was sucked back in. Maybe when Mary said Orpheus was strong, she meant he was strong enough to lose Eurydice to the Tunnels rather than watch her turn into an Everliving herself.

I didn't tell any of this to Jack. I couldn't. Not yet. He still didn't know the Tunnels were coming for me.

Jack's phone rang right then. He looked at the screen. "Will."

He started to put it back in his pocket, but I stopped him. "Go ahead. He probably needs you."

Jack pressed the button that would send Will to voice mail, and he took my face in his hands. "We have a plan, Becks. We have time. We'll do as much research as we can, find out more about Orpheus and the Daughters of Persephone, and then we'll be here next Saturday. And we'll know what questions to ask Mary."

I nodded. Now was the time to tell Jack about the mark and its meaning. We watched each other's faces, and the moment hung perched above us at the tipping point, waiting for me to spill the truth, and I didn't. Jack walked toward his car, and I told myself the moment would still be there when I saw him again.

But as I watched him drive away, the front end of his car still twisted from the wreck, I knew that there were no perfect moments left. When Jack found out the truth, it would be too late.

Jack came over that night, so we could research the Daughters of Persephone. We didn't know where to start other than Google, and the search produced just two results. The first was a bluegrass music band by the same name. Two older women who looked comfortable in overalls and who I imagined had chewed on their fair share of stalks of wheatgrass. Reading further, we discovered their mom's name was actually Persephone. Their website didn't even mention anything about a myth. It was a dead end.

The second showed a little more promise. But only a very little. It was a microfiche article about a missing newspaper reporter from 1982. The article didn't mention the Daughters of Persephone until the second-to-last paragraph, when the editor in chief said that the missing reporter had been working on an exposé of several cults, one of which was called the Daughters of Persephone.

"What do you think it means?" I asked Jack.

He shrugged. "If there's only one article out there that might have to do with the real Daughters of Persephone, it means they keep their tracks hidden."

"You don't think the reporter's disappearance had anything to do with . . ." I trailed off, thinking about the possibilities.

I typed the reporter's name and hometown into the search engine, but no other articles about her came up.

Jack pressed his lips together in a grim sort of way. "I wouldn't put anything past Cole, or anyone like him."

We also started digging deeper into the Orpheus myth, but further research turned up only slightly varying accounts of the same story Mrs. Stone had told me months ago. If there was something there, I wasn't seeing it. Maybe we'd have to find Mary. Press her for more information.

A few days passed, and Jules showed up at my locker. We hadn't spoken since that day handing out flyers.

"Hey," I said.

She smiled, but it didn't look like a smile. "You wanna go to the Ray and grab a coffee? Or are you still working with Mrs. Stone after school?"

"No. I'm caught up enough now. I could go."

She let out a breath of air. "Great. I'll drive."

The Ray was about halfway up Main Street. Jules didn't say much on the way. When we got there, several booths were filled with other students from school and the air was thick with the smell of coffee, and French toast and eggs cooking. The Ray was famous for its French toast, which was as thick as a brick and made out of coffee cake.

I followed Jules to a couple of stools at the bar and we

ordered lattes. As the waitress walked away, Jules turned to me and said, "I'm sorry things are so different now. That day with the flyers . . . That was painful."

I didn't know what to say.

"I miss my friend," she said. "I miss being able to talk about anything with you, and knowing you'd take it to the grave. I don't have that anymore. I can't talk to my mom—you remember her, she never understands anything. And talking to a boy just isn't the same as talking to my girl."

I smiled at that.

"I miss it too," I said.

The waitress returned with our steaming lattes, and we spent the rest of the time talking. Not about Jack, and not about where I'd been, but about regular high school stuff, and eventually we fell into our old conversation patterns.

I loved it. To be with my old friend, slurping coffee and forgetting about life.

For a little while.

Jules dropped me off at my car in the school parking lot, and I waved to her as she blew me a kiss. Nothing had really been resolved over our lattes, but fixing problems hadn't been the point, I don't think.

My dad was in the kitchen reading the paper when I got home. His hair looked like he'd been running his fingers through it.

"Everything okay, Dad?" I went to the fridge to get us both juice.

He grunted. "Apparently I'm not hip enough for a resort town." He shook his head and folded the paper back and kept reading.

"The paper says that?"

"It's an op-ed piece. I'm—quote—'old-fashioned and holding the town back.'"

"Back from what?"

He shrugged and put the paper down. "World domination? I don't know. Should I plug earphones in my ears and walk around looking at my iPod like all the kids do? Would that make a difference?"

"Ignore it, Dad." I poured him a cup of orange juice and set it in front of him. "You're perfect for this town."

He rubbed his face in his hands. "Thanks, Nik." And then he looked at me as if noticing me for the first time in a long time. "Thanks."

I wanted to stay that way for a few moments longer. Me and my dad. Looking at each other. Seeing each other. Grafting this moment.

Look at me, Dad.

Too soon, he turned back to his paper and the moment was gone.

Saturday morning was crisp and blue. The rest of the state was suffering from the effects of an inversion in the weather, which made the air thick with gunk, but Park City was above all that. Closer to heaven, we used to say. I showed up at the soup kitchen an hour early, and just as I swung my car into an empty spot, Jack's car pulled alongside. He gave me a knowing grin. Neither of us could wait to talk to Mary.

I unlocked my doors, and he got out of his car and slid into the passenger seat of mine. "Looks like we both had the same idea."

We waited with the heat on, watching for Mary. People started to gather near the soup kitchen door, waiting for it to open, but we still didn't see her.

"Maybe we should just go inside," I said. "She'll be here."

Jack and I went in, and Christopher put us to work at our stations. Neither of us spoke. I dripped and sloshed the soup a couple of times because I couldn't keep my eyes off the entrance.

We served up hundreds of trays. She never showed.

Christopher hadn't seen her all week.

After the last straggler made his way down the counter, Jack started to clear the dining room while I went to the closet and gathered the mopping supplies. He stacked one chair on top of another with more force than was necessary, the clanging metal providing the sound track for his frustration.

"There has to be someone else who knows about this stuff," Jack said.

I grimaced. "I'm sure there is. But how would we find them? The internet search didn't turn up—"

"Wait," Jack interrupted, pausing with a chair two feet off the ground. He set it back down.

"What?"

"Meredith said the Daughters of Persephone are raised to have no attachments to the Surface."

"Yeah?"

He tilted his head at me as if I should've seen it. "So who raised her to believe that?"

"I don't know. Her . . . *mom*," I said as it finally hit me what Jack was getting at.

Jack was smiling and nodding. "I've met Mrs. Jenkins before. Meredith used to live on the same street as Ky. It was obviously a lie that Meredith moved away. What if her mom is still there?"

I couldn't answer.

"I say we pay Mrs. Jenkins a visit." Jack grabbed another chair and flipped it over on top of the table. "Maybe she knows how we can get Cole to leave you alone."

TWENTY-FOUR

NOW

Jack's car. Three weeks left.

After we were finished with our shift at the soup kitchen, Jack drove us to a rustic ski cottage at the base of the mountain. We stood on the porch for a few moments before knocking.

"What if she really did move?" I asked.

"She lives here," Jack said with confidence.

"What if she doesn't talk to us?"

"She'll talk."

"What if—"

"Look, Becks. You want to find a way to get Cole to leave you alone, right?"

I nodded.

"Okay, then. We're doing this."

I took in a breath and knocked on the door. A few moments went by, and then a woman opened up. The same woman I'd seen at the soup kitchen, eating lunch with Meredith. She was business casual, as if she were about to leave for work at a museum. She wore a red silk scarf around her neck, and her hair was in a tight bun.

"Yes?" she said.

I opened my mouth to speak, but nothing came out.

"Hi, Mrs. Jenkins," Jack said. "We were wondering if we could talk to you for a few minutes."

"About what?"

Jack glanced sideways at me. "About your daughter, Meredith."

Mrs. Jenkins's face went blank. "Meredith lives with her father now." She started to close the door, but I stopped it with my foot.

"Please, Mrs. Jenkins," I said, finding my voice. "I know that's not true."

"Excuse me?" she said incredulously.

"I've seen her."

Mrs. Jenkins's eyes narrowed, and she pushed again on the door. "You don't know what you're talking about."

"I know she was in the Feed!" I blurted out.

Mrs. Jenkins froze, and gave me an icy glare. Jack inched toward me protectively. "How do you know?"

I took a breath. "Because I was in the Feed too."

Mrs. Jenkins's house had no decorations. No pictures on the walls. No trinkets in corners. Except for one ancient-looking jar on the mantel above the fireplace, there were no identifying features at all.

Everything from the walls to the couch Jack and I were sitting on was a different shade of beige. The place didn't look lived in.

Mrs. Jenkins appeared from the kitchen carrying a tray with a teapot and three cups on it. "Greek mountain shepherds tea," she said. "Nothing beats it."

"Thank you," I said. We each took a cup, and she sat on the chair opposite us. I couldn't wait any longer. "Mrs. Jenkins, what do you know about the Daughters of Persephone?"

I'd caught her midsip, and she raised her eyebrows and put her cup down. "You mean to tell me you *don't* know about them?"

"No."

"Then how did you—"

"I don't know. Cole just took me."

"And you survived." Even though she smiled when she said it, it came out like an accusation.

"Yes," I said.

"Tell us about the Daughters," Jack interrupted.

Mrs. Jenkins looked at Jack. "The Daughters of Persephone have a special interest in the Feed. We are taught about the Everneath, and when a Feed approaches, we prepare our children to become Forfeits." She said this as if it were the most obvious thing ever.

Jack stared at her openmouthed.

"Why?" he asked.

She looked at him like he was crazy. "Because it's a chance.

To become the next Persephone. If one of them survives and takes over the throne, it would mean eternal life for her entire bloodline. Even those who have passed on before. The queen gets that privilege. Her family is automatically welcomed into the realms of the Everneath. That means eternal life for them."

I shook my head. "You're telling me you think the queen can bring people back from the dead?" Even though I found that hard to believe, I couldn't help it when my mind flashed to my mom, and I saw how the idea would be enticing. But Cole had never mentioned anything like this.

She tilted her head. "You're obviously angry, but I don't see why. People have searched for the secret to immortality for thousands of years. This is the only way to guarantee it will happen. The Everlivings themselves have strict rules about whom they bring in, and the Shades enforce those rules. They can't let just anybody in. There's not enough energy to sustain a constant influx of people. It's a very select society. This is the only other way."

I looked at Jack, whose jaw was hard. "That's disgusting," he said.

Mrs. Jenkins turned to him. "If you think that's disgusting, you should ask your girlfriend why *she* went under. She obviously didn't know there would be a chance for exaltation, so what was her reason?"

Jack looked away.

I wasn't expecting Mrs. Jenkins to be so forthcoming, and it made me realize something I should've seen before. Our conversation might lead to mention of the Tunnels, and Jack didn't know about them. I had to steer her clear of the topic. The news of what was waiting for me at the end of my six months had to come from me, not Mrs. Jenkins.

"Mrs. Jenkins, do you know how I survived?" I asked.

She sighed and gave a slight shrug. "I only know of one person who survived like you. It happened hundreds of years ago. Adonia was her name. She Returned from the Feed, young and sane, as you did."

"How did she do it?"

"She never had a chance to tell anyone." Mrs. Jenkins gestured to the jar on the mantelpiece. "The current queen found her. Those are her ashes."

I could feel the blood drain from my face. "The queen burned her?"

Mrs. Jenkins smiled as if I were a simpleton. "No. The queen found her and stole what was left of her energy. But when a queen steals your energy, the transfer is so violent it shreds a person. *We* burned Adonia's remains."

Jack looked like he was going to be sick. I was sure my face mirrored his. How could Cole think I'd ever want to be a queen?

"So you see, my dear, even if you survive, that doesn't mean you'll be queen." My heart started to race, and I suddenly felt very exposed. Was that why Cole and Maxwell had talked about keeping my existence a secret from the queen?

"Don't worry, now," she said, noticing my expression. "I had no idea you existed. I'm sure if you were going to end up like Adonia, it would've happened by now. It would take an act of betrayal by the Everliving who Fed off you to get word to the queen." She looked at the jar. "I'm afraid Adonia was not in tune with her Everliving. He wanted her to be his queen, but she did not. So he took his revenge by telling the queen about her. And"—she paused for a moment—"where, exactly, the queen could find her."

A sound like muffled ocean waves reached my ears as my pulse quickened. Would Cole ever do that to me? Could he? Jack grabbed my hand, which I hadn't realized was shaking.

"I don't want to be queen," I mumbled.

"Well, you can just be an Everliving."

Jack sat forward. "She doesn't want to be an Everliving, either."

She frowned and tilted her head, confused, as if Jack had just told her I wanted to scratch my own eyes out for fun. *Uh-oh.*

"Don't be silly," she scoffed. "What other choice is there? You don't really think she'd—"

She was dangerously close to talking about the Tunnels. I had to shut her up, so I shot out of my seat and started coughing loudly and frantically. Jack put a hand on my back. "Do you need some water?"

I nodded, and Jack sprinted to the kitchen. I had a few seconds at the most.

"Don't tell him," I whispered to Mrs. Jenkins. "About the Tunnels."

Her mouth opened in a speechless kind of way, and then Jack was back with a glass.

"Thanks," I said, and as I sipped the water, I shot Mrs. Jenkins my most pleading look.

She tried to smile but it looked forced, and at that moment, her demeanor transformed from confused to calculating. Her eyes narrowed. "Despite how you feel now, if you *do* get to the throne one day, perhaps you'll remember this old woman, who helped you in every way she could."

Her own daughter hadn't survived the Feed, and now she saw me as a golden opportunity for her. Without saying the words, she and I had made a bargain. She wouldn't tell Jack about the Tunnels, and I would remember her when I was queen, an event she saw as inevitable.

Jack spoke up. "Is there a way we can get Cole to leave Nikki alone?"

She shook her head. "Everlivings are a tenacious bunch." She gestured to the mantel. "In fact, I would be wary of making one of them angry."

A chill ran down my back as I glanced at the urn, and I quickly changed the subject. "Mrs. Jenkins, why did Meredith Return?"

Her smile melted into a frown. "I was surprised too, although I shouldn't have been. Meredith thought that since she came from the same line as Adonia, she would have a better chance to survive and become the next queen. She was convinced. Perhaps we both were." She let out a deep sigh.

"Meredith says she came back for me. It's ridiculous, really, her attachment to me. I raised her better than that. And now I can do nothing for her. Nor she, me. The moment she left for the Feed, I let her go from my mind and my heart."

How could she be so unfeeling? Meredith was her daughter. I looked at Jack, and he nodded, probably thinking the same thing.

Jack leaned forward. "Do you know where we can find her?"

"I haven't seen her, and I've been looking."

Finally I thought I saw a sign of humanity in her, until she continued.

"She stole a piece of jewelry that belongs to me. I think she took it to get my attention."

The bracelet, I thought. Jack opened his mouth, but I shot him a look. He nodded almost imperceptibly.

"One more question," I said. "How many of you are there?"

She smiled. "You'd find us all over the world. Near every entrance to the Everneath."

"Why didn't you tell her about the bracelet?" Jack said once we were in his car and driving away.

"It didn't feel right. I don't trust her. I feel like the bracelet is the only card we have to play, although I have no idea what to do with it." I took a deep breath. "Plus Mrs. Jenkins was creepy and weird."

"She's a Daughter of Persephone. Weird probably doesn't begin to cover it." Jack allowed himself a little smile. "One thing I learned from our visit," he said, his expression serious again. "We can't let Cole know we've been digging around."

I thought back to the urn on the mantel, and I was sure Jack was thinking of the same thing.

TWENTY-FIVE

NOW

School. One and a half weeks left.

My mark reached the end of my shoulder and started to trickle down my arm, and as it did, it looked like someone had poured chocolate syrup on me and it was oozing over my biceps, gravity helping it along.

I could feel the change inside of me as well. A dark, claustrophobic feeling, as if I were trapped inside one of the musty alcoves of the Feeding cavern. I felt it even when I was standing outside on a cloudless day, as if my face would never again be warmed by the sun.

The Tunnels were getting closer.

In my art class the following Monday, Cole—in his dark-haired "Neal" disguise—turned out several watercolor paintings that the teacher, Mr. Tanner, displayed at the front of the classroom.

"Now, this is what I mean when I talk about brushstrokes." Mr. Tanner made sweeping gestures with his hands. "Where did you say you transferred from, Neal?"

"Seattle." Cole glanced at me sideways. "The suburbs."

Mr. Tanner inflated his cheeks, then blew out the air. "And this is the first art class you've taken?"

"The first one that involved paper. We were using rocks and chisels before." He chuckled, as if enjoying a private joke.

Mr. Tanner smiled like he understood, even though it was obvious he had no idea what Cole was talking about. He turned to the front of the room, where he had attached paper to the chalkboard. Using his charcoal sticks, he demonstrated his own version of the technique Cole had used, and then put us to task on our own easels.

I started drawing a house. Art never was my favorite subject, and every attempt of mine usually ended up being a house anyway. And my hands had stopped shaking. I had enough muscle control for my drawing to actually resemble a house.

Cole tweaked his easel so I couldn't see what he was working on. It also meant he could watch me work. I'd stopped caring a long time ago.

"Nik," he whispered loudly. "What's that supposed to be?"

"It's a house."

"Oh. Um . . . stunning."

I focused on my sketch, but I could feel Cole's eyes watching my lines.

"Hey, Nik!"

"What?"

"Has it started running down your arm yet?"

I whipped my head around, and the piece of charcoal I had

been using flew out of my hand and ricocheted off the back of Cole's easel. "What did you say?"

Cole held up his hands in mock surrender. "Whoa. Didn't mean to freak you out. Just wondering about your mark."

"How did you know?" And then I shook my head. "Never mind. I forget you've been through this before."

"Not like this. I've never tracked someone after the Feed. Like I said, you're different. You're—"

"I know. I know. Special." I knew the real answer now. I wasn't old and crazy. "Please draw and stop talking."

He put his charcoal on the tray of his easel and then rubbed his hands together lightly. "The Shade is getting stronger. You know the fingers of your mark? The ones that look like little breakaway lines? Those represent the Tunnels. As if the Shade is reaching out for them."

As Cole spoke, his words felt like an ice cube on my neck, shooting down my spine. I couldn't answer. Cole smiled and turned his easel so the picture he had been working on faced me.

On the canvas was a thin girl with long black hair, the ends of which were flowing behind her as if she were facing a strong wind. But as I looked closer, I realized her hair wasn't blowing. It was being sucked into a dark vortex behind her.

Cole held my gaze for a few moments. I could tell what was behind his eyes. He was saying, *Come with me and this won't be you.*

He pointed to my arm, then reached out as if he would grab it. "It's not too late."

The bell rang. I jerked my arm away. I had to get him away from me. I had to.

We stared at each other in silence for a moment. I didn't realize how much time had passed, and I started to put my tools away. The rest of the students had already done so and were filing out of the room. Cole stayed behind, waiting for me.

I packed my gear as if he weren't even there, and then I ripped my name tag off the box Mr. Tanner had given me at the start of the year. I wasn't going to waste the little time I had left in art class anymore.

Cole watched. He probably knew what I was doing. If I could wish for anything at this moment, it would be for Cole to leave. Let me have this little time to myself.

He followed me into the hallway. I turned abruptly and blurted out, "What would it take to get you to leave me alone?"

"I think you know exactly what it would take."

"What if I make you a deal?"

His eyebrows wrinkled. "A deal?"

Lowering my voice, I said, "What if I promise to go with you, but not until right before the Tunnels come?" I took a step closer in my sudden enthusiasm, and he backed up. "As long as I go with you before the Tunnels actually come, it will work. If you give me these last moments with Jack alone, I'll go with you."

I tried not to let my face show the lie I was telling.

His face went blank, then it broke out in a wide grin.

"Golly, do you *pinky swear*?" he said sarcastically. When I didn't answer, he continued, "Your little plan would involve me taking quite a bit on faith. You're not exactly a safe bet."

I guess I wasn't surprised. But I was so tired of Cole. I looked him directly in the eye. "If you can tell when I'm lying, you should know without a doubt when I'm telling the truth." I put my face even closer to his. "Here's the truth. I. Will. Never. *Ever.* Go with you."

Cole's eyes became tight, and then I saw something on his face I'd never seen before. Genuine pain.

I took in a short breath of surprise, but I stood my ground. If the hurt on his face was as real as it looked, maybe that's what it would take to get him to back down.

Cole looked over my shoulder, and his expression switched from hurt to blazing anger, the fierceness of which sent a cold shiver all the way to my fingers and toes.

I turned to see the recipient of such venom, even though I knew who was standing there.

"Jack," Cole said, his voice tense and jeering, "help me out here. Our girl is talking crazy, and I don't speak crazy."

Jack shot me a curious look. "Ignore him," I said, a pit growing in my stomach. I tugged on Jack's arm, but he didn't move.

"Oh, sure," Cole said. "Ignore the guy with the information. Speaking of information, Jack, has Nikki told you about her mark?"

The breath stopped in my chest.

"Yes," Jack said, still at a loss.

"Cole—" I started to say, but he cut me off.

"I should've been more specific," Cole continued. "I meant to say has she told you the *truth* about her mark?"

I yanked Jack's arm. "C'mon, Jack. Let's just leave. Please." Only now he definitely wasn't going anywhere.

"Did you know it's growing?" Cole took a step toward Jack and spoke in low tones. "I mean, have you seen it? The whole thing?"

Jack didn't answer. I looked at Cole. "Cole. Please." I turned to Jack. "Please," I said again, to both of them.

Cole smiled. "I'm just trying to help. He needs to know."

"He's got a life here," I said, momentarily ignoring Jack at my side. "It doesn't mean anything to him anymore." I tried the only thing I could think of. "It's between me and you. It won't matter to him."

"Between *me* and *you*? *Together?* How far are you willing to go with that, Nik?" Cole's grin widened and I knew he was calling my bluff, and before I could say or do anything else, he said, "The mark on her shoulder is like a timer, Jack. She's going away again. And soon."

I froze and closed my eyes.

"What do you mean?" Jack asked. "If you think Nikki's going to choose to go with you, I know her. She's not."

I squeezed my eyes tighter.

"Jack, she's leaving whether she decides to go with me or not. She has a debt to pay, and there's nothing you, or her dad, or her friends, or even Nik, can do about it." I heard Cole take another step closer to Jack. When I opened my eyes, Cole had a hand on Jack's stiff shoulder. "I'm sorry she didn't tell you, bro. But maybe you can help her make the right decision. You know how Nik can be . . . self-destructive. Behind one door, she faces endless pain, until she just . . . disappears. Behind the other, she'll be exalted. Help her choose eternal glory over the Tunnels of hell. She can either serve the Everneath as a battery, or rule it."

"Enough!" I stepped between them. "Leave, Cole. There's nothing more you can do."

"Is it true, Becks?" Jack couldn't look at me. "You're leaving?"

"Yes," I said. My heart felt like it was breaking.

Jack started to turn away.

"Wait, Jack." He paused, but he didn't turn. "I'm sorry. I'm so sorry, but I didn't know how to tell you."

"She's really, really sorry," Cole said, making my apology seem shallow.

Jack didn't say anything. He walked away.

Cole stood beside me as we watched Jack walk down the hall and shove open the glass doors that led to the parking lot. For a few long minutes I didn't move.

"I'm sorry, Nik. You should've known what backing me into a corner would do." His voice grew quiet. "But he deserved to know the truth."

I didn't answer. I should've told Jack. I knew this. Maybe he still would've left. But maybe he wouldn't have.

Completely numb, I started walking. Like a shadow, Cole fell into step beside me, and I let him. I was too tired to fight anymore.

We walked out the doors and into a sharp wind that carried tiny flecks of ice in it. I buried my nose in the collar of my coat. I put my key in the car door, then turned around and faced him. He had shifted back to his original self. I was surprised by how fast he could make the switch. I didn't even catch a glimpse, and he was Cole again. "Why?"

"Why what?"

"Why is it so important for you to make Jack hate me?" I closed my eyes and leaned my head back. "Please. Tell me."

"Because people in love tend to make irresponsible decisions. Human relationships—you know, the things for which you would give up your chance at eternal life—are fleeting." He was taking my own words and using them against me.

I opened my eyes and looked at him. "You're lying."

"No, I'm not."

"But there's something else too, isn't there?" There had to be another reason. Everything Cole did had a motive. He was holding something back. "Tell me."

His smile disappeared, but he stayed quiet.

"Fine. If you're not going to talk to me . . ." I jerked my car door open, but Cole slammed it shut from behind me. He kept his hand pressed against the window. I turned around, and his face was so close. "What? What do you want?"

"You, Nik." Cole took a couple of deep breaths. "I want *you*. Whether we take over the throne or not. I want you in my life, and the only way that will happen is if you become like me. We shared a heart, Nik." He touched his finger to my heart. "Your heart is in me now."

"Not my heart," I said. "Just some of my emotions."

"Same thing. It belongs to me. And so I belong to you."

I closed my eyes, but I didn't fight him. I was tired of losing everybody I cared about. Tired of being alone.

"We used to be like this, Nik." He leaned even closer, not physically touching me, but I could feel the charge between us. I knew I should've pushed away, but my stupid body betrayed me. My traitorous arms and legs wanted to tangle with Cole's again. That hundred years in the Everneath had molded us together, and our bodies had memorized how they were supposed to fit.

He lowered his head next to mine so we were cheek-to-cheek. "We were exactly. Like. This. For a century."

I couldn't move. I didn't want to.

He kept his right hand on the door, and he slipped his other arm behind me, pulling me away. "Except my hand was here." He pressed his fingertips into my lower back. "And your hand . . ." He moved his right hand and grabbed my left arm, then wrapped it around his back, soft and low, and pressed my fingers into position. "There."

With Cole so close, I couldn't help imagining leaving it all behind right now. The pain. The pungent smells of the Surface. The disappointment of my family. The heartache of Jack.

Jack.

Jack didn't give up on me when I left. Jules told me he never stopped looking. Never stopped hoping I'd come back. I couldn't give up on him now.

That's when I knew what I had to do. The only way I'd be able to think clearly would be to get Cole away from me. I pushed him away.

"I hate you."

Cole just smirked at me. "Hate. Such a strong feeling. A next-door neighbor to love."

"It will never be love. You made the only person I love leave," I said.

"No, Nik. *You* did." He opened my door for me and I drove off, leaving him standing there.

When I got home, I spent a couple of hours pacing the carpets. I couldn't let Jack let me go. Maybe at the start of my Return I would've let him alone. But we'd come too far, and I actually felt hope now. I couldn't let him give up on me. Not now. Not anymore.

I drove to his house. When I knocked on the door, Jack's mother answered. Mrs. Caputo had liked me well enough as Jack's friend, but I don't think she'd ever accepted me as his girlfriend. She'd always been civil, though, which was why her icy reception surprised me.

"Nikki. I heard you were back." She blocked the open door with her body. I was obviously not invited in.

"Yes. How are you, Mrs. Caputo?"

"Fine."

"Good. Good. Um, is Jack around?"

"No." She started to close the door.

I put my hand on it. "Wait. Please."

She held still but didn't say anything. I shivered, but not because of the cold outside. "Is he okay?"

"He and Will went out of town."

I'd just seen him this afternoon. "Alone?"

"Yes. Strange, isn't it? I can't think of what he's trying to escape." Her tone and her pointed look told me she had an idea of who was to blame. I'd run Jack out of town.

"Okay. I guess I should go."

She nodded, and then she said, "Nikki, please leave my boy alone. He's been through enough." She shut the door. Not quite a slam, but almost.

I stared at her door for a long moment, blinking back the tears. What bothered me most was that she was right. Jack obviously couldn't stand me leaving again. He didn't want to be anywhere near me when I left, so he grabbed Will and took off.

I felt sick, and I ran to my car so I wouldn't break down on Jack's front porch. I couldn't believe I wouldn't see him again. I couldn't do this. I couldn't survive what little time I had left, knowing Jack was out there somewhere, hating me.

It was time for me to do something about it.

TWENTY-SIX

NOW

Home. One and a half weeks left.

$\mathcal{I}$ was tired of hurting people. I was tired of hurting myself. When I got home, I went straight to my nightstand and took Cole's hair from the drawer. Without even stopping to think, I rushed out of the house and drove to the Shop-n-Go.

I blew past Ezra and went straight to the back, to the spot where the Everneath had spit me out.

I brought the hair up to my mouth, opened wide . . . and froze.

Just do it, Becks, I told myself.

But my hand wasn't obeying my brain. I was such a coward.

Or maybe I was my mother's daughter. Our family used to have a dog, a wheaten terrier named Bert. We would joke that Bert was my mom's lost third child. As he got older, and sicker, none of us wanted to face it. Especially my mom. We all knew he wouldn't last much longer, and every extra day he lived would be painful, but my mom just couldn't put him down. One day, he wandered away and never came back.

Here I was in the same situation. My own end was inevitable. And I couldn't pull the trigger.

I stared at the hair, wedged between my index finger and my thumb. Here it was, my chance to take control of my exit, to stop hurting Jack, to stop hurting my dad and Tommy, to stop the whole damn thing.

I brought the hair to my mouth again, and froze again. My hand wouldn't move. My breath made the hair flutter. Then I crumbled. The tears came in waves as I sank to the floor, my back against the racks that held the chocolate-covered raisins.

It was the first time I'd cried in more than a century.

Strange that I'd recovered my laughter long before my tears. Now that I'd started, I wasn't sure I'd ever be able to stop. I looked helplessly at the hair in my hand, and a couple of wet teardrops splashed in my palm.

The doors to the convenience store slammed open, and I heard frantic footsteps run toward me.

I looked up just as Cole rounded the corner of the last aisle. When he saw me, he let out an audible sigh of relief.

"Don't scare me like that, Nik."

I couldn't answer. I lowered my head and let the tears flow. Cole sat beside me and put his arm around me, and I let him. I cried into the front of his black leather jacket, my tears pooling on the chest pocket.

"Careful. I didn't bring a life jacket," Cole said.

I sniffled.

"Shh. It's okay."

I guess that was how low I'd sunk, that Cole was the one

person who could console me. We sat like that for a few long minutes, and when I finally had composed myself enough to speak, I said into his jacket, "Why won't you help me? You could be a hero for once."

He put his lips against my head. "Heroes don't exist. And if they did, I wouldn't be one of them."

My fingers had formed a tight fist around the single strand of Cole's hair. Cole took my hand and gently worked the fingers open, took the hair out, and put it in his pocket. I let him, and the tears began to flow again.

I shook, and Cole wrapped his arms around me even tighter. I buried my head in his chest, where I would've heard a beating heart if Cole were human. Of course there was no sound.

"If I went with you . . ." I started to say.

Cole tensed and waited.

"If I went with you, would I no longer have a heart?"

"Not inside you. No."

I sighed. I didn't want to admit how good the idea sounded right about now. Especially since mine was breaking.

Eventually, I disentangled from Cole. He didn't put up a fight. Maybe because he sensed victory. Everything was falling apart. What did I have left? A week, at the most? I knew my Return was approximately six months, but the Everneath had its own passage of time. One day soon, I would disappear. Maybe this time, no one would even notice.

Now that I knew I was too weak to go to the Tunnels early, I had two choices left in front of me. Fade into the background until the Tunnels came for me, or take what little knowledge I had about the whole thing and try to find an answer.

Cole had been right that first night he came into my bedroom, although it'd taken me this long to realize it. I did have hope. Somewhere, in the empty pit of my soul, I believed that I could get out of my debt. That I could stay here.

Since Jack had taken himself out of the picture, I knew this residual hope I was feeling belonged to me. I hadn't skimmed it from him.

I got to school early the next morning and went to Mrs. Stone's room. She glanced up from her seat at her desk and put down the papers she had been reading.

"Hi, Ms. Beckett. What can I do for you?"

"Have you ever heard of the Daughters of Persephone?"

Mrs. Stone's brow crinkled. "I'm not aware that she had any daughters."

"I know, but have you heard of any groups by that name?" I laughed helplessly at how nuts I sounded. "Not real blood daughters. More like . . . a society."

"No." She cocked her head at me. "Why do you ask?"

"Someone mentioned it. She said she was a Daughter of Persephone, and I wondered what she meant by it."

"Sorry. I don't know." She watched me, waiting. "Was there something else?"

"Yes. The Orpheus myth. Are there any other . . . versions of it? Any different interpretations?"

"What do you mean?"

"Any little ways it could've been mixed up or something?"

Mrs. Stone took off her glasses and rubbed them with her handkerchief. "I'm not sure what you're getting at. But if you're interested in reading more about it, take this." Opening one of the drawers on her desk, she brought out a small paperback book about mythology's greatest love stories.

"Great." I took the book and put it in my bag. I'd been reading about Orpheus and Eurydice on the internet, so I wasn't sure if the book could give me any new information. I wished Jack were here, and speaking to me. Maybe he would forgive me. But maybe when someone forgives someone else so many times, he reaches a point when he can't anymore.

Mrs. Stone leaned forward over her desk and put the glasses that were hanging around her neck back on the end of her nose. "As you read it, take note of the value the Greeks placed on love. Every decision Orpheus makes is based on love. His unwavering love nearly saved Eurydice. Remember that for your paper."

My paper. As if I'd ever finish it now.

"Thanks," I said.

She waved in response, not looking up from her desk.

After I left her classroom, I sat in my nook and flipped through the paperback. Much of the first half dealt with the great love story between Orpheus and Eurydice before she ever went to the Underworld. They were husband and wife, at the height of their romance when she was poisoned and went under.

And then, like me, Eurydice had survived.

What did she and I have in common? Cole had said I was different from the Daughters of Persephone because I had relationship ties to the Surface.

Eurydice had a tie to the Surface in Orpheus. I had Jack. Before Meredith had disappeared, she said she had a theory about anchors. What if an anchor was a tie to the Surface?

When I was in the Everneath, I thought about Jack every day. Every minute. Even after I'd forgotten his name, the image of his face made me feel whole again. Was Jack the reason I'd survived? Were our ties to the Surface what somehow kept us whole?

The one problem in the anchor theory was Meredith. She had a connection with her mom, yet she didn't survive. But then the more I thought about it, the more I realized Mrs. Jenkins didn't have a similar connection to Meredith. She forgot about Meredith the second the Feed began.

Then it hit me. Orpheus didn't forget about Eurydice. He loved her the entire time she was gone. Maybe the attachment between Forfeit and anchor worked only when it went both ways.

The drinking fountain next to me shuddered to life as a flash of intuition hit me.

I knew now that Jack never forgot about me. He'd never stopped loving me. He was the anchor that saved me.

And now he was gone.

TWENTY-SEVEN

NOW

Home. One week left.

When I got home, my dad had a "Mayor Bonds with His Wayward Daughter" dinner waiting. Chinese food. He had a few more days until the primary election, and every spare moment was spent on the campaign trail, but his secretary told me he'd scheduled in these dinners.

I followed the smell into the kitchen, where my dad was spreading out the containers from Mountain City Mongolian. "Tommy has Scouts tonight," he said.

I peeked into a few boxes. "You know there's only two of us, right?" He dished out a plate—one of everything—and handed it to me. "There's no way I can eat all that," I said.

"Nikki, I've noticed your appetite isn't what it used to be. We need to work on that."

"Sure, Dad." I scooped a spoonful of rice into my mouth.

"Your mother used to eat like a horse."

I nearly choked on my rice. He hadn't mentioned my

mother in a very long time. His face told me he hadn't meant to. Ever since I'd been back, the topic of my mother remained unexplored territory for us. The last time we'd talked about her was the day I left. I wanted to show him he didn't have to avoid the subject anymore.

"She really did," I agreed. "Remember when she used to keep the gravy boat right next to her plate, even at family parties?"

My dad chuckled. "Oh yeah. She did that when we were dating. At her first dinner with *my* family."

"Grams must've been shocked."

"She was."

Dad let out a breath, and we ate in silence for a few minutes, enjoying a level of comfort with each other that we hadn't experienced in a long time.

"How's the election coming?" I asked. I never watched the news or followed the numbers anymore. The first time he ran, I kept a chart hanging on the wall in my room, with a graph of his polling numbers. Back then he was running as a family man. This time he was a grieving widower, trying to reconnect with a rebel daughter. He was the incumbent, but the in-party challenger was putting up a fight.

"Strong. The numbers are back up." He meant after the fiasco at the Christmas Dance.

As we sat together, the two of us alone, I realized that this might be my last chance to talk to him before the election. And I might not be here for very long after.

"Dad. In case I haven't been clear, I'm sorry for all the trouble I caused you. Have I mentioned this before?"

He smiled. "Yes. You have."

"Well, I am."

"It never hurts to hear, Nikki."

After dinner, as the sun dipped lower against the mountains, I was in the driveway getting my backpack out of my car when I heard some kids yelling from up the street. I assumed it was the Scouts, maybe doing a scavenger hunt, and I started walking to the house. But then I heard a terrified scream. Tommy.

I dropped my bag and took off running toward the noise. I couldn't see very well in the dusk, but it looked like some of the kids were pelting another kid with snowballs. I was sure Tommy was on the receiving end, and it made me furious.

"Hey!" I yelled, but I was still a ways away, and they didn't hear. Tommy was getting pummeled. All I could think about was how scared he must be, and I couldn't get to him fast enough. I said a silent prayer that something would happen to distract the kids, so I could stop them before he really got hurt. Why weren't my legs moving faster?

Suddenly, as if someone had heard my prayer, a tall figure descended upon them from the other direction. He placed himself in front of Tommy and faced the attackers. "Enough!" he said.

I paused for a moment as I registered the voice. Cole's. I sprinted forward even faster. By the time I reached them, the kids who had been throwing the snowballs were wandering around as if they were lost. Two of the boys bumped into each other. They stayed silent and simply turned around, their faces blank.

Cole reached a hand down toward Tommy. "You're okay, kid."

"That was awesome!" Tommy said as he brushed the snow off his pants and coat. His cheeks were bright red, and icy snow clung to his hair. He looked up at Cole's face. "How did you do that?"

"Tommy!" I rushed over to him and put my arms around him, and Cole noticed me for the first time.

"Did you see that, Nikki?" Tommy said. "He just looked at them, and they got scared and stopped!"

Cole avoided my gaze and shifted his weight from one foot to the other.

I leaned down to Tommy. "I saw it. Dad has some leftover dinner for you. Go on home, and I'll meet you there."

"Okay. Thanks, mister!" He waved at Cole and then started walking home.

Cole waved back and then gave me a sheepish smile. "Sorry, Nik. I didn't see you coming."

"Did you . . ." I lowered my voice. "Did you . . . *Feed* off them?" I gestured to the other Scouts, who still had blank faces but were beginning to walk in the general directions of their homes.

Cole held up his hands, palms up. "A little. But don't get all mad yet. Bullies have an easily identifiable aggression layer, so it's really simple to just . . ." He sucked in a loud, deep breath to demonstrate. "And then it's gone."

I stared at him for a moment.

"I was in the neighborhood," he said, answering the question I was about to ask. His lips twitched. "You know, wandering around, trying to be a hero."

I sighed.

"Are you going to thank me?" Cole said. After a pause, he added, "Or hit me?"

I thought about Tommy, scared and cowering on the ground. "Thank you." Before Cole could say anything else I said, "But don't do it again."

He nodded.

I'd expected Cole to ramp up his efforts to change my mind, but was this his new approach? If so, it scared me more than any attempts he'd made to sway me in the past. It felt so real, and so genuine. I looked in his eyes, and I honestly didn't know what his motives were. Would he have saved Tommy if I weren't around? Would he have done it anonymously?

My love for Tommy was a weakness. I just didn't know if Cole was exploiting it. How did he have the power to confuse me still?

I had to get him away. He was more dangerous now than ever, because with Jack gone, and my time almost gone, he was more tempting than he'd ever been before.

"Cole."

"Nik?"

"You promised me you'd stay away from my house."

He frowned, and nodded again. "I'll keep my word."

We walked away in our different directions.

Just after midnight, in my room, I was printing out the latest draft of my paper for Mrs. Stone when I heard a knock at my window. It couldn't have been Cole—he never would've knocked. It was hard to see, with my bedroom light on, but as I got closer, I could make out Jack's face.

He was here. At my window.

I pushed it open, and he clambered in, panting as if he had been flat-out sprinting. His face flushed with excitement? Anticipation? I smelled the air, but his emotions were all over the place.

"Jack? What's wrong?"

He placed his hands on my shoulders and led me over to the bed. I sat.

"Becks. I found her. Meredith. Will and I have been searching for her. Asking around. We—"

"Wait," I interrupted. "You and Will?"

Jack smiled. "Yeah. Remember that day at the Kona? I guess Will was listening more than we thought."

"And he believed it?"

"Not at first. Not until we found Meredith in Blackfoot."

"Idaho?"

"We asked everyone at the shelter until this lady there said Meredith used to talk about a family cabin in Idaho and how she was going to hitch a ride there. Will has an army buddy who's doing security work on the side, and he got the address." He finally paused to catch his breath. "Will's driving to Idaho to pick her up right now. I would've gone too, but I had to see you."

See you. Those words tasted like melted chocolate to me. He hadn't abandoned me after all. He'd spent the past three days searching out our only lead. Without thinking, I leaned over and kissed his cheek. His entire body tensed. Oops. "Thank you," I whispered.

He looked at me, his mouth slightly open. Unmoving.

"No matter what it means, even if it comes to nothing, thank you, Jack."

He still didn't move. He seemed at a loss for what to say or do. Maybe I'd really crossed a line.

"I'm sorry, Jack. I didn't mean to—"

"No," he interrupted, his mouth finally moving. "It's just . . . I didn't expect . . . you . . ."

His words faded off, and we both fell silent for a few moments. I looked down.

"So, when did you get back?" I finally asked.

He seemed relieved at the easy question. "Just now."

"Why didn't you tell me what you were doing?"

He looked down. "I was . . . hurt you weren't honest with me. About your mark. Mad about the wasted time. I wasn't about to give up, but I needed to do it on my own. For a little while." His eyes drifted to my arm. "Can I see it? The mark, I mean."

I held my arm out, and he pushed the sleeve of my jacket up just past my elbow. The dark gray fingers of the mark had reached past my inner elbow and looked like veins snaking their way downward.

"It's really a Shade? An actual Shade inside you?"

I nodded.

"Why didn't you tell me the truth?"

"I wanted to. Actually, that's not true. I didn't want to. I never wanted to have to. I was hoping I'd find a way out, and if I didn't . . ."

"I'd just wake up one day, and you'd be gone again."

I nodded, looking down at the hand that still held my arm, the rough calluses there from years of holding a football.

"Where will you go? These . . . Tunnels that are coming for you. Where do they take you?"

"After the Feed, the Forfeits are used to power the Everneath. They supply the whole place with energy. Cole calls it a battery. One little cog in a giant generator." Saying it out loud sent a shiver down my spine.

Jack's voice grew even softer. "Why didn't you tell me?"

"I know you won't believe it, but I thought it would be best for you. You were doing so well until I came back. I thought you could go back to how it was. You still can."

"Don't say that, Becks. We're going to figure something out."

"I know. Even so, I understand that it would've been easier for you if I'd never come back. Maybe you and Jules . . ."

His grip on my arm tightened, and when he spoke, his voice

wavered. "Becks. I crashed when you left. Jules held together the pieces, and I will love her forever for that. But if I was with her, it wouldn't be right." He grimaced. "She told me so herself, right before I left with Will. She knew." Jack pushed my hair out of my eyes and off my forehead.

"Um, she knew what?" I could barely hear my own voice.

"It's always been you, Becks. Nothing will change that, no matter how much time has passed." He glanced down. "No matter if you feel the same way or not. You know that, right?"

I shook my head slowly, wanting desperately to believe him, but not sure if I could.

"How can you not see that? Everyone sees it." He slid his hand down my arm and grabbed my fingers, holding them in his lap, tracing them. Staring at them. "Remember freshman year? How Bozeman asked you to the Spring Fling?"

Bozeman. He was two years older than me. Played offensive lineman. His first name was Zachary, but nobody had called him that since the third grade. I'd been surprised he even knew my name, let alone asked me to the dance.

"Of course I remember. You came with me to answer him." We doorbell-ditched Bozeman's house, leaving a two-liter bottle of Coke and a note that said *I'd pop to go to the dance with you*, or something like that. Bozeman had a reputation for fast hands, but he didn't try anything with me. In fact, he barely touched me at all, even at the fling. And he never asked me out again. Or even talked to me, really. It was weird.

"Yeah, well, I didn't tell you, but Bozeman actually asked for my permission."

"Why?"

"Because it was obvious to everyone, except you, how I felt about you. And then that night with the Coke on the porch . . . after I dropped you off at home, I paid Bozeman a visit." His cheeks went pink and he lowered his eyes.

"And?"

"Let's just say I rescinded my permission. I didn't realize how much it would bother me." His eyes met mine.

I could only imagine what was said between Jack and the lineman, who was twice his size.

"Don't be mad," Jack said. Like I'd be angry after everything we'd been through. "I . . . I'm telling you this because you have to know that it's always been you. And it will always be you."

I knew then the difference between what I had with Jack and the twisted thing I had with Cole. Jack was real. Cole was a drug, artificial and simulated. My involuntary response to him was manufactured in the Everneath by a power that shouldn't even exist.

Jack was real. Tangible.

"Do you get it now, Becks?" Jack wrapped a finger around a long strand of my hair, and we were quiet as it slipped through his grip.

"You haven't moved on?"

He chuckled. "I have a lifetime of memories made up of

301

chestnut wars and poker games and midnight excursions and Christmas Dances. . . . It's all you. It's only ever been you. I love you." The last part seemed to escape his lips unintentionally, and afterward he closed his eyes and put his head in his hands, as if he had a sudden headache. "I've gotta not say that out loud."

The sight of how messed up he was made me want to wrap my arms around him and fold him into me and cushion him from everything that lay ahead.

Instead, I reached for his hand. Brought it to my lips. Kissed it.

He raised his head and winced. "You shouldn't do that," he said, even though he didn't pull his hand away.

"Why?"

"Because . . . it'll make everything worse. . . . If you don't feel—"

His voice cut off as I kissed his hand again, pausing with his fingers at my lips. He let out a shaky sigh and his hair flopped forward. Then he looked at my lips for a long moment. "What if . . . ?"

I bit my lower lip. "What?"

"What if we could be like this again?" He leaned in closer with a smile, and as he did, he said, "Are you going to steal my soul?"

"Um . . . it's not technically your soul that . . ."

I couldn't finish my sentence. His lips brushed mine, and I felt the whoosh of transferring emotions, but it wasn't as strong as the last time. The space inside me was practically full again. The Shades were right. Six months was just long enough to recover.

He kept his lips touching mine when he asked, "Is it okay?"

Okay in that I wasn't going to suck him dry anymore. Not okay in that my own emotions were in hyperdrive. Only our lips touched. Thankfully there was space between us everywhere else.

He took my silence to mean it was safe. We held our lips together, tentative and still.

But he didn't let it stay that casual for long. He pressed his lips closer, parting his mouth against mine. I shivered, and he put his arms around me and pulled me closer so that our bodies were touching in so many places.

He pulled back a little. His breath was on my lips.

"What is it?" I asked.

"I dreamed of you every night." He briefly touched his lips to mine again. "It felt so real. And when I'd wake up the next morning, it was like your disappearance was fresh. Like you'd left me all over again."

I lowered my chin and tucked my head into his chest. "I'm sorry."

He sighed and tightened his grip around me. "It never got easier. But the dreams themselves." I felt him shake his head. "It's like I had a physical connection to you. They were so real. Every night, you were in my room with me. It was so real."

I tilted my head back so I could face him again, realizing

for the first time how difficult it must've been for Jack. I kissed his chin, his cheek, and then his lips. "I'm sorry," I said again.

He shook his head. "It's not your fault I dreamed of you, Becks. I just want to know if it was as real as it felt."

"I don't know," I said. But I told him about the book I'd read on Orpheus and Eurydice, and my theory that it was her connection to Orpheus that saved her. When I finished, I asked him what he thought.

"It would make sense, I guess." He got a faraway look on his face. "I dreamed you were somewhere dark and you couldn't see."

I thought of the Cavern, and the alcove, and the Shades that bound us and shut out any light. "I don't know. So much of what happened has been wiped away." But not enough. The truth was, I couldn't see. My encounter with the Everneath had left scars on my brain, and hearing Jack talk about the darkness made them burn a little.

Jack touched his forehead to my forehead, his nose to my nose, and gave me a sad smile that was so sweet I almost forgot the spark of memory that had just been dredged up. Almost.

LAST YEAR
The Feed . . . the forgetting.

Once I'd decided to go with Cole, things happened quickly. I stayed holed up in his room for a few days, and each time I started to consider changing my mind, Cole would Feed off that top layer of energy, taking away my doubt, my pain, my foreboding, and my hesitation disappeared.

Soon, the Everlivings from the band had all gone under with their Forfeits, and Cole and I were the only ones left. Cole said this was because he needed time to prepare for the trip, and since he hadn't planned on taking me, we would be a couple of days behind. I never asked what kind of prep work he was talking about.

At the time, though, I waved aside any explanations. I was in this room of forgetting, and if the Everneath was anything like this, I never wanted to leave. He helped me out of my jacket, exposing the black tank top beneath, grabbed my hand, and I think he said, "Ready?"

I don't know if I responded, but he took my hand and pulled me under.

Like a cocoon.

The beginning of my century in the Everneath is a blur. The middle is gone entirely.

At first, I remember seeing a giant space, like an underground cave. In the rock walls were hundreds, maybe thousands, of tiny holes carved out. They reached upward, farther than my eyes could see in the dark.

I breathed in, expecting a stale, musty odor, like the

Timpanogos caves near Park City, but instead there was no identifying smell at all.

The sheer size of the place overwhelmed me, and I remembered wondering why I felt claustrophobic in a place so large. It was like the darkness itself was a physical entity, and just as that thought formed in my head, I saw the shadows on the walls begin to ripple and sway, as if a candle were flickering nearby. But there was no candle. In fact, there was no light source I could see. I moved closer and squinted, and that's when the shadows peeled away from the walls. They came over to me, snaked around my back, and guided me until I was standing in front of Cole.

Dark splotches of fluid ran down the wall where the shadows had been, as if little bubbles of oil had burst there. I reached out to touch it. Whatever it was, it didn't feel cool like liquid. It felt like air.

I turned to Cole to ask him what it was, but I didn't get a chance. The shadows surrounded us, pushing us closer together. "Just relax," Cole whispered.

The shadows began to move in circles around us, swirling, accelerating to the point where they looked like blurs of black, transforming into shrouds against my skin. They cocooned us, and the tighter they wrapped, the tighter my chest felt. But I guess I didn't need to breathe, because I didn't feel myself fighting for air.

Cole's face was at my ear. "They're Shades, Nik. They control the energy. They bind us together and they protect your energy from spilling out and wasting any."

"I don't care." And I didn't. Whatever this netting was that surrounded me, it lifted me up off the ground and held me suspended in the air, in a place where sorrow couldn't reach me. I was protected from everything that ever had, or ever would, hurt me, and I couldn't imagine ever wanting to leave. I was safe.

The Shades constricted against us, so Cole and I were as close as possible, our limbs pressed together, our arms around each other.

Looking back, I'm pretty sure we ended up inside one of the alcoves in the wall. Me, Cole, and our cocoon of shadows.

At first, my memories of the Surface began to change as I started forgetting the most recent events of my past. My mom wasn't dead anymore. She was there in our kitchen, making coffee and pancakes on a Sunday morning. And my dad wasn't forgiving the drunk driver who killed her. He was with her in the kitchen, his arms around her waist as she turned the eggs over with the spatula. And Jack wasn't with someone else. He was waiting for me beneath the trampoline, a deck of cards in his hands.

Eventually, though, my mom was in the kitchen alone, and I couldn't remember what she was doing. And Jack wasn't waiting under the trampoline. He was floating in a sea of nothing—no setting, no home.

And then there was no Mom, no kitchen. Jack's face was there, but there was no name to go with it. Everyone stopped existing. Everyone except for Jack, and even the memory of him was something I had to reach out and touch every so often, so as not to lose it.

Cole would ask me what I remembered of my former life. My answer was always the same.

"Nothing."

TWENTY-EIGHT

NOW

My bedroom. One week left.

Kissing Jack was like forgetting.

Forgetting the mark on my arm. Forgetting the Tunnels coming for me. Forgetting Cole. I realized it was probably the same for him, because he was kissing me like his lips couldn't remember how to do anything else. I was sure there would never be a reason for us to stop.

He kissed away the Tunnels, and he kissed away my doubts.

Our hands were all over each other, as if we were committing to memory every texture, every curve of the other. Jack pushed my jacket off my shoulders and down my arms and tossed it aside, revealing my tank top and my bare arms. Instinctively I tried to cover the mark on my left arm with my hand, but he wouldn't let me.

"Let me see it," he said.

I closed my eyes and rolled onto my back, but I let him hold my arm. He traced his fingers from my collarbone down my arm to where the mark stopped. He kissed my shoulder, where my mark was darkest, and then he lay down on his side next to me, facing me, his hand propping his head up.

"I'm going to kill him."

I sighed and mirrored his position. "You can't kill him. He's sort of immortal."

"Who says?"

I shrugged. "He's been around since the time of ancient myths."

"But when he's here, he's made of flesh and blood. Whatever form he takes, he is flesh. And blood."

"Even so, I don't think it's as simple as that."

His shoulders sagged a bit. "I know." He glanced down at my arm. "Do you know how much time you have?"

"No. Not exactly. A little over a week, maybe."

"What about Meredith? Wouldn't she have the same amount of time?"

I thought back to the few days I'd spent in Cole's apartment, just before he took me underground. By the time we left, none of the other band members were on the Surface. They'd all been ready with their Forfeits. "She left before me. That means she probably Returned before me."

"And the Tunnels will come for her first." Jack gave a grunt of frustration.

Something hit me right then, and a split second later I made sure the burst of intuition didn't show on my face. Even if Will returned with Mary, and even if she did know how to kill Cole,

I had no idea if my debt would be destroyed as well. What if the Tunnels were coming for me no matter what?

Jack looked like he was about to ask me what was wrong, so I brought his face to mine again.

For the first time in a hundred years, Jack's lips were against mine in a real kiss. He was mine again, and in that moment, I made a decision.

I had to find a way to stay. And I wouldn't stop searching for a loophole to my fate, until the moment the Tunnels dragged me away.

The next morning, Jack called and said Will was having trouble coaxing Meredith away from the cabin. He wanted to pick me up and take me to her.

"I can't leave right now," I said, cradling the phone.

"Why?"

"The election's tomorrow. I can't leave my family. I can't risk these last moments. I promised myself I would prepare them."

He was quiet.

"I don't mean tell them I'm leaving. But last time I disappeared in the middle of a fight with my dad. I can't leave him like that again."

"It's okay, Becks. I'll go, and I will bring her back, even if I have to force her."

I grimaced, but I knew he was telling the truth.

I promised Jack I'd do as much research on the internet as I could while they were gone, but there were only so many ways

311

I could type "how to avoid the Tunnels" into the search engine.

As my days dwindled, it was like I was living two lives. The hopeful side of me raced around, frantic to find an answer, and the reasonable part of me had settled into savoring the last moments with my family.

Trying to get alone time with my dad would be impossible until after the election, so I contacted Percy Jones and did whatever task he told me to do—passing out flyers, making phone calls—knowing the effort would eventually get back to my dad.

Cole was giving me space. I was sure he thought I was at the tipping point. He had left me alone to contemplate my future. He didn't know Jack had come back. If he did, he would've been at my window, whether he promised to leave me alone or not.

After two long days, Jack called me and said he and Will were on their way home.

My dad won by a wide margin, so when the polls closed, there was no question.

His campaign held the victory party at the Silver Lodge Hotel near the ski resort, and I put on the same black dress I'd worn to the Christmas Dance, and I cheered at the right times and hit the balloons as they fell from the net in the ceiling.

I don't know how I missed it, but I did. Even as Percy was making the announcement in the microphone, introducing the victory band, I still didn't quite get it. Even as the last of the balloons fell lazily to the floor, and the older supporters made way for the younger ones, I still didn't get it.

The Dead Elvises were about to play at my father's victory party. Surprise. I was standing there, in the center of the crowd, frozen.

One of the campaign contributors next to me said loudly to her friend, "Percy did it. He got the band to play!"

There was only one reason they'd play a stodgy election party, and it wasn't because of Percy. They were here for me. They took the stage one by one. Cole was the final one out, his entrance delayed for impact. The entire band believed what Cole believed: that I would lead them to the throne in the Everneath.

Maxwell backed Cole up, and fans who I'm sure couldn't give a rat's ass about politics swarmed the dance floor.

My dad had done it. He'd shown everyone he was the hip answer to our town's stagnant tourist industry. The Dead Elvises were playing his party. Op-ed piece be damned.

But this time I was not a starstruck fan. When the band ratcheted up the energy, I could see the traces of emotion from the people on the dance floor hanging in the air like a buffet.

As the band finished one song and began another, Cole's voice boomed over the crowd.

"This one's for the mayor's daughter." Cole used the neck of his guitar to point toward me from the stage.

A few attendees turned their heads in my direction, and I automatically backed up until I hit the wall.

Cole began to pick out a slower, discordant melody. One that almost begged for resolution. As he played, some of the lighter shades of emotions—the pleasant ones that you'd find at a victory party—wafted through the air, as if attracted to the sounds of his guitar. Cole and the band were sampling from every single person there.

The colors that sought his guitar were soft, gentle hues, and as they gathered strength above Cole they began releasing droplets, like a storm cloud's first hints of rain. The droplets danced and swayed above him and his guitar, as if they were obeying the instrument.

I glanced around at the faces in the audience. It was obvious none of them saw the colors as I saw them.

Looking back at Cole, I realized the drops were accumulating on the guitar. He made sure I was watching as he tipped his head back and inhaled deeply, sucking in much of the electric mist surrounding him.

Seeing him gorge himself on stolen emotions made me realize I was still so empty. I felt the hunger, so I started toward the exits to get away, but then something changed. Something was pulling me back. Pulling me down. My eyes lost focus, and the noise from the band was replaced by a ringing sound in my ears.

A group of campaign contributors saw that I was leaving. One of the women pulled me to her, saying she wanted to introduce the mayor's daughter around.

My heart was beating fast. Too fast, as if the blood were

spilling out of me and it couldn't keep up. As the strangers shook my hand, their faces blurred together. Somebody was asking me about college but I couldn't hear above the muffled ringing in my ears.

"Are you okay, dear?" the woman who had dragged me over asked.

"Um . . . I'm fine. I just . . ." I noticed a fog above me, larger and denser than the one from the Christmas Dance. Cole was directing it. But the energy cloud wasn't from other people . . . it was from me. The entire band was feeding off me.

Everything was blurry. I tried to reach my hand up to my head, but it wasn't obeying me. As I looked up, I lost my bearings. I stepped backward to try to balance, but I'd really stepped forward, and the red carpet came rushing at my face. Just as I expected to slam into the floor, two arms caught me around my waist.

"Okay, Becks. You're okay. Stay with me." Jack's voice in my ear. Then louder, "She's just a little hypoglycemic."

"Get me out," I whispered faintly. "Get me out." Jack heard me.

"Should I fetch some water?" one of the women asked. "Or should I get her father?"

"No," Jack said firmly. "No need to bother the mayor. I've seen her like this before, and all she needs is a little fresh air and some food." He didn't wait for protests. He scooped me into his arms and headed for the doors.

The music took on a screeching quality as if the fingers of

the sound were grasping on to my body, trying to take hold, but we were outside before anyone could stop us.

Jack set me on the bench. "Becks? Becks, open your eyes. What happened?"

"I didn't know they were . . ." I finished the explanation in my head, but the words got caught in my mouth.

"What's wrong with her?" said a voice from nearby. Will's voice.

"I don't know yet," Jack answered. He sat next to me and put an arm around my shoulders and pulled me close. "Shh. We're out now. It's okay."

"They Fed on me. The whole band."

I felt Jack's body tense. "Why would he do that? What's the point?"

"To remind me what it's going to feel like."

Jack didn't say anything. I was aware of Will sitting down near my feet. I rested there for a few long minutes with Jack holding me tight. My hands started to tremble like they did when I first Returned. Most of the energy I had built up was gone.

"Did you find Mary?" I asked in a shaky voice.

"Yes, but she didn't want to be seen here. She's waiting for us at the abandoned Firestone building."

I nodded and made a move to sit up. "Let's go, then."

"No you don't." He pushed my shoulder down so I was lying on his lap. "Rest for a little while more."

I didn't try to argue. I just nodded and closed my eyes. Jack put his hand on my shoulder, holding tight to stop the shaking.

* * *

I didn't know how much time had passed when Jack nudged me. "Becks?"

"Mmmm?"

"How do you feel now?"

I opened my eyes and slowly sat up. I brought my fingers to my face and they trembled. "I don't know. Hungry." But I wasn't as completely empty as I'd expected. Nowhere near the point I was at almost six months ago. I looked around. "Where's Will?"

"He went to make sure Mary didn't run away." Jack took my face in his hands, and before I really thought about what he was doing, he brought my lips to his. The taste of his pent-up despair left his mouth with the familiar *whoosh*, and it continued for a few long moments before the reasonable half of my brain took over.

I shoved him back. "What are you doing? You can't do that!"

He studied my face. "That's better. You look a little less . . . dead now." But his eyes had fresh circles under them, and his cheeks were noticeably sunken.

"I don't care. You know how dangerous it is?"

He didn't answer as I took in a few deep breaths and blew them out.

"I'm sorry," he said. "But I knew you'd never ask."

I could feel tears spring up in my eyes, and I rubbed my thumb under my eye and kept my head down.

Jack gathered me in his arms again. "I'm sorry. I'm so sorry." And then, in a wavering voice, "You can't go to the Tunnels."

I looked up at his face. "If I don't, then I'll have to Feed off someone else. And I will always be draining someone in order to survive. Just like I was drained."

His phone buzzed right then, and he flipped it open to read a text. "Mary's waiting. Let's go."

TWENTY-NINE

NOW

Meeting Meredith. Days left.

$\mathscr{J}$ack drove us to the abandoned Firestone tire factory, where squatters lived in between police sweeps. Will was waiting for us outside the doors.

"Where is she?" Jack asked.

"Inside," Will said. "She won't talk to me. Wanted to wait for you two."

"Okay." Jack reached for the door and Will grabbed his arm.

"Mom's freaking out. Said you're not answering your phone."

"Yeah, well—"

"Don't worry. You two have this. I'll deal with Mom."

Will took off at a jog toward his car. Jack and I turned back to the building. The wind had picked up and was blowing with such force that when we opened the large wooden door, it smacked against the wall with a loud clap. We found

Meredith in a corner. She was hunched over, rocking back and forth on her heels. Something was very wrong.

"Mary?" Jack said, crouching beside her. "What's going on?"

Meredith raised her head off her knees. "This," she said, and she held out her arm to Jack. The longest fingers of her mark had reached her inner wrist, all the way to the crease between her wrist and her hand. "It stopped just now. Stopped right at the line." She shoved her wrist closer to Jack's face.

I didn't realize it, but when she spoke I took a step back. Meredith looked frantic and despairing, and I realized that she was my future. My bleak future, with all my fears, was staring me in the face. I couldn't speak.

"What are you saying, Mary?" Jack said. "How do you even notice something like that?"

Meredith looked past Jack and spoke to me. "It'll go fast. For an entire day, it will go fast. So fast that you can actually see it move. And then it will stop."

She put her head back on her arms and continued rocking. The old building failed to keep the wind out, and the ends of her hair got caught in the draft. It twisted and curled around her face.

"Maxwell told me at the end it speeds up, and then it stops. And then the Tunnels come," she said. Her lower lip began to tremble. "I was supposed to survive. But I didn't. I didn't." She rocked back on her heels. "I shouldn't have Returned." She buried her head in her knees and started sobbing. "They're coming for me, Nikki. The Tunnels are coming and they won't stop until they have me."

"Mary, I'm so sorry," I said.

Jack stood straight, glanced at me for a quick moment, and then took hold of Mary's hand. "We're getting out of here." He pulled her up.

I could've told him right then that there was no point, but something inside me wouldn't allow it. Jack needed to see how futile it all was. And I needed to see what was waiting for me.

Jack and I flanked Mary, took her hands, and started pulling her along. Out of the building. Down the street toward the center of town. Leaves and dust got caught in the gusts of wind, making it difficult to see.

"Where are we going?" Mary asked, gasping for breath.

Jack answered. "To Cole's place. He has to see. They all have to see what they've done. You know where it is, right, Becks?"

I nodded. "It's up near the resort."

We made it to Jack's car, and Mary climbed into the passenger seat while I sat in the back. Jack shoved the gearshift and we were off. The wind picked up and the trees on either side of the street bent and swayed as if our car were going so fast the suction was affecting them.

"That's a strong wind for Park City," I said. I don't know why I said it.

Jack didn't answer, but he stepped on the gas as we turned onto the highway that led to the ski resorts.

Stray branches and twigs ricocheted off the windshield as we raced along. I glanced toward the base of the mountains, a couple of football fields away. The trees there didn't seem to be moving. Maybe it was too long a distance for me to see. We wound our way up the mountain as the strange storm brewed outside.

Jack looked in the rearview mirror, and then whipped his head around to look out the back window. "Shit."

I turned around too, trying to make sense of what I saw. A dark mass swirled behind us, as if a funnel cloud had been turned on its side and we were staring up one end. I looked at the sky. Past the debris that encircled Jack's car, the sky above was clear. The hairs on my arms stood straight, as if my body were reacting to an electrical current from the cloud, and then the mark started to spin and churn on my skin.

"The Tunnels," I said. I glanced quickly at my own arm.

Mary twisted around and caught me. "You feel it too?"

"I feel something," I said, and then I looked up and noticed Mary's hair. It was flapping against her face, as if there were a breeze in the car. But the windows were rolled up. Whatever it was, it was stronger for her.

Jack rammed the accelerator to the floor, screeching around every curve in the road until I was sure he would lose control, but the funnel cloud kept gaining on us.

Mary turned to Jack, and with a voice almost too soft for me to hear, she said, "It's over, Jack. Pull over."

"No!" Jack squeezed the steering wheel until his knuckles turned white. "We'll find a shelter. Underground or something."

"You know concrete walls won't stop it."

"Five minutes and we're at Cole's place. I want to see their faces at what they've brought here. Five minutes, Mary!"

She shook her head. I'd never seen her so lucid. "Jack, if you don't let me out, that thing behind us will destroy the car, too. You can't give up on Nikki now."

Jack's eyes flashed to me in the rearview mirror. His shoulders sagged and I could feel him let up on the gas. Moments later the car came to a stop on the side of the road.

"Thank you," Mary said. She paused. "Do you still have the bracelet I gave you?"

Jack and I both nodded.

She closed her eyes and let out a long breath. "The bracelet holds a secret the Daughters of Persephone have been protecting for centuries." She opened her eyes and looked at Jack. "By telling you that, I've betrayed all of my ancestors."

"What secret?" Jack said.

She shook her head. "I don't know."

She pulled on the handle and cracked open the door.

"Wait!" I blurted from the backseat. "What about Orpheus and Eurydice? What did you mean, Orpheus was strong?"

She looked at me for a moment. "Poor Nikki. You won't like the answer." Then she leaned over the seat and whispered in my ear, "You have a debt to the Tunnels. But the secret is, it doesn't matter who fills it, as long as the debt is paid."

She kissed my cheek, and then, with the dexterity of a teenager, Mary threw the door open and sprang out of the car.

All we could do was watch. Once she was out of the car,

and waiting, the Tunnels didn't hesitate. The funnel cloud was on her, and then she was gone. And everything went quiet.

Jack clenched the steering wheel tightly until I was sure he would rip it off. "How long?" His voice was barely audible.

I knew what he was asking. "Meredith left two days before me."

He leaned his head down on the steering wheel. "How did this happen, Becks?" Then he seemed to remember I was in the backseat. "Would you please get up here and talk to me?"

I climbed into the front.

"What did she say to you about Orpheus?" Jack asked.

I looked him in the eyes. *It doesn't matter who fills it, as long as the debt is paid.* Orpheus was strong. He took Eurydice's debt. He went to the Tunnels in her place. I knew without a doubt that's what Mary was telling me.

But Jack could never know that. "She told me Orpheus stayed strong to the end, and helped Eurydice choose the Tunnels over her Everliving."

Jack narrowed his eyes. "We already knew that."

I looked out the window. "I know. She was only reminding me that no matter how enticing Cole makes it sound, we can still make the right choice."

Jack sighed. "I should've found you, Becks."

"When?"

"That night at the dorm, when you drove off, I thought I'd still have time to explain. I didn't know about the Kevin

Reid verdict. I thought tomorrow morning would come, and then I'd talk to you and everything would be okay." He rested his head back on the steering wheel. "I should've chased you down. It's my fault you went with Cole."

"No, it's not."

"But Lacey was in my room." And there he said it. The thing we'd never talked about.

He kept his head down on the steering wheel. "I was asleep, and I didn't know she was there. One of the guys helped her get in. Nothing happened, but it could've. I thought if I could just talk to you, I could make it all okay."

I turned my head to look out the window. The last bits of debris from the Tunnels were settling to the ground. "It doesn't matter anymore. I made the decision to find Cole. I talked him into it. You need to remember that, because when I'm gone—"

"You're not going!"

I inhaled a long, deep breath and lowered my voice. "That night, when I left the dorm, I could've gone home and shut myself in my room. I could've faced you and yelled at you. But I didn't. I took the easy way out. I begged for the easy way out. Cole took the pain away, and I didn't care that it would ruin everything in my life, because I was stupid enough to think I had nothing else to lose."

I watched in the reflection of my window as he slammed the heel of his hand down onto the steering wheel over and over, so hard it cracked the plastic covering at the base.

Watching the Tunnels absorb Mary, I lost that niggling

little scrap of hope inside me. But Jack hadn't. I knew I could take his despair and make him focus. "Jack. What are we going to do about it?"

It worked.

He raised his head. "It all comes back to the bracelet. The Daughters were protecting a secret for the Everneath, and I can only think of one secret worth protecting over all the others."

"What?"

He held my gaze. "How to bring them down."

THIRTY

NOW

My house. Forty-eight hours left.

Jack and I ended up at my house, at my desk, while we tried to figure out where to start. My dad and Tommy were renting a room at the Silver Lodge after the win, but I begged him to let me stay at home instead. Jack and I had the house to ourselves.

I bent the desk lamp down as close to the bracelet as I could. The markings on it were worn with a patina, so I grabbed a rag and a tube of toothpaste from the bathroom and dabbed a little dollop on the silver.

"What's that for?" Jack asked.

"It's a trick my mom taught me. In a pinch, if you need your silver polished . . ." I rubbed the toothpaste onto the brace-let until the entire surface area was covered with a thin layer. "And then when you rub it off"—I swiped it with the clean part of the rag—"you get this."

I dangled the bracelet in front of Jack's face. The worn,

smudged parts were clear of dirt, and we could get a better look at the shape of the markings.

"It doesn't look like a language," Jack said. "It looks more like pictures. Or symbols."

I nodded. "Maybe like hieroglyphs. We are talking about mythology, after all." Jack's leg was bouncing up and down. "Jack, go grab a pencil and a paper. You're better at drawing."

He rifled through the top two drawers of my desk until he found a notebook and a pencil. He set the paper on the desk and then looked from the bracelet to the paper, drawing what he saw. The first shape looked like a pot. The second like the outline of a person, only shaded in black. The third like a bird with a human head.

I opened my laptop and searched for "hieroglyphics bird with a human head," because that was the only symbol for which I could imagine search terms. There were a few that didn't make sense at all. But about halfway down the first page, I saw a similar image to the one on the bracelet.

I read off the screen. "Bird with a human head can mean 'ba.' Or soul."

"Try the other two," Jack said.

I typed in "hieroglyphics pot." The search came up with thousands of entries. No pattern as to what it meant. I tried the human figure next. "Hieroglyphics man shaded." Nothing. I tried "hieroglyphics human form" and other descriptive terms for the outline of the person, but it didn't help.

"It's not going to work because I'm not describing the

symbols right. I'm saying 'human shape,' but it's too general, or completely wrong, because I'm not getting any answers."

"I know, Becks." He rubbed his chin with his fingertips. I smiled. Another typical Jack Caputo move. "The bird with the human head was specific enough. 'Ba,' right? So let's look up 'ba' and see if anything else pops up."

I typed "ba" into the search engine, but the first few entries were for British Airways. So I added "hieroglyphics," and that's when I saw it. An article titled "The Five Elements of the Egyptian Soul."

Jack read over my shoulder. "'The human soul is made up of five parts: the ren, the ba, the ka, the sheut, and the ib. Also known as the name, the personality, the life force, the shadow, and the heart.'"

Each part had an associated symbol pictured next to it. "The bracelet shows all five symbols." I looked at Jack. "The five parts of the soul. But what does it mean?"

"I don't know." We sat quiet for a moment, staring at the strange bracelet. "I thought it would be something obvious," Jack said.

"Like a recipe for a poison apple?"

He gave me a wry smile. "Something like that." His smile gave way and he picked up the bracelet and held it closer to his eyes. "It's there. We're just not seeing it."

I wasn't so sure. Jack noticed my skepticism.

"It's there, Becks. Why would Mary spend her last moment aboveground leaving us this clue if she knew it would come to nothing? One last practical joke she wouldn't be around to see? I don't think so. It's valuable enough that the Daughters of Persephone went through a lot of trouble to keep it. It's gotta mean something."

"I hope you're right. So what do we do now?"

Jack pointed to my computer. "We start showing it around. Somebody out there knows what it means."

I thought about the missing reporter. "That could be dangerous."

He just shrugged. "What do we have to lose?"

Jack took a picture of the bracelet with his phone and emailed it to both of our accounts. He folded the paper with his own drawings. "Come to school with me tomorrow."

"Jack, I have two days left at the most. Why—"

"Just to Mrs. Stone's class. She's a mythology geek. Maybe she can help, or point us in the right direction. She took those classes in college, the one where that professor was nuts for this stuff. I don't know . . ." Jack covered his mouth as he tried to stifle a yawn. I glanced at the clock. It was nearly two in the morning.

"You're tired," I said. I reached out and traced the circles under his eyes. "You should go and get some sleep. We're both going to need it."

Jack looked down, and when he spoke again his voice was gruff. "I don't know if I can say good night."

I could see the little divot appear in between his eyebrows. I wanted to smooth it out. Smooth away the worry there. "I'll still be here tomorrow. I promise." He was waiting for me to disappear again, and it killed me.

He nodded like he believed me, but he didn't move. I leaned toward him and kissed him on the cheek. He held perfectly still.

"You need sleep," I whispered, my lips at his ear.

I saw his cheeks pull up into a grin. "If this is your way of convincing me, it's not working. How about I just stay here?"

"You know if you stay here, we won't be able to sleep."

He sighed. "You're right. I know you're right."

He left before either of us wanted to part. I fell asleep quickly, the effects of the band's meal robbing me of energy, but when I woke up I knew it was too early to actually get up. I looked out the window to see if there was any sign of the day beginning, and saw Jack's car parked alongside the curb outside our house. Fog on a couple of the windows obscured a peek inside. I checked the grass. The tips were white with an overnight frost.

I put on a thick robe and my slippers and grabbed a couple of blankets from the linen closet. Outside, I took a breath, and it felt like dry ice making its way down the back of my throat.

I picked up the pace to the curb and knocked on the driver's-side window.

The indistinct shape inside jumped, and the door cracked open. Jack sat up. He rubbed his hands over his arms and then curled his fingertips and breathed on them. "What time is it?"

I threw a blanket around him, tucking it in on the sides. "It's five thirty."

"Oh." He closed his eyes again and started to curl back up against the seat.

I rolled my eyes. "You never were a morning person. You can still sleep, but not in the car. Come inside."

I thought he'd put up more of a fight, but he followed me silently into my house and into my room. I shut the door behind us, and Jack curled up on the floor in the corner under the windowsill.

"Jack, sleep on the bed."

"Nope. I'm good here." His eyes were still closed. I didn't think he'd opened them once yet.

I was about to insist, but he was already snoring softly, so I draped the blanket over him and climbed back in my bed and drifted.

Jack woke me up about an hour later, fully dressed, hair combed, breath smelling like toothpaste.

"Let's go, Becks. Time to make our last stand. I'll be in the living room."

I threw on some clothes, brushed my hair and my teeth, and met him inside our entryway.

On the drive to school, Jack held my hand. "It's not going to come for you, Becks. We'll figure this out."

I nodded. I couldn't say anything for fear of breaking down completely. He held my hand as we walked into Mrs. Stone's classroom.

Mrs. Stone was there, marking some papers at her desk.

She looked up. "Ms. Beckett. Mr. Caputo. You're both early. What can I help you with?"

Jack tossed the bracelet so that it landed on her desk, right in front of her. "We were wondering if you could tell us anything about the markings on this. Anything at all." Jack was trying to keep his voice even.

Mrs. Stone put her reading glasses on and studied the jewelry. "It's hard to see what the figures are . . ."

Jack pulled out the paper with his drawings on it and put it in front of her. "Maybe this will help. They're my own drawings, so they're not, like . . . professional or anything. But we think they're hieroglyphics."

She looked at us both for a few seconds. "Why would you have a bracelet with hieroglyphics on it?"

I was about to say something, but Jack beat me to it. "That new store on Main is selling them. Each bracelet is supposed to mean something different."

"Oh. Then do you think this could wait until after school?"

Jack switched on his most charming grin. "I sorta bet my friend we could figure it out before he did. Please?"

She gave a half smile and looked at the paper with his drawings. "Well, I know the pot is the symbol for heart. That one's sort of universal. But the others . . ."

I looked at Jack and shook my head. This was going to be a waste of time if all she could do was confirm what we already knew.

Jack leaned against her desk. "I was doing a little research, and the other symbols might have something to do with the parts of the soul . . . or something?"

She shrugged. "That sounds familiar."

"Do you know of any books we could check out? Maybe at the library?"

"Library . . ." Her voice trailed off and she held a finger up in the air. "One of my old professors at the university would be the one to talk to. He's the one who convinced me to use myths as a basis for my creative-writing projects, but of course, I never got into it so much that I would know how to read hieroglyphs. . . . When I get home tonight, I'll see if I can find some contact info for you—"

"It'll be too late tonight," Jack interrupted. I put my hand on his arm, and he took a breath. "I mean, my friend is really close to . . . Look, Mrs. Stone. Can we just straight-up ask it as a favor?" She gave him a curious look and let him continue. "If he's a professor at the university, that means his email's probably on their site. I have a picture of the bracelet. We could email it to him. It's important." Jack looked down, and when he spoke again his voice was anguished. "It's everything to me."

"Do you promise to turn in your scholarship applications by next week?"

Jack cracked a grin. "Whatever you want."

"That's what I want."

* * *

Mrs. Stone followed us to the computer lab, and she logged on to her email while Jack found the university's contact page on another monitor.

"I'll send the email from my account," Mrs. Stone said, "but I'm sure you realize Dr. Spears is probably really busy. He may not get the sense of urgency you seem to have."

"I understand," Jack said. "But we have to try."

Mrs. Stone typed out a quick message, even telling Dr. Spears he would be doing her a huge favor if he looked at the picture of the bracelet as soon as possible and helped decipher its meaning.

"You know, if you two hadn't been putting in your time for my class every day, I wouldn't be doing this."

"Thank you," I said.

Mrs. Stone cc'd Jack's email address, attached the picture, and then clicked send. She sat back in the lab chair. "Okay. We'll see what happens. Mr. Caputo, I expect your scholarship papers by the end of the week."

"Done," Jack said.

We had only a few minutes before the start of class, so we hurried back to Mrs. Stone's classroom. After I took my seat, Jack scooted his desk a couple of inches closer to mine. I smiled.

He leaned close and said, "Becks, all we need is one little spark. One little push in the right direction. I don't think that's too much to hope for, do you?"

I shook my head.

"If we don't hear anything by lunchtime, I'll start posting it on boards. Classifieds. Everywhere."

About ten minutes into Mrs. Stone's lecture on Walt Whitman's *Leaves of Grass*, Jack's phone vibrated in his hand, indicating a new email. He read the screen, and as he did his left foot started tapping.

"What is it?" I whispered.

"Professor Spears. Requesting an immediate phone call. He left his number."

I drew in a deep breath. I couldn't believe he had responded so quickly. This was it. Whatever that bracelet meant, it was important enough to warrant an immediate phone call with the head of the anthropology department at the university. Jack kept his eyes on Mrs. Stone as he typed a response under his desk.

"I told him we'd call at the end of class," Jack whispered. "Doesn't Mrs. Stone have her second period free?"

I nodded.

"I want her here for this so she can back us up if we need it."

The minute hand on the wall clock decided to take the long way around, and the rest of class dragged. When the bell finally rang, Jack and I sprinted to Mrs. Stone's desk.

"Professor Spears wants to talk," Jack blurted out, his thumb already on the keypad of his phone. "I'm calling him."

Mrs. Stone pulled her eyebrows together and said, "I don't think—" She didn't finish, because Jack had pressed send and it was ringing.

"You talk," Jack said, handing the phone to Mrs. Stone. "Please."

We were silent as we listened to Mrs. Stone's end of the conversation. Jack nearly ripped the desk in half as Mrs. Stone asked about the professor's current research, but then it sounded like Professor Spears cut it short. Mrs. Stone stopped talking and handed the phone to Jack. "He wants to talk to you."

Jack took it. "Hello, Professor Spears. Thanks for calling—" Jack looked at me as he listened. "Okay, do you mind if I put you on speaker?"

He put the phone down on the desk between us.

"You were saying?" Jack said.

Professor Spears's voice crackled through the line. "I'm wondering where you got this bracelet. It's a copy, correct?"

"A copy of what?"

"I know of only one like it in existence, and it's in storage at the Smithsonian. The design is not something you'd expect everyday jewelers to replicate." He paused and sounded a little like he was chuckling. "It's just that your picture almost makes it look authentic—or, at the very least, an expensive replica—and I wondered where you got it."

Jack ignored his question. "We thought the symbols had something to do with the five parts of the Egyptian soul. Is that right?"

"Yes, but that's only the beginning of the meaning behind the markings. It's the position of each picture on the bracelet that tells the story. The bracelet refers to an ancient civilization called the Ring of the Dead."

"What does that mean?" Jack interrupted.

"I'm getting to that. Do you see how the sheut, the ren, and the ba are grouped together?"

We were both silent, staring at the picture. "Um . . ." Jack said.

"The sheut, the shadow figure. The ren, the name. And the ba, the personality. Got it?"

"Yes," I said. I didn't think we had much choice in the matter.

"And in the center, we see the ib, or the heart; it looks like a pot." Jack and I both nodded, even though Professor Spears couldn't see us. "And on the other end is the ka. The life force. The entire picture represents those humans who have discovered the key to eternal life, by giving up their own kas, or life forces, and stealing the kas of others. So the bracelet has to do with the royalty of the Ring of the Dead. The Akh ghosts. Or Everlivings, as some more contemporary studies have deemed them. Of course, these are all fringe theories."

My heart sped up. *Everlivings.* I couldn't believe there were actually people out there who knew about them. "Keep going, please, Professor Spears," I whispered.

"You see, ancient myth has us believe death can occur only when the ka leaves the body. Akh ghosts replenish their kas constantly, and therefore the ka never leaves their bodies and death cannot touch them."

My mouth opened a bit, and I looked at Jack. Even Mrs.

Stone had taken an interest in the conversation. She sat in a desk behind Jack, listening.

"Akh ghosts are sort of a popular legend in anthropology circles." He chuckled softly. "Some of my own colleagues believe Akh ghosts wander the face of the earth today. I think it adds to their zeal for our area of study . . ."

I stopped listening as Professor Spears told of the quirks of some of his colleagues. I only tuned in again when he said, "Where did you get the replica, by the way? Its likeness to the one stored at the Smithsonian is extraordinary. If possible, I'd love the chance to have a look at it."

"Tourist knockoff," Jack said.

"You're in Park City, are you not? Why would a town focused on a tourist trade of American Indian artifacts have a bracelet with ancient Egyptian roots?"

"Because tourists don't know the difference."

"Maybe," Professor Spears conceded. "But I'd still like to talk to the shop owner. Perhaps he received inspiration from something else in his possession, and maybe he doesn't know what he has. Museum artifacts are found this way all the time. Someone buys a house and finds something in the attic, or buried in the backyard." He paused, waiting for an answer.

I narrowed my eyes at Jack, and he raised his eyebrows and shrugged.

I answered. "I got the bracelet from a friend, so I'll have to ask her."

"One last question, if you have a moment . . ." Jack said.

"Shoot."

"How do you kill an Akh ghost?"

There was a pause on the phone line. "Uh, are you serious?"

"It's for a paper." Jack sounded so convincing, even I believed him for a second. "Theoretically, how would it happen?"

"Joyce, what kind of assignments are you handing out these days?"

We both looked at Mrs. Stone. She leaned toward the phone as if it were a microphone. "It's extra credit. Trust me, Jack needs it." She winked at Jack.

"Well, as the image shows, the Akh ghost existence is based on a perfect balance, this exact configuration of the five elements. If one of them were to throw the others out of balance . . . if the Akh ghost no longer had access, say, to other people's kas. Other people's energy."

I felt my shoulders sag. There was no way we could prevent Cole from Feeding off others.

Jack must've thought the same thing, because he asked, "What about the heart? Why is it separate but in the middle?"

"Because it's not part of the being, but it's nearby."

"Can they live without it?"

I jerked my head at Jack, but he was staring intently at the phone.

The line crackled, as if Dr. Spears had breathed deeply into the receiver. "I guess not. But you must find out where the heart beats first. Hypothetically."

We were all quiet for a moment. Mrs. Stone looked at Jack

and he nodded. She leaned forward again and said, "Thank you again, professor."

"Of course, Joyce. And, kids, if you find out where exactly the bracelet comes from, please do let me know."

We hung up the phone. We were going after Cole's heart.

THIRTY-ONE

NOW

Jack's car. Thirty-six hours left.

We walked out of the school and straight to Jack's car. He turned on the engine and the heat. I looked back at the school, aware that I probably wouldn't set foot inside it again.

"What do you think, Becks?" Jack said.

I turned away from the building. "Cole always tells me he has a heart, but it's not inside him. I've even listened to his chest. There's nothing there."

"If it's not inside him, it's gotta be near him. We just have to figure out where it is. Professor Spears was right about the life force stuff. We have to assume he's right about the heart, too, which means it's valuable to Cole. So valuable that he would protect it with everything he has."

"Maybe it's locked away in a vault or something? Like in an urn." I could only imagine a shrunken actual heart, but perhaps I was being too literal.

"But the band moves around so much," Jack countered.

"I'd guess it would be in something portable. Not as fragile as an urn."

"Wait," I said. Something portable. Something valuable. Something he protects and keeps with him always. Something as important to him as my own hands were to me. "His guitar." I got excited thinking about it.

"His guitar." Jack repeated the words, as if trying them out.

"He takes it everywhere. And once, when I touched it, he freaked out." I remembered the day in my bedroom when I'd clawed at the strings. "I should've seen it before. He uses music to stir the emotions and circulate the life force of the audience, just before he steals energy. It's like an actual heart; the center of the circulatory system. Pumping the nourishment. I watched him do it. It's his guitar . . ." I stopped talking. Jack was staring at my arm, his eyes wide.

"What?" I demanded.

"The fingers. I can see them moving."

I looked down at the mark, which was visible beneath the thin cotton of my shirt. It was halfway between my elbow and my wrist. I didn't see it at first, but as I stared, I saw the line creeping.

"Mary said it would speed up," I said.

Jack was quiet for a moment, staring at it. Then his arms were around me and he crushed me into him. "I can't lose you again, Becks."

"You're not going to."

This time, though, I actually believed it might be possible.

Jack drove us to Grounds&Ink. His left leg never stopped bouncing. When we found a booth, he ordered two coffees.

"Make them decaf," I said to the waitress.

Jack nodded. When the server left, he said, "We've got to figure out a way to separate Cole from his guitar." The words spilled out of his mouth and ran together.

"Do you think it's just a matter of getting it away from him?" I asked.

"We find it, steal it, and then smash it."

I laughed a desperate sound. "So all we have to do is find Cole, get close enough to him that we can steal his guitar—without him knowing it—and then smash it. And we have twenty-four hours." I tilted my head back and looked at the ceiling.

"I know how we can get close to him," Jack said quietly.

"How?"

"We give him the one thing he wants." He was staring at his hand as he flicked his ring finger with his thumb.

"Me."

He nodded, still not looking at me. "And then I think I know someone who would love to smash a guitar."

We left the coffee shop and Jack drove me to my house. We had decided to wait until the next morning to go to Cole's place. It was my idea, in case we failed. I couldn't stand the thought of waiting those last few hours for the Tunnels. If our plan didn't work, I wanted the Tunnels to get me that very instant.

Jack pulled over in front of my house. My dad's car was in the driveway. He and Tommy were home from the Silver Lodge.

"Um . . . where will you . . ." I bit my lip.

"I'll be in your room. Don't lock the window." He touched his lips and then touched my hand.

I nodded and got out of the car. My father, Tommy, and I ate a simple dinner that night. French toast. Breakfast for dinner. Just what the mayor needed after a tiring campaign. When I first got to the Everneath, I sometimes pictured what I would say to my dad and Tommy if I had the chance. But imagining the scene was very different from living it.

Tonight I had nothing to say. No wisdom to impart. No tearful good-byes. I had once had the words, but now they fell through me, as if I were a defunct sieve. Just one more ordinary dinner, in our ordinary kitchen, under ordinary circumstances. As if nothing were different.

I realized then that my Return had been painful. More painful than I ever could have imagined, with birthdays of Tommy's that I'd never get to see, and the inauguration of my dad that I wouldn't be able to attend, and good-byes I'd never be able to say.

But it'd been beautiful, too. The moments I could cling to, like the touch of Tommy's golden hair beneath my fingers, and the sound of my dad's voice as he talked to my mom when he thought no one else was listening.

When we were done, I hurried and did the dishes, and then I hugged Tommy and said good night.

"You never hug," Tommy said.

I kissed the top of his head, scruffed up his hair. If this worked, I would do everything I could to make life normal for my little brother. I headed down the hall to my room, opened the door, and shut it behind me.

Jack was lying on his back on my bed, his hands behind his head, staring at the ceiling. Without a word, I laid down next to him, facing him. He turned to look at me.

We were quiet for a moment. I studied his face—the bend of his cheekbones, the curve of his lips. Softly, I touched the post in his eyebrow.

His eyes crinkled in response.

"When did you get it?" I asked.

"A month after you left," he said, "my mom told me to forget you. That you were gone, and you were never coming back, and that I was better off without you." His lip quirked up in a half smile. "I knew she would hate it."

I smiled, then leaned in and kissed his eyebrow.

His eyes flicked to my arm. The mark crept along, unstoppable, and as I watched it, the weight of all the things I couldn't change came crashing down on me. This was the last night. Our last night. The last time I would feel his calloused hands on my skin. I looked at his beautiful face, and I couldn't bear it.

Every breath I took meant another grain of sand in my hourglass disappeared, and I only had a few left. I tried not breathing. I was losing it, and I turned away.

Jack put his arm around my waist and pulled me tight against him, so my back was cradled against his chest. He knew exactly what I was feeling. He breathed slowly, deliberately near my ear, willing my own breathing to mirror his.

"Do you want to know the first time I ever saw you?" he said with his lips at my ear.

I knew the story, but I nodded anyway, frantically.

"Your family had just moved in. You were . . . how old were you, Becks?"

I shrugged, and he ran his fingers over my head, calming me. He knew the answer.

"You were eleven," he said. "I was twelve. I remember Joey Velasquez talking about the pretty new girl in the neighborhood. Actually his exact words were 'the hot chick.' But I didn't think a thing about it until I saw you at the baseball field. We were having practice at the park and your family showed up for a picnic. You had so much dark hair, and it was hiding your face. Remember?"

I nodded. "I know what you're trying to do."

He ignored me. "I had to see if Joey was right, about the *hot chick* part, and I kept trying to get a good look at your face, but you never looked over our way. I hit home run after home run trying to get your attention, but you couldn't be bothered with my record-shattering, superhuman performance."

I smiled, and breathed in slowly. I'd heard this story so many times before. The familiarity of it enveloped me with warmth. "So what did you do?" I asked, fully aware of the answer.

"I did the only thing I could think of. I went up to bat, lined my feet up in the direction of your head, and swung away."

"Hitting the foulest foul ball anyone had ever seen," I continued the story.

I felt him chuckle next to me. "Yep. I figured in order to return the ball, you'd have to get really close to me, because . . ." He waited for me to fill in the blank.

"Because someone made the mistake of assuming I would throw like a girl," I said softly.

He pressed his lips against my head before he went on. "Which, of course, was stupid of me to think. You stood right where you were and chucked the ball farther than I'd ever seen a girl, or even any guy, chuck it."

"It was all those years of Bonnet Ball my parents forced on me."

"The entire team went nuts. You gave a little tiny shrug, like it was no big deal, and sat back down with your family. Completely ignoring me again. So my plan totally backfired. Not only did you get the attention of every boy on the field— which was *not* my intention—but I got reamed by the coach, who couldn't understand why I suddenly decided to stand perpendicular to home plate."

It'd worked. My breathing was slow again. I turned against his body, so I was facing him, and wrapped my arms around his back and tangled my legs up with his.

I'd spent a hundred years with Cole, in a similar position, but this was nothing like it. There were no outside forces keeping us together. No otherworldly powers interfering with this simple act.

No. Jack wanted me close because he wanted *me*. Separating from him now would be worse than anything I'd felt before. Separating from him now would make me bleed, and I would never stop.

I didn't tell him this. I didn't have to.

We stayed like that for hours—my head on his stomach—trying so hard not to fall asleep. As if we could stop time.

THIRTY-TWO

NOW

My house. Hours left.

In the morning, Jack left to go pick up Will, and I went to my kitchen and took out a pen and two pieces of paper. My dad and Tommy deserved letters this time. They were the closest thing I had to a real good-bye. In the letters, I tried to explain that I was gone, and that I wasn't coming back. I tried to express my love. I tried to make it all okay. I tried.

When I was finished, I folded up the letters and placed them under the milk carton. Except for the rare dinner of French toast, the only time my family ever drank milk was at breakfast, so I was pretty sure my dad wouldn't discover the letters until tomorrow morning at the earliest. If I made it back, I could get them before they were ever read.

Jack was back on my porch within the hour. "Sorry, it took me a little while to find Will."

"Is he sober?" I asked.

He nodded. "Mostly. Enough to drive his own car. You ready?"

I glanced behind me, toward the empty house and the letters to my family, and then I turned back to Jack. "Yes."

Jack took my hand and pulled me toward his car. I looked up at him as we walked. The sun was behind his head, burning through his hair, and I had the feeling that the way he looked right then would be the picture in my head forever. "Jack, do me a favor?" I said.

"Anything, Becks."

"Don't let go of my hand. And if the Tunnels come for me, don't let go until the last moment."

"If the Tunnels come for you, I'll hold on, and they won't be able to take you."

I smiled at the sentiment, even though I knew that no one would be able to hold on.

Jack and I drove toward the condo in a new state of mind. We'd both been stripped of all the evasiveness, all the lies, everything we'd ever kept from each other. Layer by layer, we had given up our defenses and our excuses and our demands for whys and hows, and what was left were two broken beings. Clinging to one last shred of hope. Tethered to each other.

I couldn't speak as to what occupied Jack's mind on that drive, but I knew what I was hoping for. That Jack would be able to recover. That he would heal. That those who loved him would soon repair the broken sheathing around his raw soul, and that his memories of me, while tender, wouldn't define him. I couldn't tell him this, because then he would know the doubt in my mind, and now wasn't the time for doubt.

First, I hoped we would succeed in destroying Cole's guitar. The other things were a silent prayer, kept close to my heart, for just in case.

As we got closer to Cole's condo, Jack and I went over our plan again. It wasn't very complex. I would let Cole believe I'd chosen him over the Tunnels, and then when we found the guitar, we'd make a break for it and toss it off the balcony and into the cement courtyard. Or smash it against the floor. But tossing it sounded better, because then nobody would be near enough to fight us.

We didn't talk about my dad, or Tommy, or Jules. We didn't talk about failing. We didn't talk about how the mark was about a finger-width's distance from my wrist line.

I remembered the bend in the road that would reveal the massive condo on the hillside closest to the resort ski lift. I'd made this drive almost exactly one year ago. That time, there'd been an early spring, and the road was clear. Now it was covered with a couple of inches of packed snow.

Jack parked as close to the door as possible, and we climbed the stairs. Outside the front door, I looked at Jack and he nodded. I knocked. Maxwell opened it, and I shoved my way past him.

"Where's Cole?" I said. Before he could answer, I raised my voice. "Cole! Get down here."

"Nik?"

I looked up in the direction the voice came from. Cole was leaning on the second-floor railing that looked over the spacious living room. I couldn't see his guitar.

I held up my arm. "I'm out of time, Cole."

"I know. I'd almost given up." He looked from me to Jack, and his forehead creased with pain for a flash, and then it was gone. Replaced by a calm expression, his eyes suddenly dark. "I hope you didn't come here to ask for my help. You know I have no power over the balance of the Everneath." He glanced at Jack. "Sorry, bro. Even with your biceps, we can't fight the force of nature."

Jack's mouth tightened, but he held back his response.

"Cole, look at me," I said. Cole hesitated for a moment and then swung his gaze back to me, and I met his stare. "I'm going with you."

He froze. Didn't move for a full thirty seconds. Maxwell and Gavin appeared from the back room, silently watching.

Cole stood up straight. "I'm not buying it." He turned around.

"Wait!" Jack called. Cole stopped. "It was my idea."

Cole turned to face us slowly.

"I convinced her to go with you. She's going away anyway. Better to rule hell than serve it."

I stepped forward and raised my arm, showing my wrist. "Cole, please come talk to us."

He narrowed his eyes, skeptical, and I thought it was over then and there. But then he said, "Be right there."

He turned back and disappeared down the hall that would lead to the stairs. I looked up at Jack. He whispered, "Let's hope he brings the guitar."

But when Cole descended the last flight of stairs, his hands were in his pockets. No guitar strap over his shoulder. I tried not to let even a hint of disappointment show in my face. We had a backup plan.

Cole followed us outside to the balcony of the condo, and we made sure that his back was to the front door. The air outside stirred with a rush of unseasonably warm air. I looked at my wrist. The marks had stopped moving. I pulled my sleeve forward to cover it and stared at Cole's face. I had to focus extra hard on watching Cole, so my eyes wouldn't flick one bit when Will made his move.

Will knew exactly what to do. The army had trained him for this. When he appeared in my peripheral vision, behind Cole, he was wearing his army fatigues and camouflage. I fought a smile as he slipped inside the open condo door. He would be in and out before the rest of the band even knew what was happening.

Jack stepped aside, shuffling his feet against the wood to mask any noise, and leaned back against the wall. He looked away as Cole spoke to me.

"What's this all about, Nik?" Cole said.

"I'm going with you. I don't want to be in the Tunnels."

"But you'll have to Feed."

"I know. Why are you being like this?" I said. "I thought you'd be happy."

"Because it seems so unlike you. I've never followed someone during the Return, but I know for a fact nobody would choose the Tunnels over the Court. Except you. You're stalwart in your selflessness, to the point of self-destruction, which is why I'll ask you again. What are you doing here?" Softer, he added, "You would never come with me."

Behind him I saw movement from the doorway of his condo. Will was at the threshold, Cole's guitar in his hand. I grabbed Cole's arm to stop him from going any farther.

"I didn't think I would. But there's nothing I wouldn't do for Jack," I said. Cole looked at Jack and then back at me. "I'm scared, Cole."

Cole's expression immediately softened, and he blinked quickly a few times.

I kept going. "I promised Jack you'd take care of me. That I'd be safe with you."

"Of course, Nik. I won't let anything bad happen to you ever again. You'll be a queen. You'll be safe. And you'll live forever." He reached for my hand.

Out of the corner of my eye, I watched Will step quietly out the door. He had four feet to go to the railing, where the cement below would ensure the guitar's destruction. Three feet. Jack shifted his stance and looked back at Cole. But before he did, his eyes flicked for the tiniest second toward Will.

Cole whipped around as Will reached the edge.

"Will! Throw it off!" I screamed.

Will hoisted the instrument over the side of the railing an instant before Cole charged him and tackled him. He went flying back and landed with a thud on the ground, Cole on top of him.

But it was too late. I heard the crunching sound from down below of a guitar exploding on the cement.

I yanked up my sleeve. I didn't know what was supposed to happen, but the mark was still there. Still frozen at my wrist line.

The wind picked up, twisting my hair into a spiral that lifted off my back.

Cole pushed himself off Will and stood. His eyes cut over to me and he reached into his pocket. "Were you looking for this, Nik?" He took out a tiny triangular piece of plastic. His guitar pick. "My heart. You missed." He frowned, his eyes sad. "You'd actually kill me?"

I held my breath and put my hand over my wrist, rubbing the skin. Jack stepped in front of me, blocking Cole.

"Becks," Jack said. He was staring behind me with the most pained expression I'd ever seen. I knew what he saw there.

I had seconds left. Seconds.

Cole raised his voice over the sound of the rushing air. "This is it, Nik. You have nothing, except for one last chance to come with me." A small trickle of blood escaped the corner of Cole's mouth and ran down his chin. He wiped it with the back of his hand and looked behind me. "Decide, Nik. It's coming for you."

I turned around. A dark mist was forming behind me. At first, it had no distinct shape, but then it started to swirl in the air, forming a giant spiral, the center of which was far away, darker than everything around us. It began to look like the funnel cloud that had taken Meredith.

"No!" Jack growled from beside me. "This wasn't how it was supposed to happen."

Cole held out his hand toward me. His voice turned pleading. "Please come with me, Nik. Rule with me."

"You can't let it have her," Jack said to Cole. He lowered his voice. "I know how you feel about her."

Jack told me he knew what loving me looked like on a person. Cole stared at me with an expression that seemed almost vulnerable. His lips were parted and his mouth was open, and with each breath, his shoulders trembled. His hands were clenched in fists at his sides, as if he were ready to hit someone if it would help. "I can't feel," he said, but his words betrayed the obvious emotion painted on his face, as if he had never felt anything so deeply before in his life.

Jack shook his head and looked away, incredulous. "How can you watch it take her?"

Cole didn't answer right away. His gaze shifted to the Tunnels. "I have no power over it. I tried to make her see." He shook his head and looked back at me, new fire in his eyes. "It's not too late, Nikki. It's not. As long as you're still here, you can change your mind." He took a step closer. "Come with me."

Jack turned to me, and I could see the defeat in his eyes. He took a deep breath. "If it's better than the Tunnels . . ."

"What?" I said.

He grabbed my shoulders. "Meredith wanted this chance. She died for it. There's a whole culture of girls who would give anything for it."

"Why are you saying this?" I searched his face.

Cole stepped forward. "I know her. She'll never do it." Jack shoved Cole hard against the condo wall and then turned to me again. The roar around us seemed to dampen everything except Jack's voice.

"Because, Becks. I don't want to see you suffer." He looked at my wrist. The one with the mark. He raised it to his lips and kissed it. "If it's better than hell, go with Cole."

I put my hand on his cheek and urged his face toward mine. "Never. That would mean selling my soul." I pulled his head toward me so our foreheads were touching. "If there is an afterlife, I want my soul intact. And then maybe I'll see you there." I smiled, somehow calm now that I was facing something inevitable. I was getting the good-bye I'd always wanted. Jack's face was in my hands. He was mine again at last, and it was more than I could've hoped for.

I could feel the suction at my back growing stronger. It flicked a few strands of hair around my face. "Jack. You should leave."

Jack clutched my hand in his. "I told you I wouldn't let go. We promised Meredith we wouldn't let anything separate us." He blinked right then and tilted his head. Something seemed to click for him. "Meredith. She told me to be strong like Orpheus. She said it was his choice . . . to be a hero."

"It's over," I said. I started to turn toward the Tunnels, but Jack's hands kept me facing him.

"I love you, Becks."

"I love you too."

"Do you remember in Mrs. Stone's classroom how you said there's no such thing as redemption?" His voice cracked a little.

I shook my head. "Forget about what I—"

"Do you still believe it?"

"Yes."

He looked past me. I could feel what he was staring at. The growing tunnel. The suction was so strong that the hood of my jacket was perpendicular with the ground. It was almost ready. Will and Cole watched silently from a few yards away. Cole had the strangest look on his face, unbelieving, as if he were watching something he'd never seen before.

Jack pressed his lips against mine one last time. He pulled back and looked at me, as if he didn't know what else to say. There wasn't anything else to say.

"Will you look after my family?" I attempted a smile. "Tommy's going to need a . . . big brother. Someone to fish with." It seemed stupid to be talking about this stuff, but there weren't any words for the bigger stuff anymore. "He makes his own flies." Jack already knew this.

"Becks—"

"And make sure he doesn't play football." Jack tilted his head at this. "I mean, football's fine, but it's dangerous. I don't want him concussed—"

"Becks, stop."

"Just tell me you'll do it." I closed my eyes. "Tell me."

There was a long pause, and I wasn't sure there'd be time for him to answer anymore. But after a few moments, he did. "No."

My eyes shot open. "What?"

His eyes were tight, his expression on fire with blazing determination. "You watch over Will."

"What are you . . . ?" My voice trailed off as it dawned on me what was going on. "No!" I tried to wriggle my hands free from his grip. "Don't you dare, Jack Caputo!"

But I couldn't break from his strong grasp. I twisted and thrashed but that only made Jack hold on tighter. He closed his eyes and said, "Stay with me, Becks. Dream of me. I am *ever yours.*"

"No! I will never forgive you!" I tried to pull back. Tried to get close enough for the Tunnels to suck me away instantaneously. But Jack had to be about twice my weight and pure muscle. "Let me go!"

He ignored me. In the quickest, strongest move I would ever know, Jack yanked me toward him and threw me to the ground behind him. Away from the Tunnels.

By the time I realized what he had done, it was too late. He still held my hand, but the rest of him was covered in the dark smoke of the funnel. He had jumped in, feet first.

"Jack! No!" I screamed as I dug my fingers into his hand. As if I could pull him out. As if I had the power over the light and the dark. The balancing forces of the universe.

But I didn't. I held on to his hand, and as I did, I caught a glimpse of the mark on my wrist. It didn't disappear. It just slithered down to my fingertips and then leaped over onto Jack's hand. I said a prayer inside my head. I begged whatever being was in charge of all this to give me back my mark. But it was gone.

Jack was gone.

He let go first.

I knew the instant his touch left me. Our fingertips separated. Even with all the commotion going on around me, I could only think about how his fingers slipped away from mine, and I didn't have the strength to hold on and I would never feel them again.

I started counting the seconds. Perhaps if I kept track of the seconds, somehow he would still be connected to me.

But it was difficult to concentrate on sequential numbers, because someone was shouting in my ear. I tried to swat the voice away.

"Becks!" Will's voice was urgent. "Becks, I'm getting you out of here. Now!"

I closed my eyes and shook my head. "Shhh. Twenty-five. Twenty-six. Twenty-seven . . ."

Arms circled around me, and my feet left the ground.

SOPHOMORE YEAR
Before he was mine and I was his. . . .

"You weren't in the lunchroom today," Jack said, coming up behind me at my locker. "Jules says you're never in the cafeteria on Wednesdays."

I tried to calm the flush to my cheeks before I turned around to face him. My crush on Jack was getting ridiculous. Pretty soon I would be nonverbal. Just because he noticed, for the first time, that I wasn't at lunch, it didn't mean anything.

I tried to keep my tone light. "Sounds like you guys had a very intriguing conversation."

"Oh, we did." Jack fell into step beside me, and we walked down the hallway at a slower pace than everyone around us. "She said you avoid the cafeteria on Wednesdays. And she said you like me."

I heard myself gasp, and I came to a stop.

I'm gonna kill Jules, I thought.

"So, is it true?" Jack said.

I could barely hear him with the crashing waves in my ears. I started to turn away, embarrassed, but Jack stepped sideways so he was in front of me, and there was nowhere else I could look.

"Is it true?" he asked again.

"Yes. I hate hot-dog Wednesdays, so I don't go to the lunchroom. It's true."

"That's not what I meant, Becks."

"I know."

"Tell me. Is it true? Do you *like* me?"

I tried to roll my eyes, and promptly forgot how. So I just looked at the ceiling. "You know I like you. You're one of my best friends."

"Friends," Jack repeated.

"Of course."

"Good friends?"

I nodded.

"More than friends?"

I didn't say anything. I didn't move. Jack reached toward my hand and tugged gently on my fingers. The movement was so small, I wouldn't have seen it if I hadn't felt it.

He leaned forward and said, "Tell me, friend. Is there more for us?"

I looked into his eyes. "There's everything for us."

THIRTY-THREE

NOW
Still counting.

The sun touched the tops of the Wasatch mountain range behind Tommy's head, illuminating the errant clumps of his blond hair sticking out in all directions, typical from a day of fishing the Weber River. He cast another line, then another one.

"There!" he said, pointing downstream where the surface of the water broke and a fish darted toward his bait. "That's ten for me. Eight for you."

I smiled and sent another cast over the running water. We never fished with hooks anymore. We couldn't be bothered with the pain of catch-and-release, for us or the fish, so we just counted the number of fish who jumped for the bait.

Tommy eyed my next try. "Ten and two, Nikki. Flick the pole between ten and two."

He was talking about the first rule of fly-fishing, repeating the same phrase my dad had said to me over and over when I was a little girl.

I sighed. "Hey, I'm the one who taught you how to fish in the first place."

He gave me a sheepish grin. "I wasn't sure if you remembered."

The sun dipped a little lower, and I glanced at my watch.

"We're not going, are we, Nikki?"

"Sorry, bud. I still have homework to do for tomorrow." It was partially true. School would be out in a few weeks, and I had several final projects left, one of which was the thesis paper for Mrs. Stone's class. But really I looked forward to the end of every day, always anticipating the evening, when I could finally close the door to my bedroom and fall asleep. And dream.

Tommy and I packed up our gear, and I drove the car while he recounted every "catch" he'd made that day. I smiled at the simple routine of it all.

Since the night at Cole's condo, I had tried to stop counting the seconds. But the numbers relentlessly filed past my vision, coming to rest in my head. Eventually, they were no longer numbers. Just flashes. Sparks of light, shooting across the horizon in my mind, ticking away the moments since I had last touched Jack.

And that was how the seconds evolved into minutes. Then hours. Then days.

What Jack did for me splintered me, and I wondered how my body stayed together each day instead of falling apart into the thousands of little pieces it should've been. Each time I looked in a mirror, I was surprised the cracks didn't show on my face. With every smile, I should've shattered.

When we turned the final corner to my street, I saw a big black motorcycle parked alongside the curb. The sun glinted off the mirrors, making me squint and question whether or not what I was seeing was really there.

"Who's that?" Tommy said.

I shielded my eyes with my hand. A figure in the shadow of the neighbor's oak tree moved, catching my eye.

Cole.

"It's no one, Tommy." I pulled the car into the driveway, and out of the corner of my eye I saw Cole take a step forward. "Listen, I want you to go inside and wait for me," I said as I threw the gearshift into park.

"Why?"

I kept my eyes on Cole. "Just do it, okay? Please?"

I turned off the car, and we both got out. A passing cloud blocked the sun, erasing the shadow of the tree. Tommy threw the gear bag over his shoulder and made a move to grab one of the fishing poles.

"Leave the poles," I said. "I'll get them."

He nodded, and hesitated for only a moment before he walked away. Once he was inside, Cole came toward me. I met him halfway.

Cole looked changed. He still wore the same clothes; his hair was still the same sandy blond. He hadn't changed in any tangible way. But the difference was there, in the way he walked. No swagger. And the way his lips weren't pulled up in a smug grin.

"Hey, Nik."

I stopped a couple of feet away from him and folded my arms. "What are you doing here?"

He shifted his stance, his hands shoved in the pockets of his leather jacket. "We both lost here."

"So, what, you're here to commiserate? Don't even pretend we've been through the same thing. You lost some game. I lost . . ." My voice caught as if on a fishing hook.

"Whether you like it or not, you're still my future. I have to know . . ." He stepped closer and grabbed my hand. "You have to tell me, how did you do it? How did you stay young during the Feed?"

I twisted my hand out of his grasp and took a couple of steps back.

"Even if I knew, what makes you think I'd tell you?"

Finally a hint of his smirk danced on his mouth. "Because I have ninety-nine years until I have to Feed again." He stepped forward. "I have all the time in the world. What, in your infinite knowledge of me, makes you think I'd ever give up?"

I squinted at him in the sunlight. "Cole, do you feel anything for me?" I don't know what made me ask this, except that Jack had asked him the night of the Tunnels. It obviously surprised him.

He backed up. "What?"

I inched forward, not quite sure where I was going with this. "Do you feel . . . something for me?"

He was quiet, still as a statue, so I moved even closer.

"Don't, Nik." His gaze dropped to the ground.

"If you feel *anything*, please leave me alone. I don't know why I survived. I don't have your answer. Shadowing me will get you nothing."

Then he did something unexpected. He backed down, and as he turned around to his motorcycle, he shook his head and mumbled, "What have you done to me?"

"I don't know," I said. "But you have ninety-nine years to figure it out."

He kicked it on and revved the engine, and at the sound, he found his cocky smirk again. "That's a long time, Nik. Jack is gone, and I'm here. Let's see who gives up first."

I stayed there until he drove away, his tires screeching against the asphalt, then I let out a sigh. The sun had set and I felt that familiar tug pulling me to my bedroom. My tether to Jack coaxed me there every night, just like a rubber band drawing me in.

The thing was, I knew exactly how I had survived. Mary had been on to something with her anchor theory, but she was a little unclear on the logistics. Jack told me he dreamed of me every night, and it was as if I were really there. I was in a dark place, and he helped me see.

Now Jack was invading my dreams every night. Not a dream Jack, but the real thing.

I know this because during one of the first dreams, he told me what the tattoo on his arm said. *Ever Yours*. The next morning, I rushed to draw the image from memory, and then I researched it.

The symbols were artistic versions of ancient Sanskrit words. They stood for eternity and belonging. *Ever Yours*, just as Jack had said. There was no way my subconscious could have come up with that explanation on its own.

I'd finally found the connection Meredith had longed for, the tether from an anchor that kept a Forfeit alive. They were bound together through their dreams, sustaining each other during sleep.

When I was asleep, Jack would come to my bedroom and sit on the end of the mattress and face me. He came to me every night, talking about his uncle's cabin, the Christmas Dance, how my hair hides my eyes, how my hand fits in his, how he loves me. How he'll never leave. I spent the first few dreams saying "I'm sorry" over and over and over, until he threatened to stay away if I didn't stop.

My dad wondered why I couldn't wait to go to bed every night. "You sure you're feeling okay, Nikki?" he would say. "I've never seen someone sleep so much."

"I'm good, Dad. I'm probably just making up for all those sleepless nights."

Since Jack left, my dad had been trying to spend more time with me, going out of his way to relate to me. Maybe he was worried I might leave again.

I wasn't going anywhere. The Tunnels had forgotten about me. Jack's sacrifice meant that I had my family back, and even though our fractured relationships had a ways to go, my home life was suddenly a stronghold in my otherwise messed-up world.

I had escaped the Tunnels. I had my family back. And in a way, I had Jack, too. The pain of loss was fresh every night, but I no longer begged to have it taken away. I owned it.

I revised my paper for Mrs. Stone's class. I'd found my redemption, and my hero. And I was going to get him back.

AT NIGHT
My bedroom, as I drift.

Every night, Jack is with me.

He lies down on his side, lengthwise on my bed, and props his head up on my pillow. I mirror his position. He places his hand over mine. I see it, but I don't feel it. We discovered long ago that we can't touch, even in our dreams. I am as much of a ghost to him as he is to me. We are a breath away—and a world apart—from each other.

He doesn't know where he goes when he's not with me. He doesn't think he exists anymore, except for in my dreams.

I think he is right. And I tell him to hang on. I will never stop dreaming of him.

I will find him.

ACKNOWLEDGMENTS

*B*race yourselves: This is going to be long. It takes a village to raise a novel, and this book owes its existence to one giant, crazy village.

First off, a big, sloppy kiss on the cheek to the folks at DGLM, especially my agent, Michael Bourret, who is one-half advocate, one-half shrink, and the other third kindred soul. Thank you for seeing the beauty in the beastly draft that I sent you, and for talking me down from the ledge on a regular basis. And for loving tennis just as much as I do. Added kisses for Lauren Abramo and her stellar work abroad on behalf of *Everneath*.

Next, high fives all around to the entire team at Balzer + Bray and HarperCollins. Special thanks to Sara Sargent and my editor, Kristin Daly Rens, who fell in love with the story of *Everneath* months before it was even submitted. You taught me to never stop asking questions and digging deeper. The Everneath came to vivid life because of you. Also thanks to the many people behind the scenes, including even more editors, copy editors, and the enthusiastic sales, design, and marketing teams.

Slaps on the bums (football-team style) for my writing group, the SIX (aptly named because we are all six feet tall): Bree Despain, Emily Wing Smith, Kimberly Webb Reid, Valynne Maetani Nagamatsu, and Sara Bolton. Without your brilliant critiques, endless readings of crappy drafts, and emergency runs to In-N-Out Burger, this book would be a flaming pile of goo.

Hugs all around for friends who have helped me through the madness of trying to get a book published, either by reading early drafts or providing emotional support and chocolate: Amy Jefferies, Diane Adair, Anne Petty, Matthew J. Kirby, Alissa Owen, Raina Williams, Debbie Lambson, Jenni Elyse, Robin Weeks, Karin Brown, Amy Weech, and especially Dorien Nielson, who read the earliest version when it was only twenty pages long and I was getting it ready to be critiqued at a conference.

Thank you to Martine Leavitt and the rest of my WIFYR 2009 workshop group for their insights. Thank you to many more blog friends, Twitter friends, real-life friends, and book bloggers who have watched my journey from the beginning and thrown their enthusiastic support behind this book. You know who you are!

Chest bumps to my extended families, including Frank and Kathleen, the Johnsons, the Otts, the Jacksons, the Ellingsons, and the other Johnsons, and endless nieces and nephews who also were subjected to early drafts. Special thanks to Eden Ellingson, who gave me the idea to write a book in the first place.

A noogie on the head for my sister, Erin, who shouted the praises of crappy first drafts and was ready with a pair of brass knuckles for anyone who thought differently. I'd want you on my side of any battle! Extra noogies for her husband, Dave.

A kiss on the forehead for my mom and dad, who raised me to believe I could do anything and celebrated every step of the journey, from false starts and rejections to that magical day when I got THE CALL.

A pinch on the cheek for my boys, Carter and Beckham, for reminding me there is life outside of my books.

Most of all, a smack on the kisser for Sam. You never let me give up. You believed in me when I didn't believe in myself. You are the best man I know. It's you and me against the world. Love you.

Praise for EVERNEATH by Brodi Ashton

"Enthralling and suspenseful, EVERNEATH is pure indulgent escapism!" Becca Fitzpatrick, New York Times bestselling author of HUSH, HUSH and CRESCENDO

"I was pulled under by this bittersweet, beautiful retelling of the Persephone myth. Wonderful!" Allie Condie, author of the MATCHED trilogy

"In terms of originality, pacing and plotting, this book is flawless . . . *Everneath* gets all the stars from me. Thanks, Brodi Ashton, you ripped my heart right out with this book, and that ending left me in tears. If I could rate this book ten out of five, I would. It's perfect." *Daisy Chain Books, 3rd February 2012*

"This book should come with the book equivalent of a Nicotine patch though – it's THAT addictive!!!" *District YA, 6th February 2012*